Francesca's heart stopped beating

It simply plain stopped right in her chest. Jack was ignoring everything she'd told him, all the boundaries she'd set. She had no reply, nothing but that swelling feeling in her chest, a feeling of such excitement that she had to consciously remember to breathe.

"Francesca, Francesca," Jack said in a voice that told her he knew exactly the effect he was having on her, told her he had no intention of playing by her rules. "Just because *I'm* under your spell doesn't mean I'll throw the investigation."

Then he laughed softly, a sound that filtered through her like the warmth from the fire, and Francesca knew right then and there that she was in trouble. Deep, deep trouble.

Dear Reader,

Where is Bluestone Mountain? In my imagination it's a picturesque town sandwiched between Woodstock and Bearville in the Catskill Mountains. In my heart it's the place where I explored my imagination and learned to dream.

I was born and reared in New York City and spent my youth running back and forth between Brooklyn and the Mid-Hudson Valley. When the time came to create a whole new world… I returned to my roots.

Frankie's Back in Town is my first title for Harlequin Superromance, and I'm thrilled to be writing stories that reflect situations and struggles most women know intimately. For Francesca, returning home means not only facing the past, but taking a few chances on the future. She rises to unexpected challenges, learns a few things about herself along the way, and finds love where she never expected. Not so different from real life, is it? Hence my new catchphrase: *Ordinary women. Extraordinary romance.* Sigh. Life is good.

I hope you enjoy Francesca and Jack's love story. I love hearing from readers. Visit me at www.jeanielondon.com.

Peace and blessings,

Jeanie London

Frankie's Back in Town
Jeanie London

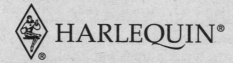

HARLEQUIN®

TORONTO • NEW YORK • LONDON
AMSTERDAM • PARIS • SYDNEY • HAMBURG
STOCKHOLM • ATHENS • TOKYO • MILAN • MADRID
PRAGUE • WARSAW • BUDAPEST • AUCKLAND

Recycling programs
for this product may
not exist in your area.

ISBN-13: 978-0-373-71616-6

FRANKIE'S BACK IN TOWN

www.eHarlequin.com

Printed in U.S.A.

ABOUT THE AUTHOR

Jeanie London writes romance because she believes in happily-ever-afters. Not the "love conquers all" kind, but the "we love each other so we can conquer anything" kind. Which is why she loves Harlequin Superromance—stories about real women tackling real life to fall in love. She makes her home in sunny Florida with her romance-hero husband, their two beautiful and talented daughters and a menagerie of strays.

Books by Jeanie London

HARLEQUIN BLAZE
153—HOT SHEETS*
157—RUN FOR COVERS*
161—PILLOW CHASE*
181—UNDER HIS SKIN
213—RED LETTER NIGHT
 "Signed, Sealed, Seduced"
231—GOING ALL OUT
248—INTO TEMPTATION
271—IF YOU COULD READ MY MIND

*Falling Inn Bed...

HARLEQUIN SIGNATURE SELECT SPOTLIGHT
IN THE COLD

Don't miss any of our special offers. Write to us at the following address for information on our newest releases.

Harlequin Reader Service
U.S.: 3010 Walden Ave., P.O. Box 1325, Buffalo, NY 14269
Canadian: P.O. Box 609, Fort Erie, Ont. L2A 5X3

A very special thanks to Wanda ;-)

CHAPTER ONE

JACK SLOAN, CHIEF OF POLICE, set the phone back in the cradle then reached for the intercom that connected him directly to his assistant.

"The mayor's on his way over," he said. "Just tell him to come in when he gets here and hold my calls."

"You got it, Chief," the upbeat voice shot back.

Jack got up from the desk and went to stretch before the window. He had a view of a street lined by shop fronts whose colorful awnings were now indistinct beneath a leaden gray sky. Mounds of dingy snow covered the curbs and spilled over onto sidewalks of the main street that wound through town center and bisected with Route 45, the primary highway into the valley.

Once a quarry town, Bluestone Mountain was now a fair-sized community, popular with writers, artists, musicians and sports enthusiasts because it lacked the commerciality of the nearby, and more widely known, hamlets of Woodstock and Bearsville.

Even now, in the dead of winter, folks came to town to enjoy some of the best skiing around. When the ice finally melted, Bluestone would attract people from all over who wanted to enjoy a renowned Catskill summer.

A good portion of his town's population consisted of part-timers from Manhattan—business people eager to escape the city for densely wooded hillsides and mountain-tops, sports and outdoor activities, all only a convenient few hours north.

Another portion of his town's demographic was made up of deeply rooted locals. Well over a century ago, people had surged to the area when miners had discovered feldspathic greywacke, the rare, dark blue sandstone that made Bluestone Mountain unique, and wealthy.

Even now, when the whole Catskill region had been earmarked as part of New York's Forest Preserve, not all the land around here was publicly owned, which made Jack's jurisdiction an interesting mix of big- and small-town politics. A mix that had its share of plusses and minuses. A plus was the freedom to run his department the way he saw fit. A minus was being at the beck and call of the good old boy network. Some folks considered themselves the local monarchy.

Like the mayor.

Gary Trant was Bluestone homegrown—Ashokan High class of '92, a year Jack's senior and, also like Jack, an alumnus of the football team. Those were the kinds of ties that bound tight. Since the mayor had appointed Jack, he could pick up his phone any time and inform his police chief he'd be dropping by to discuss whatever was on his mind.

That was how things worked in Bluestone.

Fortunately, the timing was good. Jack had just returned from observing a SWAT class at the police training academy and wasn't due to meet with the assistant chiefs of the Professional Standards Bureau for another forty-five minutes. Plenty of time if Gary didn't get waylaid by folks who recognized the mayor's smiling face. No question whether he'd stop and chat.

Jack didn't have to wait long, though. He'd barely sat back at his desk to review some proposed changes to the departmental budget when the door opened and Gary strode into the room, hand extended.

"Good to see you, Jack."

Gary Trant radiated the kind of energy and personality that played well to the media. On the football field, too. Jack knew exactly how well because he'd followed in Gary's wake and had found the helmet a challenge to fill.

"Have a seat," Jack said. "What's on your mind?"

Gary didn't sit. He only cocked a hip against the desk, folded his arms across his chest and leveled a serious gaze Jack's way. "Heard about the trouble at Greywacke Lodge. Credit card fraud, is it?"

"We're not sure what we're dealing with yet."

"I pushed hard for that senior-living community to be built. Folks get old. Made sense to bring in developers to provide facilities instead of forcing people out of Bluestone to retire. Don't want anything to reflect poorly on that decision."

Not with reelection around the corner and Kevin Pierce looking to step up from the town council. Pierce was already generating buzz about the town needing a change. Since the *Bluestone Mountain Gazetteer* was giving him ad space, Jack knew which way that wind would blow.

"I've got people on it," he said. "No need to worry. You know as well as I do in this electronic climate, credit cards get stolen all the time."

"Agreed," Gary said. "But that's what I wanted to talk about. *Who* you've got on the case."

"Randy Tanner. Assigned him when Chuck Willis realized there was a problem with a routine stolen wallet report."

"You think Randy's the best man to put on this?"

"Randy's the best I've got."

Gary nodded. "I know. I know. No question there."

"Then what's your concern?"

"Randy isn't a local, Jack. You have half a force made up of people born and bred here. Couldn't you assign one of them?"

"How does being homegrown factor?"

Surprisingly, the answer didn't come fast. In fact, Gary hesitated so long Jack guessed he couldn't find any diplomatic way to say what was on his mind. Not a good sign.

"You heard that Frankie Cesarini's back in town."

Jack had heard all right. Frankie hadn't been in town for twenty minutes before he'd gotten his first phone call reporting the news—from his long-ago ex-girlfriend. And Karan Kowalski Steinberg-Reece didn't pick up the phone to call him without a reason. Not since their second year of college when he'd disappointed her by realizing his calling wasn't law, but law *enforcement*. A huge difference in Karan's book.

"I heard," he said.

"Then you know she's running Greywacke Lodge?"

"I also know that the man who reported the missing wallet lives there. Are you saying Frankie has something to do with my investigation?"

Gary pushed away from the desk with a sharp sigh, and Jack stared at him, waiting. Call him stupid, but he just wasn't making the connection here.

"There's speculation Frankie is involved with the crime."

Now it was Jack's turn to sigh. "Do you mind telling me how you heard there was a crime? To my knowledge Randy and Chuck haven't even determined that yet."

"How can you *not* know?"

"We have suspicion of a crime." Jack tried not to sound impatient when Gary had sidestepped his question. "Hence the investigation. Until we determine whether or not an actual crime has been committed, we can't determine jurisdiction. Credit card fraud goes to the Secret Service. Identity theft stays with us."

Gary closed his eyes and groaned. "Secret Service? Jeez, Jack. That's the last thing we need. Can't you keep the outsiders away from this?"

Not unless he wanted to commit a crime of his own. "Don't you think you're putting the cart before the horse? All we have right now is an elderly man who misplaced his wallet and a string of hits on his credit report."

"Credit card fraud, then." Gary looked sick.

"Maybe. Maybe not. Like I said, I got my best man on it. We should know something soon."

Gary seemed to reconsider. "Okay, the sooner the better. This is a delicate situation. I think it'll be best handled that way. The rumor mill is already grinding."

"About Frankie Cesarini?"

"She goes by Francesca Raffa now."

"Married?"

Gary shook his head. "Divorced. Has a teenage daughter."

"Anything else I need to know?"

"Just buzz. But don't you think it's awfully coincidental the town bad girl comes home and now we have a crime?"

"We don't know that we have a crime yet, remember?" Jack sank back into his chair and rubbed his temples. "And the town *bad girl,* Gary? Since when do you deal in melodrama? I don't remember Frankie ever doing anything all that bad."

"What do you call tear-assing down Main Street on a stolen tractor?" Gary snorted.

"The tractor wasn't stolen. Not exactly. She worked for Ray Hazzard at the farm for a summer."

Gary's eyebrows shot halfway up his forehead. "What does that mean? She *borrowed* it for a joyride? She was like the Harriet Tubman of Ashokan, Jack. Every slacker in high school used to pay her to get them off property when they wanted to skip class. She knew every crack and crevice in the place and exactly who'd be monitoring the halls and when. She ran that racket for the better part of my junior year before Happy Harry finally shut her down."

"One could call it enterprising." Jack knew his fair share of students who'd paid big bucks for the service. "Frankie Cesarini never touched the juveniles this precinct deals with now. Curfew infractions. Skipping class. Leaving campus to smoke. I should be so lucky." He'd take Frankie's sort of rebellion any day compared to the middle school kids Randy Tanner brought in when they busted a meth cookhouse last week.

"You're defending her?" Gary looked genuinely surprised.

"I'm not defending her. I didn't know her. Hell, Gary, I wouldn't have even known she existed if not for Karan and her cheerleading posse. They obsessed over everything Frankie did."

Gary rolled his eyes. "You know what I'm talking about, Jack. She ran off to some third-world country with a guy two days before graduation, never to be seen or heard from again…until a few months ago. It's no wonder people are talking."

Folks did too much talking around Bluestone, as far as Jack was concerned. "Even if Frankie had been on the wrong road in high school, she must have cleaned up her act. Unless your developer hires felons for upper management. They must run background checks. If she'd been in any trouble—"

"My developer doesn't hire anyone for anything. They partner with a management company who does that."

"So Frankie works for the management company?"

"Same company Susanna has been with for years."

Bingo. Mystery of the rumors solved. And Jack glanced at the clock, wondering if he had time to kill one hen-pecked patrol cop before his appointment with the assistant chiefs. He knew exactly where the rumors had started.

The cheerleader connection. Susanna Adams had been close friends with Karan since high school. If she'd mentioned to Karan that the police had come to Greywacke Lodge asking questions about the missing wallet report, then Karan would have been all over the news because of Frankie. Karan had probably called her buddies from the cheerleading squad—most were still friends—and started up the gossiping. The only way they could have known of any potential crime meant that Becca had grilled her husband, and that henpecked patrol cop had dished out enough details to satisfy his wife.

Damned small town.

"Listen, Jack." Gary spread his hands in entreaty. "I'm not saying Frankie has done anything wrong, then or now. But I don't like the way people are talking."

"You've got that right. First and foremost, no one should know about this investigation. And I don't like that people are placing blame. I can't even say a crime's been committed yet."

If life didn't dish up enough drama, then some folks weren't happy unless they manufactured their own.

Frankie's return was news to warm up a cold winter.

"High school was a long time ago, Gary. What do you know about Frankie now?"

With a frown Gary settled back against the desk. "She's been running Greywacke Lodge since the doors opened and must be doing a decent job. I worked closely with the developer when they were putting together the deal for the property. The management company is top-notch. The investment bankers, too. I had no idea senior living was such big business."

"Makes sense," Jack said. "Baby boomers grow up."

"As far as I know they're running a first-rate community up there. Really, Jack, Frankie is the director of operations. The whole property answers to her. Including Susanna. Frankie must know what she's doing or we'd have heard something."

"You'd think."

Jack tried to remember back to the "good old days," when he, Karan, Susanna and her then-boyfriend Skip had been a frequent foursome. Susanna hadn't seemed much for instigating gossip, but as a member of Karan's cheerleading squad, she'd been part of a group that obsessed about Frankie.

Jack had never understood why. In fact, he really didn't remember much more about Frankie than she'd been orphaned young and reared by her grandmother. With the obtuseness of a teen who'd been more interested in football than girl drama, he'd only listened hard enough to figure out how to shut them up.

Especially Karan. When she started to rant, she could go on for hours, working herself up so much that nothing he did could bring her down again. That much he remembered.

The *good old days*. A chill ran down his spine.

"All right," Jack conceded. "I know why you don't want to add any more fuel to the fire, but I still don't understand your concern about Randy running the investigation."

"I *don't* want to add any more fuel. That's the whole point. Randy's the best you've got, no question, but that doesn't change the fact he isn't local. If people are on fire already, I don't want to give them anything else to speculate about. If you put another detective on the case with

Chuck, say Rick or Brett Tehaney, then no one can say your people didn't cover all the bases. Rick or Brett knows the history around here. They're not likely to miss anything."

"Neither is Randy." To hell with anyone who even thought his department wouldn't run a tight investigation.

"I'm not telling you what to do, Jack. Just consider what I'm saying. Greywacke Lodge is a draw to Bluestone. Half the movers and shakers in this county have sent their old folks to live there. Kevin Pierce called my office an hour ago asking if he should be worried about his grandfather. He didn't come out and question my integrity, but he made it loud and clear that he knew something was going on up there."

Bull's-eye. The real reason for this visit.

Pressure from the competition.

"I hear what you're saying," Jack said. "And I'll take another look at the situation, but I can't jeopardize an investigation—"

"I don't want a few malcontents who can't get their heads out of the last millennium starting up bad press about Greywacke Lodge." Gary checked his watch. "I've got to go. So as long as you know you're sitting on a powder keg here, I trust you'll deal with it. Do me a favor, though. Keep me up on what you learn. I don't want to be sideswiped by anyone else."

"No problem."

"Good luck then."

The door had barely shut behind Gary before Jack followed.

"I'm heading over to Professional Standards," he told his assistant, without adding that he'd be making a pit stop on the way. If he managed to restrain himself from throttling a patrol cop who couldn't keep his mouth shut, he would at least insist on some answers from his best detective.

Chuck was off duty, but Jack found Randy working at his desk. "Where are you on the Hickman case?"

"You got ESP?" Randy leaned back in his chair and tilted the computer monitor toward Jack, who glanced at the display.

"The Federal Trade Commission. You got something." It wasn't a question. The FTC's Identity Theft Data Clearinghouse ran a complaint database that catalogued identity theft victim and suspect information nationwide.

"Not yet, and let's hope I don't. Just got a call from one of your council members who heard we were up at Greywacke Lodge. Says his grandfather is there, and he'd appreciate it if we'd keep him up on how the investigation is going."

Jack winced against the dull ache starting in the recesses of his head, the foreshadowing of what promised to be a headache unlikely to go away any time soon. "Kevin Pierce."

That also wasn't a question.

"I gave him your cell number," Randy said with a chuckle. "But I'm guessing I better not drag my heels on this."

Randy didn't know the half of it.

"Don't worry, Jack," Randy said. "Natural for folks to worry after that grocery chain got hacked. Two-hundred-and-fifty-thousand debit card numbers. Friggin' nightmare. I'm heading back up to the lodge. I've got more questions for Hickman. If this does turn out to be identity theft, I'll walk him through the process. He'll have to file a fraud alert because I'll need his help to have a shot at nailing the perp."

When Jack didn't reply, Randy kept going.

"If he'll give me authorization, I can get his theft-related transaction records from creditors without a subpoena, which will save me some time. We need a list of the places where he's used his cards recently. But I'm putting a Clearinghouse Alert out first since we're dealing with national transactions. Maybe another agency can help me fill in the blanks."

"Sounds good," Jack finally said. "Any clue what we're looking at yet—credit card fraud or identity theft?"

"No. But I should know after looking at Hickman's records. A lot will depend on who had access to his credit card."

Precisely the problem. Jack already knew of one person who had access—the Greywacke Lodge employee who had found the missing wallet. That employee would be seen as an obvious connection to Frankie Cesarini. Throw Kevin Pierce into the mix, and this situation could become a train wreck fast.

But neither Rick nor Brett Tehaney would be effective—either at getting answers or as damage control. They were good cops without question, but neither had Randy's experience at producing the sort of results that routinely blew open cases.

Still, Gary was right about one thing. A trusted local would go a long way to reassure folks the BMPD had the situation well in hand. A trusted, high-profile local, who could appease folks both in the cab and the caboose.

With a sigh, Jack lay across the tracks. "Randy, looks like I'll be working this case with you."

CHAPTER TWO

IT WAS ONLY TUESDAY, and already the piles on Francesca Raffa's desk were so high she would need the rest of the week to dig her way to the bottom. *If* she took work home.

Six months had passed since she'd become director of operations at Greywacke Lodge. She oversaw the three-hundred-plus-employees who made retirement living in Hilton style grandeur a daily reality. She liked the position. But, quite honestly, her years of experience in healthcare had helped her juggle the demands of upper management so she'd had some quality of life. This move was proving a real challenge. What had she been thinking?

That, at least, was no mystery. She'd been thinking about doing what was necessary. As usual.

One of the job perks had resolved her grandmother's living situation. After Nonna had spent her eightieth birthday rehabilitating a broken hip, it had been obvious that she couldn't live alone anymore. Not when she'd grown so forgetful that Francesca feared her grandmother might forget to turn off the stove. Now Nonna was safely ensconced in her own apartment on-site.

Another job perk was leaving behind the big city of Phoenix for the smaller town of Bluestone Mountain, where Francesca had grown up. And a dose of small town would—hopefully—be good for her daughter, who'd taken an interesting turn after starting high school.

By the end of Gabrielle's freshman year, the circle of friends who once competed for ranking in the National Junior Honor Society had morphed into a group of teens who competed to see who could pierce the most body parts. Gabrielle had passed her AP Algebra class by .8%.

Francesca suspected the problem had a lot to do with her ex-husband, Nicky, who'd barely made time for his daughter after the divorce. Not because he didn't love Gabrielle, but because he was too busy sneaking around town with his girlie-girl so he wouldn't have to answer his daughter's questions about why their family had broken up.

Francesca hadn't seen fit to share the grisly details. Their fifteen-year-old hadn't needed to know that her father had thought it morally acceptable to cheat on his wife with their daughter's teacher in the very school he worked at and their daughter attended. To Francesca's knowledge, Gabrielle had never suspected, which she was eternally grateful for.

Thank God for small favors.

The move was both necessary and good, Francesca reminded herself. If she could survive the first year, she'd get her feet under her again. Just the way she had as a single parent. It was only a matter of time.

Time that obviously wasn't on her side this morning because she didn't get a chance to dive into that pile of work when her administrative assistant's voice sounded over the intercom.

"Ms. Raffa, June just called. The BMPD is on their way up to see the Hickmans."

Bluestone Mountain Police Department.

So they were back to the Mystery of the Reappearing Wallet. "Thanks, Yvette. I'm on my way."

Casting a bleak glance at her desk, Francesca headed out the door. She bypassed the corridor leading from the administrative offices to the main lobby and made for a service elevator and a ride to the sixth floor, where she immediately spotted two men. They stood at the far end of the spacious hallway, where each recessed doorway was embellished with decorations that reflected both the season and the occupant.

For Valentine's Day, Mrs. Humble of G-611 had a Victorian theme, complete with a designer topiary and a wreath of bright red hearts and sparkling angels.

Mr. and Mrs. Butterfield of G-610 had gone Western. Cutouts of cowboys with lassos had been artfully arranged with hearts and roses on a large bulletin board. The centerpiece was a glossy eight-by-ten photo of themselves in younger years astride horses.

All in all the effect made for a festive, if quirky, stroll. Francesca usually admired the creativity that went into the doorway displays. Today's stroll was a little different.

The men in front of the Hickmans' door seemed to swallow up the hallway. She assumed they were from the BMPD although neither wore a uniform. One wore a fashionable, and obviously expensive suit, while the other was more casually dressed in blue pants and a sport coat.

As she approached, she heard a door creak open and an elderly voice say, "Hello."

The man in the sport coat flipped open a badge to reveal his credentials, a flash of gold that Francesca caught even from several feet away. "Are you Mrs. Bonnie Hickman?"

"Yes."

"Detective Tanner, ma'am. And this is Chief Sloan. Is your husband at home?"

"Is this about his wallet?" Mrs. Hickman's voice faltered. "We cancelled the report."

"What's that, Bonnie?" a gruff voice boomed from inside the apartment. "Are you going on about my wallet again?"

The detective peered into the doorway purposefully. "Sir, we need to ask you some questions."

"What's that?"

"Questions," the detective repeated louder this time. "Chief Sloan and I need to ask you some questions about the wallet you reported missing. But first, sir, I need to see your identification."

The door of apartment G-606 opened, and Mrs. Mason popped out her coiffed blond head and glanced curiously around. Both detective and chief gave her casual glances before turning back to the Hickmans.

Francesca strode toward the men, extending her hand.

"Hello, gentlemen. I'm Ms. Raffa, the facility director."

The men turned to greet her, but Francesca only had eyes for the one in the expensive suit. For a protracted instant, she could only stare. Deep russet hair, an unusual color that made dark eyes seem almost black. The hard lines of a face she remembered from high school, an older version of a face no less striking today than it had been all those years ago.

Jack Sloan.

He swept a gaze over her, one of those classic law-enforcement looks that summed her up in a glance. He didn't register any recognition, but that didn't surprise her. She hadn't exactly been part of his crowd back then.

When her brain finally kick-started into gear again, she connected the man in front of her with the introductions she'd overheard. *Chief* Sloan was a blast from a long ago past, a memory she hadn't even realized had still been inside her brain until coming face-to-face with the grown-up version of a boy who'd been legendary in Ashokan High School.

Jack Sloan—valedictorian, quarterback, prom king and voted most likely to succeed.

And here he was, wearing an expensive suit that show-cased shoulders even broader than they'd been in high school, padded as they'd usually been by football gear. He'd been gorgeous all those years ago and was no less gorgeous now. More so, if that was even possible.

It was, she decided. Definitely. He towered over her, ex-tending his hand…. She mentally shook herself and slipped her fingers against his. "Is there anything I can help with?"

His grip was warm and strong. "We're here to ask the Hickmans some questions."

Jack raked his dark gaze over her again, taking in every-thing from the top of her head to the hand she had to remind herself to release.

She greeted the detective, relieved for the distraction, and glanced at his credentials before smiling through the open doorway. "How are you today, Mrs. Hickman? Captain?"

"Just fine, dear. I'm so glad you're here." Maturity had honed Mrs. Hickman's femininity to a soft patina, and when she met Francesca's gaze with faded blue eyes, the worry eased. "You can explain to these police what happened to Joel's wallet."

"We already did," the captain said in nothing less than a dull roar as he offered the offending wallet to the detec-tive.

"Why don't you invite us all in?" Francesca suggested. "We can find out exactly what these gentlemen need?"

Captain Joel Hickman had once been a man who'd stood taller than six feet, evidenced by his photo in full military regalia that hung beside the door's nameplate.

Now extreme age had bowed him until he wasn't much taller than his wife. He gave a nod, stepped back from the doorway with a shuffling gait and held the door for his guests.

Mrs. Hickman led them into an apartment with windows that overlooked the mountain and a living room filled with family photos and mementos from love-filled lives.

Francesca stepped inside and found herself so close to Jack that she could smell his aftershave. Just the barest hint of something fresh and masculine. She eased back on her heels a bit to put some space between them, but there was barely room to move in the small foyer.

She wasn't the only one who'd noticed their proximity. A quick glance brought her face-to-face with Jack's dark gaze and the amusement softening the edges of his chiseled expression.

Oh, he'd noticed their proximity, all right.

And it looked as though Jack Sloan was the same charming rogue he'd always been. Not that he'd ever turned his charm her way. She hadn't been worthy of his notice back in high school, but a girl would have had to be dead not to notice him. And everyone in Ashokan High, whether on top or bottom of the food chain, had known about Bluestone's golden boy.

"Please make yourselves comfortable." Mrs. Hickman finally cleared the foyer and motioned toward the sofa.

"No, thanks, ma'am." Detective Tanner stood his ground on the edge of the living room. "Our questions won't take long."

"What questions?" The captain's raised voice rebounded off the walls in the apartment's confines. "I already told your desk sergeant the report was a mistake. I only called the police because that television program… What's the name of that program, Bonnie?"

"*Dateline,* dear."

"*Dateline.* Those folks had a program on identity theft. They said the only protection a person has is to file a police report. My driver's license was inside my wallet. My Social Security card, too. So I filed a report."

"Then your wallet turned up?" Jack asked.

The captain nodded.

Detective Tanner pulled a notepad from inside his jacket and jotted down a note. "How long was your wallet gone?"

"Less than a day. I already told the desk sergeant."

Detective Tanner nodded. "Humor me, if you don't mind, sir. You noticed your wallet missing right away then?"

"Of course I did. Well…" The captain narrowed his eyes, clearly reconsidering. "I didn't actually need it until we were at the mall in Kingston. But I'm sure it was in my pocket before then." He raised a hand that trembled slightly and motioned to the coatrack behind the detective. "I keep it in my jacket pocket right there."

Mrs. Hickman didn't look so sure, and both Jack and Detective Tanner appeared to notice.

"Had you used anything in your wallet during the week prior to the mall trip?" Jack asked. "Your driver's license or a credit card maybe? Is it possible your wallet had been missing before you noticed?"

"No." The captain shook his head emphatically.

Mrs. Hickman backed him up. "I bought peach preserves at church on Sunday. He used his check card to pay."

Francesca knew what Jack was looking for—a time discrepancy. She'd reviewed the reports herself, but before she could think of a diplomatic way to mention that there had been one, Jack asked, "So you didn't actually look for your wallet after you used your check card at church on Sunday until you were at the mall on Thursday?"

"That's right."

"The report stated you found your wallet here at the lodge on Friday, is that correct, sir?"

Another nod.

Detective Tanner scribbled a note on his pad. "Have you ever misplaced your wallet before, sir?"

That was a loaded question. Sure enough, the captain sputtered his response, bristling, and Mrs. Hickman cast a worried gaze Francesca's way.

That was her cue. She needed to cut off this questioning before the captain got upset. He'd just completed a stint at the lodge's nursing center, weeks of physical and occupational therapy to declare him fit enough to return to independent living after a flare-up of a heart condition. He'd been home only a few days before the wallet incident.

Accidents happened. It wasn't easy to make peace with the physical limitations of aging. Francesca hadn't even crossed the hump to thirty-five, and she was getting a glimmer. Those extra five pounds she was suddenly unable to starve off had made her a target for her daughter's comments about "muffin tops."

For this once-vital man to admit, let alone accept, that he needed help with routine daily tasks couldn't possibly be easy. So Francesca sidled close to Jack, leaving the detective to his questioning, and whispered in a voice she hoped the captain couldn't overhear. "He has misplaced his wallet before."

Understanding flared in that dark gaze, and Jack lowered his own voice to a throaty whisper. "Often?"

"Just once. An employee found it."

"You have that employee's name?"

The warning bells in her head starting clanging. "I'll give you a copy of the report before you go."

"You'll tell us who has access to this apartment?"

"Of course." Those alarm bells were shrieking loud enough to kill off brain cells now. More was going on here than these men were sharing. A lot more.

He inclined his head then asked, "Captain, we need to know if you've made any trips out of state recently."

The captain reached for his wife's hand and muttered

something Francesca couldn't make out. Mrs. Hickman seemed to understand, though, and asked, "Detective, is my husband in some sort of trouble?"

Even Francesca found herself awaiting that answer. Neither Jack's nor Detective Tanner's expressions gave anything away. But Jack produced a business card. "We just had some questions that needed answers, sir. We'll be back in touch."

"And if you wouldn't mind," Detective Tanner added. "Will you make us a list of all the places you've used your debit and credit cards recently? Online purchases, too, if you've made any. Call the number on that card when you get the list together. I'll swing by to pick it up."

Francesca was *not* happy with that answer, which said nothing and everything all at once, and left a nice couple looking confused and worried.

"Ms. Raffa." Jack turned to her.

He didn't need to say another word. Reaching for the door, she politely refused his bid to hold it for her. She waited while both men strode through then used the moment to address the Hickmans. "Don't worry. I'll see what I can find out."

She slipped into the hallway and shut the door behind her. Neither man said a word while awaiting the elevator but, once the door hissed shut and the elevator began its descent, Francesca took advantage of her captive audience.

"Frankly, gentlemen, you've got me worried. I can't imagine the police department has the time or staff to investigate every reappearing wallet. I assume you're concerned about something else."

What other explanation could there be? True, Bluestone Mountain hadn't grown up all that much in the sixteen years she'd been away, but she read the papers. There was enough crime in and around town to keep the police force busy.

"I'm sure you understand we can't discuss an open investigation, Ms. Raffa." Jack sounded cordial enough.

"Precisely the problem since the investigation had been closed the last I heard." She wasn't going to be sidetracked. "We outsource our personnel screening with a highly reputable firm. I've worked with them in the past with another management company. I need to know if you're concerned about theft, Chief Sloan. I'm responsible for ensuring the residents' safety."

"Do you have reason to suspect any of your employees of dishonesty?" Jack asked.

"If I did, the party or parties in question wouldn't be on my staff."

The corners of his mouth twitched as if he was holding back a smile. "You have to do a lot of documenting before you can let an employee go."

"True enough." That thought was enough to distract her from his almost grin. Terminating an employee potentially opened up the property to a claim with the Equal Employment Opportunity Commission. Defending one claim cost nearly eighty person-hours in information gathering alone. Greywacke Lodge was a well-staffed facility, but administration had enough on its hands without that additional workload.

"Let me rephrase," Detective Tanner said. "Are you in the process of documenting to terminate any of your employees for suspicion of theft?"

"No, Detective, I'm not."

"I understand your concern," Jack said, and something in that whiskey-warm voice assured her he did. "You have my word that if suspicion falls on any of your staff, you'll be the first to know."

"Thank you."

"Will you tell us about Greywacke Lodge," Jack asked as the elevator stopped at the first floor.

Francesca moved through the lobby, catching June's inquisitive gaze as she circled the desk and led the way down the administrative corridor.

"What exactly would you like to know?"

"Who lives here?" The detective cast a meaningful glance around. "Looks like a hotel."

Francesca smiled. "Greywacke Lodge is a senior-living community, upscale as far as these communities go. Seniors come to enjoy their retirement years in comfort and convenience, and we provide long-term housing and a level of assistance tailored to their individual needs."

She filled them in on the stats of the property and the lodge's mission to provide a healthy, successful environment. Residents were kept active under the supervision of medical, lifestyle and activities' coordinators. The calendar was so full that Francesca had to check it daily to keep up.

"When independent living is no longer a viable option," she explained, "we also provide assisted living in a nursing center nearby. It's staffed to meet the more demanding needs of aging and provides rehabilitative services for our residents recovering from hospital stays."

Detective Tanner took notes as they strolled toward her office, but Jack gave her his undivided attention. The man had a knack for making it seem as if he was hanging on to her every word. A knack that must serve him as well in local politics as it had way back when every high school teacher and coach had adored him. Was he still Bluestone Mountain's golden boy? She wouldn't be at all surprised to learn he was.

Striding through the reception area outside her office, Francesca instructed her administrative assistant to make copies of the missing wallet reports. Then she ushered the men into her office and offered them seats.

"The copies won't take long," she said.

"Thank you." Jack smiled, nothing more than a courteous response, but somehow one polite smile reflected charm that could be wielded like a weapon.

Detective Tanner set his notepad on her desk. "Who owns this place?"

"There is no one owner," she explained, grateful for an excuse to look away from Jack. Honestly, she might have been seventeen again. "It's the product of a collaborative partnership of companies that specialize in senior living."

"Their names?" Poising his pen above the notebook, he waited.

Francesca wondered if this was some sort of test. This information was a matter of public record. "Lakeland Developers, University Realty Associates, Northstar Management and Rockport Investment Banking."

"And you're with the management company?"

She nodded. "Northstar Management. We staff over two dozen properties around the country."

The intercom beeped. "That'll be the copies, gentlemen."

Jack rose, the sleek gray lines of his suit enhancing the athleticism of the motion. Francesca wondered if the high school football star still played. Was he a coach for his kids? Did he even have kids? Just the thought of this gorgeous man reproducing with the bullying bitch he'd once dated was enough to make Francesca twitch.

"We appreciate your help, Ms. Raffa." Jack extended his hand. "We'll be in touch."

Francesca had been helpful. She'd given a lot more information than she'd gotten in return. Now it was his turn to repay the favor. "What can I tell the Hickmans, Chief Sloan? They'll be worried, and the captain really doesn't need any stress right now."

"Why's that?" he asked.

"Heart trouble. He spent some time in our nursing center after a hospital stay. He wasn't home long before he misplaced his wallet."

"Tell them not to worry. If there's a problem we'll advise them on how to proceed."

Not exactly what she was hoping for, but it wasn't her place to push. She'd leave that to the Hickmans' daughter. So she ushered the men from her office, picked up the copies from Yvette before escorting them back to the lobby.

They exchanged polite goodbyes. Francesca waited while they got into an unmarked car. As Jack slipped into the passenger side, he glanced over his shoulder and caught her gaze. And smiled that smile.

Then he slid into the car. The door closed behind him, and the tinted windows shielded him from view. He could be staring right at her for all she knew, so Francesca stood her ground until the car pulled away, refused to give a man with law-enforcement vision the slightest indication that her heart was pounding double-time.

Honestly.

"Never a dull moment around here," June commented drily when Francesca finally returned to the lobby.

"That's the truth." She shrugged off the cold. "Now it's time to get back to work."

But as she strode toward her office, she couldn't stop thinking about Jack. Police chief? She'd have pegged him for a world-class surgeon or a high-powered attorney or some other similarly affluent career. He'd been A-list back in high school. His future had looked like the land of opportunity from where Francesca had been standing.

Then again, when she remembered the way he'd listened to her talk about the lodge, she wasn't surprised he'd gone into a career that relied heavily on his people skills. Even she, in the seventh circle of social hell, hadn't missed out on the whole Jack Sloan mystique. How such a guy had been involved with Karan Kowalski… Francesca shook off the thought, determined not to let the past impact her present. No one knew better than she did that people grew and changed. For all she knew, Jack could be married to Karan now and have six kids. But he hadn't been wearing a wedding band.

Which meant exactly nothing, she thought stubbornly. Her ex-husband, Nicky, had taken off his ring when it had suited him, as she'd learned too late.

Jeez. What was it about a charming man that melted her from the inside out? One might think her years with Nicky Raffa would have made her immune. Apparently not.

CHAPTER THREE

THE SUN HAD GONE DOWN hours ago, but Jack was only now getting around to a workout. Not his preference, but it beat missing one for the third day in a row. He'd just left the office, which was late even for him, and he was no slouch when it came to long days. All the law-enforcement agencies in the area worked closely with the sheriff and the state troopers to keep the Catskills safe. Since crime happened around the clock, Jack had to be available the same.

But he enjoyed his job. The flexibility. And the surprises. No two days were ever alike. Every time he walked through the door or his cell phone rang, some new challenge forced him to juggle commitments with crises in the inadequate amount of time available.

Who'd come up with a twenty-four-hour day, anyway?

Left to Jack, he'd have added at least six more hours— enough for some decent shut-eye.

He wiped the sweat from his neck before moving to the bench for some barbell curls. One nice part of a night-time workout was that he practically had the gym to himself. No waiting for equipment, which was exactly why Tom Censullo, the owner of Pit Bull Gym, kept the place open 24/7. For some diehards, workouts were like crime.

"You do know that normal people are at home watching the news right now?" The familiar, but unexpected voice broke into Jack's thoughts.

Surprised, he glanced in the direction of the sound to find his dad heading toward him. "You're telling me you're not normal?"

His dad tossed a towel on a nearby bench. "That's news?"

"Maybe not."

Shrugging, his dad propped a water bottle against the leg of the bench before sitting.

When he'd been younger, Jack had thought his father was the most conventional, and humorless, parent on the planet. Only maturity had helped him appreciate his father's finer points.

A corporate attorney for a Fortune 500 company, Richard Sloan was as no-nonsense and traditional as his wife was avant-garde. Jack had come to think of them as *big business meets the debutante.* His mother and father were an unusual combination, but they complemented each other in their surprising ways.

His mother had grown up on the Upper East Side. She was the daughter of privilege who cared more for her current crusade than for what might be printed on the society page.

His dad was privileged in his own right. Bluestone Mountain royalty descended from one of the founding miners of the area. As a young man he hadn't been able to blow out of his hometown for civilization fast enough. He'd headed to Manhattan, where he'd earned a law degree, an enviable job with a company he was still employed by some forty years later, and a wife who'd insisted they rear their only son in the Catskills' fresh air.

His father commuted to this very day.

"Why are you here so late?" Jack asked.

"Your mother had a fundraiser tonight. She stayed in the city."

"But you came home?"

His father rolled his eyes, a look Jack knew meant he hadn't made the trip willingly. "Gus-Gus isn't doing so well."

That explained it. Gus-Gus was the patriarch of his mother's hoard of Maltese dogs. Eighteen years old if he was a day. "Michaela couldn't have kept an eye on him?"

"Your mother would have cancelled the whole event if she could have gotten away with it. The governor doesn't have another free slot in her schedule for six months."

"She didn't want to leave Gus-Gus at Michaela's mercy." The family's live-in housekeeper didn't have the same soft spot for dogs that Jack's mother had. "She's afraid Michaela won't hear him if he has trouble breathing. And if he does go downhill, she *knows* Michaela won't usher him from life in the style to which he's accustomed."

"She trusts you?"

"I have detailed instructions."

Maltese dogs, both old and young, were serious business in the Sloan house. His mother drove a gas-guzzling Suburban just so she could transport her dogs back and forth between Bluestone and the family apartment in the city. She'd mentioned on several occasions that Gus-Gus didn't travel as easily as he had in his youth, so Jack knew it must have killed her to leave him behind with one paw in the grave. "If you're on death watch, then what are you doing here?"

"He was breathing fine when I left," his father scoffed. "Just don't mention you saw me."

"No problem."

His father adjusted the pin on the weights and got down to business. "What about you? Shouldn't you be with Jessica Mathis at the gallery opening? I thought your mother said it was tonight, which is why she didn't ask you to babysit the dog."

Jack supposed it was good to know she'd have trusted him. "Had to cancel. Working an investigation with Randy."

His father gave a low whistle. "Better come up with a better reason than that. Your mother will be asking how your date went. Trust me. She likes Jessica."

"Don't want to hear it."

His father chuckled. "A heads-up then because if you think your mother is ever going to back down, think again."

"She says she wants me to be happy," Jack said.

"You're thirty-four, Jack, and single. She doesn't think you *can* be happy."

"Run interference for me. Remind her that she wouldn't settle for coming in second to your job."

His dad shook his head. "Don't know a woman who would."

"Don't kid yourself. Lots of women don't mind the trade-off. Otherwise no doctor on this planet would be married. Pastors or professional athletes, either. She's out there. Trust me. I just haven't found her yet."

"So I should tell your mother to cool her jets because you're looking for the perfect woman."

"Yeah."

Something about that seemed to amuse his dad, who smiled and said, "I'll do what I can, but I'm not sure anything will work. Your mother's biological clock is ticking."

"What started all this up again?"

"Kelly had twins. You'd think those babies were our grandchildren with the way your mother's been shopping. She even had a sign made for Kelly that reads Twins and Another. What a Lucky Mother!"

Jack sighed.

Kelly was a long-time family friend, a car pool buddy from elementary school. There was no way Jack could compete with Kelly's ten-year marriage, three kids and white picket fence.

His dad knew it, too. He set the weights into place with a light clank and faced Jack. "Maybe I'll try the doctor angle. Sacrificing yourself for the good of mankind should appeal to her."

"Sounds noble." Jack chuckled. "Protecting the streets is saving lives. Trust me."

"That's what you're doing over at Greywacke Lodge? Saving lives?"

Jack paused midcurl and let the barbell rest on his thigh. "How'd you hear about Greywacke Lodge?"

"Your grandfather is close friends with Judge Pierce. Remember, they're both past Grand Knights?"

"Got it." Bluestone's good old boy connection.

"So does your grandfather. He's decided your investigation is another reason not to consider senior living."

At eighty-two, Jack's grandfather was definitely past the point where living alone was good for his health and everyone else's stress levels. If his mother and Michaela didn't bring food every day, the stubborn old guy would starve.

He couldn't get out much anymore. His failing eyesight made driving unsafe even when the roads weren't half iced over in the dead of winter. Jack squeezed in time for visits whenever he was in that part of town, but he could tell by how reluctant his grandfather was to let him leave again that those visits weren't nearly enough.

"So what's Granddad waiting for?" Jack asked. "You to invite him to move into your place?"

"Already did. Makes sense. At least we'd have Michaela to keep her eyes on him. It's not like your mom or I are around enough to get in his way."

"What's the problem then?"

"Doesn't want to lose his independence. If he gives up

the house…" He let the thought trail off. "But from what I'm hearing about theft at Greywacke Lodge, maybe that isn't the answer, either."

"Theft?"

His father paused in between reps and leaned back on the bench, dragging the towel across his face. "Isn't someone stealing the residents' credit cards?"

"Granddad said that?"

They exchanged a glance. "Then you're not investigating the woman who runs the place?"

Jack shook his head. "Haven't even ruled out the card owner."

"Oh. Your grandfather must have misunderstood. Not like that hasn't happened before."

"Maybe not. You're not the first person to mention this."

"Didn't you go to school with the woman who runs the place, Jack?"

"Yeah. Same year, anyway."

"So you weren't friends? She never came over to the house?"

"No, Dad. She never came over to the house."

His father nodded, looking relieved. Too relieved. This, to Jack's surprise, annoyed him. A lot. A woman whose name hadn't yet come up in this investigation shouldn't be speeding into first place on his suspect list.

"What did Granddad say about her?"

"Not much. Just that she'd been a troublemaker, so no one's surprised there's trouble now she's back. I can't imagine your grandfather knew the girl. I assume the judge said something."

Jack set the weights on the rack and took a moment to stretch out his upper back. He let the quiet of the gym, marked only by the rhythmic whisper and clang of the weights and his father's controlled breathing, deflect his irritation.

"Like I said, we haven't even ruled out the card owner yet. I'd appreciate it if you'd keep all this to yourself. This fire doesn't need any fanning." He leveled a meaningful gaze at his dad. "You're getting that straight from the horse's mouth."

"Understood."

Good enough for Jack. He'd do his bit to knock down speculation about Frankie. A lot of years had passed since high school, and the woman he'd met didn't strike him as a criminal. He had a good gut instinct, one he trusted.

Frankie might have been a troublemaker once, but she'd been helpful and professional when he'd been at Greywacke Lodge. He liked how she'd handled the Hickmans, clarifying details and reassuring them when they'd been unsettled. She was also unexpectedly beautiful, and he hadn't been able to resist digging out his old high school yearbook to jog his memory.

Everyone of the class of '93 had looked ridiculous in their senior pictures. Himself included. A rite of passage, he guessed. Frankie's young face had been framed by fuzzy hair, the same caramel color it was now—not quite blond, not quite brown, but somewhere in between. But that was where the similarities had ended. Her gaze had been narrowed and her mouth set tight. As if she hadn't had all that much to smile about.

But now she was full of easy smiles, courteous professional smiles for him and Randy. Warm, reassuring smiles for the Hickmans. Appreciative, friendly smiles for the assistant who'd made copies at her request.

Jack wasn't sure why he'd noticed, except that he'd been on red alert because folks were already implicating her. Or maybe he'd been reconciling the beautiful professional with the girl who'd once sold forged hall passes.

He reached for the barbell when a cell phone rang. Jack

didn't recognize the ringtone. His father set the weights down too fast, and the resulting crash echoed through the quiet gym. He fumbled for the phone buried beneath a sweaty towel.

"I hope this isn't the damned dog." He snapped open the phone and said, "Hey, what's up?"

Jack realized his mother must be on the other end when his father said, "No, he's hanging in there, hon. Don't worry. I'll text you if anything changes, but it won't. Not until you get back. Gus-Gus is tough."

Jack couldn't help but smile, which earned a scowl from his father. "Just enjoy the night and give my regrets to the governor. I'll see you in the morning."

After disconnecting the call, he dropped the phone on the bench. "I'd better not push my luck. She'll probably call Michaela to double check."

"I hope Gus-Gus doesn't bite it on your watch."

"For real." Swinging his legs around the bench, he stood. "This was good. We should meet here more often. You hear me?"

"I hear you." Jack factored a few more hours into his perfect day. "I'll make time."

"I'm serious, Jack. There's more to life than work."

So he'd been told. But right now all Jack could think about was work, and the woman that too many people were convinced should be his number one suspect.

CHAPTER FOUR

ONLY ELEVEN O'CLOCK AND Francesca already knew this day was on its way downhill. Forcing a smile, she slipped the neatly stacked papers back into a folder and said, "Looks like you've covered everything with the proposed change to the cable service provider, but I'd like to take some time to consider any hidden overhead before making a decision."

"I've defined all the costs in the budget narrative," Susanna Adams, chief financial officer, said. "I know the property is new, but now the cable company has installed this far up the mountain, they can offer us a bundled service package that will reduce our overhead considerably. They're eager for our business and will make the hardware changes without cost to us. Switching only makes sense."

"I just want to look at the learning curve for a new system. I'm not worried about our staff, but the residents…" She smiled. "It's phone, TV and Internet. Some can barely work the existing system after six months of living here. I'm sure you'll have answers to all my questions here, so I'll make reviewing this a priority."

"Thank you," Susanna said politely, but there was no missing that she wasn't happy with this.

Figuring out ways to streamline costs was part of Susanna's job. She'd done the research and wanted to act. Francesca understood, but that didn't change the fact that she needed to consider the effects of those changes everywhere on the property and the way maintenance could support the services. She would need a little time and a few more brain cells than she had to spare right now to consider those effects.

To Susanna's credit, she didn't argue, but disapproval was obvious in her brisk motions as she collected her copies and tucked them neatly away.

In any other situation, Francesca wouldn't be mentally rationalizing her decision. But Susanna Adams had once been Susanna Griffin and Karan Kowalski's best friend. So instead of being two professionals who'd spent the past six months learning to work together for the benefit of Greywacke Lodge, Francesca and Susanna had been dancing around the past.

Francesca was all for letting bygones be bygones. She'd come back to Bluestone fully aware the past would have to be dealt with, and she worked hard to keep an open mind and let each day be a new day. A courtesy she hoped would come back to her in time. Truth was, she'd been very impressed with Susanna's work. But the ugliness of long-ago just wouldn't allow them to be normal around each other.

Shoulders back, chin up. Ever forward.

A heavy silence followed them to the door of the conference room, where they found a surprise awaiting them.

"Jack." Susanna greeted the man in the reception area with genuine pleasure.

Jack turned at the sound of his name, that smile transforming his face, proving beyond any doubt that he cared very much for Francesca's CFO. Susanna tossed her arms around his neck, and he gave her a good-natured squeeze.

He met Francesca's gaze over Susanna's head and nodded a greeting before asking Susanna, "How are the kids?"

"Hanging in there, thanks." She stepped back and gave a shrug. "Brooke's fifteen. What else can I say?"

His laugh was throaty and low. "What about you? Are you hanging in there?"

"Yeah." Susanna rose up on tiptoes and planted a kiss on his cheek. "And you're a sweetheart for asking."

Francesca guessed Jack referred to how Susanna was holding up after her husband's death. According to her personnel file, he'd only died last year. Skip Adams had been another of the high school "in" crowd. A close friend of Jack's, if memory served. And since their daughter was in the same grade as Gabrielle, they must have married around the same time Francesca had married Nicky.

"You wouldn't even recognize the kids, Jack," Susanna said.

"It's been too long."

"Always is." She laughed. "No one sees you anymore. Not since you became chief."

Francesca stood in the doorway to avoid intruding upon this blast from the past. Her high school years had been filled with similar meetings, and here she stood, many years later, still on the outside where she'd always been.

Feeling the same uncertainty. Feeling the same need to prove that being on the outside was infinitely better than being on the inside when watching Jack and Susanna really made her feel the urge to step back inside the conference room and close the door.

Francesca inhaled deeply, surprised and annoyed. She'd known what coming back to Bluestone would entail. But apparently knowing didn't necessarily mean she'd be prepared.

She made a break for her office, but Jack's smooth voice stopped her before she'd even reached the door.

"I was hoping for a few moments of your time, Ms. Raffa," he said.

"Of course." She didn't turn around, not sure whether the heat currently suffusing her entire body was making her blush. "I'll be in my office."

She beat a hasty retreat to allow Jack and Susanna to finish up their visit, and closed her office door just as Susanna was promising to give Karan Jack's regards.

Francesca hightailed it toward her desk and sank into her chair, fanning herself to disperse the effects of a hot flash that had zero to do with menopause. She was such an idiot. Why should she care that Jack hadn't married Karan after all?

She didn't. Not one way or the other. She'd decided after the divorce that she was putting the "woman" part of her life on hold until after Gabrielle went off to college. She had so little time—with her daughter, who was growing up so quickly, and with Nonna. Add to that her challenging new job, and there simply weren't enough hours in the day.

Francesca was at peace with that decision. For the time being she was reveling in motherhood, making up for lost time as a granddaughter, too.

A sharp knock signaled the opening door, and Jack appeared.

"Hello again." He motioned her to remain seated as he sank into a chair before her desk.

He raked his gaze over her, those black eyes taking in everything in a fast glance, and Francesca, idiot that she was, could suddenly feel the heat of the climate-controlled air through the sheer silk of her blouse.

"I received a message to pick up the Hickmans' list."

It took Francesca a moment to wrap her brain around that. "Their daughter mentioned she was coming by to help them get it together."

He was so tall that she could still meet his gaze above the file folders that seemed to have taken up permanent residence on her desk. Edging a pile to the side as nonchalantly as possible, she cleared space between them.

"So what else can I do for you today, Jack?" she asked.

"I'm wondering if you're having the same problem I am."

"What's that?"

"Too much discussion about what happened to Hickman's wallet."

"One of the reasons for the meeting you caught me and Susanna leaving." She gave a dismissive wave. "It's not really surprising considering the collective nature of our community. Who's talking on your end?"

"The friends and relatives of your residents. Any attempts at damage control?"

"I believe wholeheartedly that a strong offense is the best defense. We've been reassuring residents that we're doing our part to protect their personal information and offering them tools to protect themselves."

"Like what?"

She motioned to a folder on top of a stack. "We feature an ongoing lecture series here on Thursdays, so Rachel, my activities director, is putting together talks about today's electronic climate. Tips to protect against credit card fraud and identify telephone hoaxes. Stuff like that. We're hoping to get someone in to address phishing scams, too, since a surprising number of our residents are computer literate." She paused and took a deep breath, not sure why she sounded so breathless. "She's working with the Identity Theft Resource Center to schedule speakers who'll gear topics toward seniors."

"Excellent. I can put in a mention with our crime prevention task leader. He could get someone out here."

"Wow. That would be great. I'll tell Rachel. Thanks."

"No problem. Now before I go see the Hickmans, I'm

hoping to get your authorization for a walk-through of your common areas. I have a list of items and I'd like to see if any turn up around here. It would save me from going to a judge for a subpoena."

Francesca frowned, concern finally managing to wipe away every shred of her ridiculous reaction to this man. "You promised I'd be the first to know if I needed to worry about my staff. Is it time to start?"

He shook his head. "Not yet. This is just a formality."

"Then take your walk-through. Would you like an escort?"

"If you'll do the honors."

She was surprised when she really shouldn't have been. Once charming Jack Sloan, always charming Jack Sloan. "Of course."

She didn't waste a second, but hopped up and led him from the office, eager to escape his dark gaze. Even if only for the time it took her to get to the door.

She didn't make it. Jack stood and withdrew a long envelope from an inside jacket pocket.

"I understand you have a vault on the property." He unfolded the papers and closed the distance between them. "Any possibility of finding out if any of these items are in it?"

Francesca stood her ground until he was close enough for her to read his list. And inhale his aftershave. The same fresh scent she'd noticed before. But the effect dispelled fast when she saw the items on his list. "Whoa."

"Recognize anything?"

"Can't say I've noticed the captain wearing a Rolex that cost more than my Jeep." She took a discreet step back, found a few inches between her and this man made it easier to think.

"Jack, our residents don't normally walk around wearing

their Sunday best. I can check the log but anything more won't be possible without a subpoena, I'm afraid."

"Good enough."

Francesca led Jack the short distance down the hall to the vault's anteroom. He surveyed the small room, no bigger than a standard walk-in closet with the wall vault on the far end.

"Who has access?" he asked.

"Myself. My assistant director. Susanna. Head of Security. Human Resources. That's it."

"What about assistants? Do you or any of your managers ever authorize support staff to handle the deposits and withdrawals?"

"Only the paperwork. Otherwise, I'd have to turn over the key and security codes. The vault runs its own security log, so I can always check who accesses."

Moving in front of the computer, she brought up the program and entered her password. "My staff is well-versed on the protocol, Jack. We can't offer security if we're not willing to provide it. And, honestly, it's not as if overseeing this vault is a full-time job. It's only a courtesy for residents who haven't made personal arrangements for security in their own apartments."

"Some of the residents have their own vaults?"

"All apartment designs offer the personal security feature. Some opt for it before they move in, but it's available as an add-on afterward, as well."

Jack nodded and held up the list for her to read. The program had a search function, where Francesca inputted brand names of watches and descriptions of various pieces of jewelry.

No matches.

"Doesn't look like anyone has us hanging on to any six-carat pink diamonds, either," she said to break the silence.

Jack looked amused but didn't get a chance to reply before his cell phone vibrated audibly.

Glancing at the display, he smiled apologetically. "I need to take this."

Francesca only nodded, relieved for a break from him standing on top of her.

Get a grip, Francesca! Back in high school, she'd prided herself on being different from the rest of the female student body who drooled every time Jack walked down the hall. She'd thought he was drop-dead gorgeous like the rest of them, true, but as far as she was concerned, something had to be wrong with any guy who dated Karan Kowalski.

Now she had to wonder. Even if she was interested in dating—which she was not at this time of her life, thank you very much—Jack was exactly the sort of man she'd vowed to steer clear of. A charmer. And after thirteen years of marriage to a man who could make the polar ice cap melt with one smile, Francesca could spot a charmer a mile away.

Forcing her fingers to fly, she typed descriptions into the search function even faster, racing against the clock—or his phone conversation as it was.

No matches.

She wanted out of this tiny room, where Jack seemed to steal all the air.

No matches.

Finally, she entered the last one…

"I'm sorry about that, Francesca," Jack said, flipping his phone shut and stepping back into the room.

No matches.

She smiled and hit Print. "No apology necessary."

"Any luck?"

"Depends on your interpretation of luck. No matches, so I'd say my luck is holding. Not sure about yours." Still not meeting his gaze, she willed the printer to produce quickly, then whisked the report off the tray before the ink was dry. "So, where are we off to next?"

"Housekeeping." He scanned the document, not appearing in any hurry to move his broad-shouldered self out of her way. "I need to know how you work things here. Do the same staff members regularly service apartments?"

"We assign certain groups to certain quadrants to keep traffic in and out of the apartments to a minimum. Doesn't always work as we intend, but it's a pretty solid system."

"I need to talk to the folks who serviced the Hickmans' apartment during this time frame." He finally lifted his gaze from the report and reached into his pocket for another list, which he held out for her.

One quick glance at the list and she saw the possibility for escape. "Let's go then."

Jack stepped aside to allow her to precede him, and Francesca resisted the urge to bolt. Leading him down the hallway, she reached for the radio that was a permanent fixture at her waist. "Kath, is Emelina in the laundry today?"

"Yes, Ms. Raffa."

"Thanks. On my way." She ended the connection and found Jack staring down at her.

"Do you know where everyone works around here without looking at a roster?"

There was a compliment in there. She could hear it in his deep voice, knew it would be all over his smile if she looked at him. So she didn't look. "I oversee the scheduling."

"And have a photographic memory, it sounds like."

She was saved from a reply when they reached the elevator and the doors slid wide to showcase Mrs. Talbot.

The woman wore a badge with the lodge logo and her

name imprinted to provide easy identification for staff and residents. And visiting police chiefs.

"Good day, Mrs. Talbot," Jack said.

She nodded politely before asking Francesca, "You're coming for lunch today, aren't you? It's Tasty Thursday."

Francesca glanced at her watch. "Fingers crossed. I can't promise."

"They're featuring my squash casserole, so do your best." Mrs. Talbot moved along with another polite nod to Minnie Moorehead, who shuffled up aided by an electric-blue walker.

Jack reached above Francesca's head and held the elevator door.

"More like Tasteless Thursday," Minnie said as she stepped inside.

Francesca followed, unable to hold back a laugh. "I don't know about tasteless. Her four-bean salad was so good Chef Kevin added it to the menu."

Minnie made a moue of distaste. "Gave me gas."

Francesca wasn't sure how to respond to *that* but enjoyed Jack's surprised response. Nice to know the man could be taken off guard.

To his credit, though, he didn't miss a beat. Stepping into the elevator, he asked, "What floor, Ms. Moorehead?"

"Fourth." She eyed him curiously. "This your man, Francesca?"

"Minnie." Francesca warned and hurried on before Jack could introduce himself. The last thing Minnie needed was anything more interesting than Mrs. Talbot's squash casserole to discuss over lunch. And another visit from the police chief definitely qualified. "How did you ever find a shade of lipstick to match that beautiful sweater?"

Flattered, Minnie launched into a discourse about her particular shade of Cherries in the Snow until the elevator ground to a stop on the fourth floor.

Disaster averted. *Whew!*

Jack held the door until Minnie was into the hallway before letting the doors slide closed again. He depressed the button for the basement.

"We're riding the local today," Francesca said to fill the quiet.

"An interesting ride."

"Usually is," she agreed.

"I've got a question for you, Francesca."

"Shoot."

"You mentioned that you'd spoken to the Hickmans' daughter about the list. Do you always liaise for the residents?"

She shrugged. "Not always. Company policy is to notify family members whenever anything out of the ordinary comes up. Unfortunately, we can't be everywhere at once."

His visit to the Hickmans was a prime example. She'd barely made it upstairs in time to intervene. "If we can't notify a family member, we try to make someone from the lodge available. We have a patient care consultant on staff for that purpose, but any one of the management staff will do."

"It isn't always possible?"

"Afraid not. Try though we might. This is a senior-living community. We don't oversee every aspect of our residents' lives. Our involvement is like our security vault—a courtesy."

"But your company still has policy in place?"

Hmm. How could she phrase this delicately to a man who clearly wasn't grasping the whole concept of senior living? "We deal in aging services here, Jack. Double-checking details usually works to everyone's benefit."

"Got it." And something about that quirk at the corners of his mouth told her he did.

They found Emelina in the laundry, but after Jack introduced himself, she eyed the nattily dressed chief of police in horror and launched into a stream of Spanish that had Francesca scrambling to keep up.

"There's nothing wrong, Emelina," Francesca said. "Chief Sloan just wants to ask you a few questions."

Jack stepped in, turned on the charm and soon had Emelina eagerly looking over his list. *Anything* to help out the police chief. Francesca tried not to be impressed—by the effect of his manner or his fluent Spanish. She tried to find something off-putting in the way he used his charm.

Nada.

But she did find herself distracted when he showed Emelina an entirely different list, one that itemized costly sound systems, hi-definition televisions and computer equipment.

Could all these purchases really have been made on one credit card?

Francesca was getting a really bad feeling and pretended to watch linens being fluffed, folded and tossed into carts while listening to Emelina's replies.

No, she hadn't seen a notebook computer in bright pink in any of the apartments she cleaned.

Maybe, she would notice a new flat screen TV since it was her job to dust it. Maybe not. TVs all looked the same since she never had time to watch them.

Yes, there was an apartment she cleaned that had an expensive-looking electronic keyboard.

Francesca knew for a fact that Mrs. Hickman had brought a keyboard as a compact replacement for the baby grand piano she'd played most of her adult life. But that keyboard had moved in with them. Long before the captain had misplaced his wallet.

This time.

Jack thanked Emelina and looked to Francesca for an escort to the next place on his list.

"The residents' parking garage," he said. "Would you like to grab a coat?"

"Only if you're planning to keep me outside a while."

"Just a walk-around."

"Then I'll be fine."

Better to get this tour over with as quickly as possible rather than delay with a trip back to her office. Besides, some cold air might help clear her head. Of course, the instant Francesca got a blast of a Mid-Hudson Valley winter, she was thinking twice about her clever idea to force Jack to hurry.

She watched him scan the rows of cars on both sides of the garage and had to ask, "Did these suspicious purchases on the captain's credit begin the first time he misplaced his wallet?"

"I'm sorry. Can't answer that yet."

Okay. She understood he couldn't discuss the details of his investigation, but she didn't like being in the dark. She tried a side-door approach. "If you tell me what you're looking for, I can help you look."

"A 2009 Ducati Desmosedici RR."

Francesca stopped short. "Ducati? As in *motorcycle?*"

"A limited edition. Red. We'll check with gatehouse security, but I wanted to walk through in case it was brought onto the property and not registered."

"Jack?"

He glanced around, obviously just realizing she hadn't kept up with him. "Francesca?"

"You're looking for a Ducati, *here?* But these cars belong to residents who can still drive. There aren't many. Trust me. Even if the captain bought a Ducati, why would he park it here?"

A frown furrowed his brow. "I have no way of knowing."

The wind picked up, whipping her hair into her face, blowing through her hose and freezing away any reaction she once might have had to this man's charm. Now he was just obtuse. "You met the Hickmans, Jack. These lists of yours make it sound as if you think they went on some Bonnie-and-Clyde style shopping rampage. I understand you can't discuss the details of your investigation, I honestly do, but can't you be a little clearer on exactly what you're looking for?"

That black, black gaze bored into hers for a long time before he said, "Evidence linking the suspect charges to the person who made the purchases. I need to confirm whether or not Captain Hickman made these purchases before I can know if I need to keep looking at whoever has access to his credit cards."

"Like my staff."

"Like your staff," he agreed.

"So we're not talking about a little crime your department will solve quickly? We're talking about a big messy crime that keeps my residents worrying and every red flag I have flying."

A crime that would keep the too-charming chief of police dropping by her office whenever he had a question.

"I'm afraid we are," he said.

"Damn." Francesca exhaled a frigid breath. "And it's only Thursday."

"Tasty Thursday." He reminded her.

She didn't need a reminder, thank you.

CHAPTER FIVE

"HANG ON," SUSANNA WHISPERED into her cell. "I can't talk here."

Hurrying from the lobby, she bypassed her office to step inside an exit stairwell. Easing the door closed, she shut out the familiar sounds of the administrative wing. The drone of the copier where Yvette was printing the latest edition of the residents' activity calendar. The electronic hissing and beeping of the fax machine. The intermittent ringing of the switchboard. Once the door clicked shut, the silence enveloped her in a calm that she welcomed with a deep sigh.

"That's better," she breathed into the phone. "What's up?"

"Dish," Karan's voice shot back over the receiver. "Becca told me that Chuck is off the case at your place, and *Jack is on.* Have you heard?"

Not even a "Hello, how's your day?" Classic Karan. But Susanna didn't mind. Despite Karan's obvious quirks, she'd always been there when it counted. Like during Skip's long battle with the non-Hodgkins lymphoma that had finally taken his life. Karan had put to work her connections with the medical community and those connections had been considerable—compliments of two ex-husbands.

"No, I hadn't heard," Susanna said. "But Jack has been by a few times. I assumed he was helping out."

"A few times? And you haven't called?"

Susanna propped the phone against her ear, reached for the handrail and began to climb in her version of a power walk. Well, *power* wasn't exactly accurate, since she was wearing a business suit and practical pumps. But she might as well settle in for the long haul because Karan wasn't going to hang up the phone until she'd been dished all the details.

If it hadn't been twenty-six degrees outside, Susanna would have preferred to be on the par course. She'd settle for hoofing it up and down the stairs. Good exercise for her butt which, according to her daughter, was showing the effects of too much time behind a desk.

Thank you, Brooke.

"No, I didn't call. It's been crazy around here."

"Susanna, we're talking about *Jack*." Karan's tone scolded for breaking an all-important, if unspoken, rule.

Karan was always interested in Jack, regardless of who she was married to. "I was getting there. Between this place and all the nonsense going on with the police investigation, not to mention Brandon made the play-offs—"

"Stop right there, Suze. I do not want to hear your litany of excuses. Just tell me what's going on with Jack."

Susanna took the next few steps. "I really don't know anything."

"But you said he's been by a few times."

"He has. I saw him this morning. He asked me to give you his regards."

"Really?"

"Yes, really." She didn't admit that she'd had to wheedle the courtesy out of him. Jack never so much as mentioned Karan's name. Not in all the years he'd been dropping by the house to watch football with Skip. He'd moved on with his life, unlike someone else who would remain nameless.

"How does he look? I haven't seen him since we ran into each other at Gary's last five-hundred-a-head dinner."

Not exactly a surprise. Karan might officially live in Bluestone, but she'd been spending more time in the city, avoiding the gritty reality of her latest marriage meltdown. "No obvious gunshot wounds."

"Susanna!" came the exasperated reply.

Susanna snickered away from the phone's mouthpiece then said, "I really don't know anything else. Jack's been by a few times. That's all I know. Frankie doesn't share that sort of stuff with me. Or anyone else for that matter. She's professional. *Ultra* professional. I've told you that before."

"Humph. I know what you've said, but I still have trouble believing it."

"Hard to believe, I know, but there you have it," Susanna agreed automatically, confirming her position on the right side of a line that had been drawn in the sand years ago. "They did tour the property together this morning, though. I overheard her assistant telling one of the other managers."

"Really?" Karan's interested tone reassured Susanna that all was forgiven. "A tour of the property? Wonder what they were looking for. Probably where she stashed the body."

"Karan." Susanna winced. "That's awful."

Laughter chimed over the line like silver against crystal. "Perhaps, but this is *Frankie* we're talking about."

As if that explained everything. Honestly, some days Susanna wished with all her heart she'd have listened to Skip when he'd wanted to accept the job promotion that would have taken them to Napa Valley. Then, of course, they'd have been clear across the country when he'd gotten sick, with no family or friends as a support system, *alone....*

"I have no clue what they were looking for," Susanna said. "The missing wallet that started this whole fiasco turned up a week ago. That much I know for sure. But Becca told you Chuck was off the case. I find that curious."

"Isn't it, though? Doesn't Jack let his minions do the grunt work nowadays?"

"Like I would know. I don't see Jack that much anymore." Not since Skip.

"From what I hear, no one sees him much anymore. Makes you wonder what he does with his free time, doesn't it?"

Susanna sighed. "Not really."

"Jack's working this case for a reason. I know it. Unless he's itching to get his hands dirty again."

There was no missing the sarcasm. Karan might not admit it aloud, but she still hadn't forgiven Jack for veering from the path she'd had mapped out for their future. And from the day she'd set her sights on Jack in the tenth grade, Karan had been mapping. She'd intended to become the wife of a high-power attorney from a Bluestone royal family that had deep ties in Manhattan society. That life would have fit her to a T.

Obviously not Jack, though. He'd surprised them all by rolling up his sleeves and diving into law enforcement. Conversely, no one had been surprised at all when Karan dumped him for the first wealthy medical student she could get her perfectly manicured nails into.

Susanna was about to tell Karan she'd keep her informed when the sounds of young laughter and loud music distracted her.

There was an activity lobby on this floor, but the music wasn't anything she'd expected to hear for line or ballroom dancing. More like something she'd have told Brooke to turn down. Better yet, turn *off*. What sort of dance class happened on Thursdays? She tried to remember. The activity calendar was so busy she didn't know how Rachel kept up.

"Hang on a sec," she whispered to Karan, pushing the door open to get a peek of what was going on inside.

Windows spanned an entire wall, and bright afternoon sun streamed over the wide expanse of carpeted lobby where nearly four rows of residents stood in lines. It was a nice turnout, over twenty people in all, male and female, all casually dressed. Susanna expected to find Roberto, the lodge's physical therapist and dance aficionado leading the group in the slow motion steps of some dance. Instead, a young girl stood at the front of the group, a lanky young girl wearing tight jeans, layered shirts and a nose ring.

Frankie's daughter.

Gabrielle was a pretty girl, close in age to Brooke. But that was where the similarities ended. Everything about Gabrielle screamed "Attitude!" From the artfully arranged chunky silver jewelry to the Converse All Star sneakers that looked as though they were the ones her mother had worn twenty years ago. For all Susanna knew they were.

The music stopped abruptly, and Susanna pulled her eye away from the crack in the door, not wanting to be caught.

"Let's try it again," Gabrielle said. "Think superhero. Y'know a dude in tights who can leap tall buildings."

Susanna risked another peek to see Gabrielle demonstrating a dance move vaguely reminiscent of a horizontal swan dive.

Mrs. Gunderson made a valiant attempt, a slow-motion stretch of arms with gracefully pointed fingertips.

"Yeah, that's it," Gabrielle said with a straight face. "You've got it."

Paquita Escabar, Auntie Pippa as she liked to be called, didn't fare so well. She was a tiny woman, who was a lot older than most people knew, and she would have landed on her face had Mr. Patrick not gallantly steadied her.

Exactly why a licensed physical therapist should be teaching this class.

Susanna opened her mouth to tell Karan she'd call back as Mrs. McIlhenny stopped her attempts at the dance moves and waved her in. "Susanna. Come in. The girls are teaching us the Soulja Boy."

The girls? Susanna stepped inside the lobby, and sure enough another girl was working the boom box and demonstrating the same dance move...*Brooke.*

"Got to run," Susanna said and snapped the phone shut.

"Hi, everyone." Shoving the phone in her pocket, she made her entrance. "So what's going on?"

A chorus of replies came from the group, but they barely registered as Susanna glanced at the girls. Gabrielle cocked a hip against the windowsill, folded her arms over her chest and bristled with attitude. Brooke, on the other hand, looked as if she wished the floor would open wide and swallow her whole.

"What do you think of our featured instructors?" Roberto strode in from the direction of the elevators.

"Interesting." Susanna forced a smile.

"They're wonderful," Auntie Pippa said. "Thank you so much, young ladies."

"They promised to come back next week," Mrs. McIlhenny added, glancing at Roberto for approval.

Like the girls would have had a chance to say no with this group. Roberto graciously smiled. "The Soulja Boy, hmm?"

"I don't polka," Gabrielle issued deadpan.

"We've had it with Lawrence Welk," Mr. Shaw said. "You need to keep it lively or we'll all drop dead right here."

Roberto spread his hands in good-natured entreaty. "No arguing with that. How about you, Brooke? Are you in for another session next week?"

Brooke glanced at her mother uncertainly, but Susanna left her to make her own bed. "I'll have to get back to you on that."

Smart kid.

Undeterred, Gabrielle instructed the group, "You keep on practicing that superhero move, okay? You'll get it and we'll put it all together."

"That we can do," Roberto agreed. "We'll work on it."

"Well, have fun, everyone." Susanna circled the group and attached herself to her daughter for an escort downstairs.

Brooke headed for the elevator behind Gabrielle, but Susanna steered her to the exit door instead.

"The stairs?" Brooke winced. She'd be a captive audience in privacy.

Susanna just opened the door and, once inside, demanded, "You're supposed to come to my office after school. What was this all about?"

All the previous uncertainty vanished. "Nothing. I just saw Gabrielle going upstairs."

"So you followed her?"

That one question effectively ended the conversation. Her daughter shut down in the blink of an eye, expression going blank, gaze hardening, and her entire body tensing for the fight. Susanna knew the drill. Brooke was going to stonewall her, likely for days.

Damn.

Her husband had been the patient one, the calm in the storm when life got chaotic. Teenagers were chaos.

All right, Skip, she sent up a mental plea. *What now?*

She knew no answer was forthcoming and forced herself to breathe deeply and keep her mouth shut, hoping that a floor or two of silence might give them a chance to start over. She wasn't surprised Brooke was fascinated by

Frankie's daughter. Gabrielle stuck out like a beach umbrella on a ski slope. She'd transferred in from a big city school and the aura of urban cool radiated off her, in her appearance and her demeanor. Brooke had been reared in Bluestone Mountain with virtually the same group of kids since birth.

The Soulja Boy. Honestly. Susanna didn't even want to know how Brooke knew that dance.

Another deep breath then Susanna said, "You're going to run into Gabrielle around here. That's unavoidable, but I really think you should give some serious thought to pursuing a friendship." She made a supreme effort to sound respectful of Brooke's ability to make choices.

"I wasn't pursuing a friendship. I was helping her with *your* old people. Mr. Roberto had to leave for a few minutes. He asked us to babysit."

"Where did he go?"

"I don't know. He probably had to pee. He's as old as everyone else around here."

Roberto was a good two decades younger than Greywacke Lodge's demographic, but Susanna wasn't about to waste her energy explaining. At Brooke's age, old was simply old.

Instead, Susanna watched her daughter in her periphery as they rounded the stairwell to the sixth floor, tried to gauge Brooke's expression.

Closed for business.

Great. Just great. Here was a problem Susanna couldn't have foreseen. She'd recently celebrated her thirteenth anniversary with Northstar Management, so when they'd offered her the chief financial officer position at Greywacke Lodge, she'd jumped all over it. The promotion had been an answer to a prayer. It ended her commute into Saugerties, a distance that had made her so inaccessible to the kids after Skip had died.

Ashokan High School was within bike-riding distance of Greywacke Lodge and shuttling Brandon from school to ball practice was a simple matter of taking a late lunch. Quality of life had improved dramatically for all of them. And she enjoyed the pace of the lodge. *Hectic* made the day go by much more quickly. A huge improvement over years spent in the financial office on her last management gig— just Susanna, a massive payroll and an assistant who'd been allergic to laughter.

Who could ever have guessed that Frankie would return to Bluestone? Or sign on with Northstar for that matter? Not in a thousand years would Susanna have ever imagined that the class of '93's rebel would wind up as *her* manager.

"Another of life's little surprises," Skip would have said.

Susanna wasn't sure how many more she could take.

CHAPTER SIX

JUST WHEN FRANCESCA HAD the end of this all-important project tantalizingly in sight, she couldn't stuff one more piece of china into the plastic storage box. Not one.

Nonna was expecting to be reunited with her china this morning, and Francesca didn't have the heart to disappoint her again. Nonna was already having a hard enough time settling in at the lodge, which shouldn't be coming as a surprise. Nonna had lived in her three-story Victorian since the day she had married some sixty-odd years before. A lifetime.

This china had traveled with her on a ship from Italy, a wedding gift from her parents. Nonna might not have the room to display the set in her apartment now, but she wasn't about to part with it, either. She'd passed along the set to her own daughter-in-law as a wedding gift, but then inherited it back—along with Francesca—after the auto accident that had killed her only son and daughter-in-law. Since Nonna was a big believer in family traditions, she continued to break out the dishes on holidays, and promised to pass the set along to Francesca as a wedding gift.

If and when she married someone worthy.

Nicky Raffa hadn't counted as far as Nonna was concerned. Not only had he convinced Francesca to leave Bluestone to see the world, but he'd also committed the ultimate sin by convincing her to elope at the courthouse, which had meant no wedding dress. That had been incomprehensible to someone who had made a living beading wedding dresses and ladies' formalwear.

But Nonna's hope sprang eternal. Patience, too. She was still waiting for Francesca to find a china-worthy man. That legacy had grown in importance now that age had robbed her of the eyesight and motor skills needed to create those beaded masterpieces that had defined her life's work. Even if Francesca did find a worthy man, she wouldn't be wearing one of Nonna's fantasy wedding creations as her own mother had.

Such was life. Not always fair. Rarely easy. Yet Francesca was learning that those imperfections made it possible for the good times to stand out and shine all the brighter. The love she knew for her daughter. The second chance she had with Nonna.

Besides, on the positive side, the family china hadn't become another casualty of her errant youth. Without question she would have sold off the whole set when Gabrielle had gotten sick in Guatemala City and she and Nicky hadn't had the money to pay for a doctor.

That had been one of those mixed blessing situations so prominent in her life. A turning point because had she not had such an awakening to the responsibility of parenthood, she might never have shaken off the rebellion of her youth and grown to functioning adulthood.

But she had, thankfully, which was why she'd awakened early today. And she would be finished with this project already, if not for being short a storage bin.

Glancing at the clock ticking methodically away on the mantel, Francesca calculated the time. Barely five. A twenty-four-hour Wal-Mart Supercenter store was practically in her backyard so she could go for her morning run, buy a bin and wrap up this project if she got a move on.

In Phoenix, she wouldn't have considered running before the sun came up, but in Bluestone… In less than ten minutes, Francesca was telling a sleepy Gabrielle that she was leaving, locking the front door and heading outside.

Her breath burst in white clouds in the frigid air, so she wrapped her scarf around the lower half of her face. She remembered this cold from her childhood, but the cold was about the only thing recognizable about Bluestone anymore.

The town had grown so much that the sprawl had reached Francesca's childhood home. What had once been a quiet residential street was now zoned commercial, with Nonna's home sandwiched between an automotive repair shop and the loading docks behind the Supercenter.

Francesca took to the predawn streets and let physical exertion empty every thought from her head until she could hear nothing but blessed silence.

Five miles later, she was blinking against the fluorescent glare of the store's interior. Fortunately, it was quiet this time of the morning, mostly employees scrubbing floors, stocking shelves or serving the few other early bird customers.

Francesca headed straight for the storage department, grabbed a plastic container, and headed to the checkout. As she cleared kitchen appliances, she nearly collided with a man who'd emerged from pet supplies in as much of a hurry as she was.

"Oh, I'm so sorry—" She came to a tottering stop, grateful for her running shoes on the freshly mopped floor. Had she been in heels, she'd be on her butt right now.

"Forgive me, Francesca."

She glanced up in surprise. "Jack?"

"My fault entirely." That smile. That totally *to-die-for* smile.

He appeared to be in uniform, although she couldn't see

much more than the gold stars at his throat. The black wool
duster he wore made him look big and imposing and completely out of place in this friendly neighborhood Supercenter.

She was in a waking nightmare. Her cheeks felt freezer
burned, and Jack could probably smell her. Her hair, well,
that wasn't a total tragedy as it was frizz on a *good* day.
"Please tell me you're not here to bring me up to speed on
the Mystery of the Reappearing Wallet."

His smile widened. "You'll have to call it the *Case* of
the Reappearing Wallet if you want to be official."

"Can't be unofficial in that uniform."

He laughed, an easy sound in that deep voice that rocked
the quiet and told her he liked that she'd noticed him. He
liked it very much.

Nightmare? No. Francesca was in hell. No question.

"Still shopping?"

She shook her head, afraid to open her mouth again lest
more stupidity tumble out.

He nodded, and they fell into step together toward the
front checkout. When she didn't say anything, he held up
a bag of rawhide bones. "For Gus-Gus."

She did *not* want to ask, but there was simply no way
around it. And no question in her mind that he'd set her up,
either. He wanted to chitchat. What was with this man?

"All right. Who's Gus-Gus?"

"My mother's dog. He's failing, and she's upset. Thought
I'd drop by on my way to an appointment to bring a conva-
lescent gift. Not that I think there's much hope of convalescing."

"That's really depressing, Jack."

"Sad, yes. But not too tragic. The dog has lived a long
and privileged life. My mother's pets are official family
members. Gus-Gus is the brother I never had. So what
about you? What brings you here at this hour?"

"Never-ending storage needs." She glanced down at the plastic container she held, so big he couldn't have missed it even if it hadn't almost taken him out when they'd collided. "Packing up my grandmother's place."

"The Victorian on Third." It wasn't a question.

"So you do know who I am." The words were out of her mouth like a horse at the gate. Damn it. Why didn't mouths come with padlocks? "I mean, that I'm from around here."

"We went to school together, Francesca."

"I know." She forced a laugh, backpedaling. "Long time ago. I didn't think you'd remember me."

He came to a sudden stop and arched a dark eyebrow, looking thoroughly charming and thoroughly amused.

"Okay, not much hope of that. I was pretty memorable." Especially since *his* girlfriend had been captain of the anti-Frankie squad. How stupid could she be? *Stupid. Stupid. Stupid.*

"That's not why I remember you." His voice was throaty and low, his admission oh-so personal in the quiet of this early morning. Too personal.

"Oh." She didn't have a clue what to say to *that,* but she wasn't about to ask him why. She didn't want to know.

All Francesca knew in that moment was that she wasn't the only one noticing the chemistry between them. She'd been telling herself that Jack had been pleasant and friendly, his usual charming self, but right now, standing in front of aisles filled with tabloids and impulse buys, she knew this man *noticed* her, even though she must look like the Bride of Frankenstein.

She did the only thing she could think to do.

"My daughter and I are staying at Nonna's house until we can pack everything and get it on the market," she said, babbling about the first thing that came to mind. "But I'm afraid with the way the neighborhood has gone, I'll sell the house and they'll bulldoze it to build a drugstore."

Jack's gaze never wavered, but his smile did. Damn man was so used to women tripping over themselves for him that he could spot one a mile off. He knew exactly what she was up to. Oh, he knew all right. She could see it in his face, feel it in the pit of her stomach.

"That doesn't seem right." His smile widened. "Seems like there should be some loophole for historical significance."

It took a moment for his words to register, to realize he'd let them segue through the moment and ignore this awareness between them. This awareness that shouldn't be happening.

"You know, I hadn't thought of that," she said in a rush. "Nonna's was one of the first residential houses around here. I should check with the town historical society."

"Good idea. So what happens after you sell the place? Do you and your daughter intend to buy something in the area?"

Danger. Danger. Danger.

The warning blared inside her head. She *should not* be feeling this crazy pleasure because Jack was interested in her plans. Maybe he was being polite. Or his interest was strictly professional. But she could hear that warning inside her head, *feel* it straight to her toes. So much more was happening here.

She forced herself to reply casually. "That's the plan. Not sure where we want to live yet, though. Haven't had much time to look between getting settled at work and school and pulling the house together."

"That must be a job. The house looks huge, and I know you're busy working and solving mysteries and…" Dragging his gaze down the length of her, he didn't miss an inch in between. "You're a runner."

She nodded.

His smile widened. "So am I."

Three little words that closed the distance between them in a very personal way.

Francesca was saved from having to reply as they reached the express lane. Jack took her storage container and placed it on the conveyor then stepped aside, allowing her to move ahead.

Get a grip. Get a grip. Get a grip.

She reached inside her pocket for her debit card and didn't say another word as they made their purchases and headed outside. She didn't trust herself to open her mouth just yet. Not with this man oozing his charm all over her. Not with her immunity to charm in desperate need of a booster shot.

The predawn cold went a long way toward diffusing the warmth that had everything to do with the handsome man beside her. Francesca set down her bin to bundle up for the walk home.

Jack watched her wrap her scarf around her neck, and the charm vanished in the blink of an eye. The smile disappeared and there wasn't a hint of flirting in his voice when he asked, "You're not walking, are you?"

"I'll cut through the parking lot."

His brow creased as he narrowed his gaze over the vast and mostly empty parking lot that suddenly seemed like a hotbed for potential crime beneath the suddenly scowling expression of the police chief. "I'll give you a ride."

"That's not necessary, Jack. I'll be home in a heartbeat."

He held her gaze steadily and repeated, "I'll give you a ride."

Mr. Take-Charge wasn't leaving her any way to decline politely. Francesca wasn't sure what she thought of that. It was a new experience. That much was for sure.

She resisted the urge to point out that she'd just survived a five-mile run, and said, "If you insist."

"I do." His voice was a husky whisper between them as he slipped a hand around her elbow and led her toward an occupied space.

The next thing Francesca knew, she was being ushered inside a late model Crown Victoria that screamed unmarked car with its darkly tinted windows and nondescript design. Taking her storage bin, he held the door while she slipped inside. He settled her purchase in the backseat then slid in beside her, filling the close quarters with his presence, so completely masculine with his determined manner.

The glow from all the electronic displays cast his profile in glowing relief, and the moment became surreal, an intriguing glimpse of a Jack she hadn't met yet. A Jack who wasn't the thoroughly charming police chief, but a law-enforcement officer who dealt with a side of life she tried her level best to avoid.

"So this is what the inside of an unmarked car looks like," she commented as he turned over the engine. "Not as high-tech as I would have thought."

He gave a nod and steered the car toward her street.

"So, any new developments on the investigation?" she asked, needing to get them back on familiar footing, to help her reclaim her equilibrium around this man.

"Progressing, I'm happy to report. And you don't have to worry about your personnel yet. So what about things on your end? Calming down?"

She shrugged. "A little maybe, but let me take this opportunity to say thanks for the way you've been handling the Hickmans. Their daughter appreciates it, too."

He shifted his gaze off the road. "You mean handling their case professionally and thoroughly?"

How could she *not* smile at that? "And thoughtfully. This situation is unsettling. It's tough enough to misplace things, but with the situation dragging on…"

Jack gave a quiet laugh. "Oh, I hear you, Francesca. I've got a grandfather of my own."

That was all he needed to say and, honestly, she wasn't surprised. Not when he'd treated the Hickmans, and the other residents they'd encountered, so easily. "Well, I wanted to say thanks. We all appreciate what you're doing to reassure the Hickmans you have everything in hand."

He flashed a smile that gleamed white in the dimly lit car. "That's because we do."

She couldn't help but laugh, although she wanted to resist this man. With every ounce of reason, she wanted to resist. But she sat so close, lulled by the breaking dawn and the stillness broken only by the steady hum of the powerful engine. She was glimpsing sides of him that she'd never met before, and that only deepened the intimacy of the moment. He was Jack Sloan, after all, she reminded herself. And she was only human.

CHAPTER SEVEN

AFTER WATCHING FRANKIE disappear inside the dark house, Jack had to remind himself to put the car into gear and reverse out of the driveway. What was it with this woman? She continually caught him off guard. If he wasn't noticing how beautiful she was, he was noticing how easily she laughed.

Frankie wasn't what he expected, which made him question when he'd formulated those expectations. Truth was he didn't know much about her. Except that she was attracted to him.

As attracted to him as he was to her?

Jack could only hope. And he did.

That surprised him.

So as he drove to his parents' place, he considered what he actually *knew* about Frankie, not what he'd *heard*.

A few obvious things stood out. She took her job and her responsibility to Greywacke Lodge's residents seriously. She had a sense of humor about life and herself. She hadn't gone to pieces or made excuses about her appearance today. And though she was obviously post-workout, she'd made windblown and breathless a striking combination. Exercise had brightened her gray eyes and flushed her cheeks. And her mouth…the cold had made her mouth look like it might after she'd been kissed.

Jack hadn't thought about kissing anyone in a while.

So, as he pulled into the driveway at the home he'd grown up in, he evaluated whether or not he needed this investigation to continue indefinitely so he had access to Frankie or conclude quickly so he could ask her on a date.

He wouldn't break any real rules by asking her out. She was a contact person on this investigation, not a suspect, but Jack knew how things worked in Bluestone. With the rumor mill already grinding, any personal interest he expressed in Frankie would only fuel the talk even more. And undermine the very reason he worked with Randy on this case.

Damned place was a fishbowl.

He no sooner shoved open the door when he heard a familiar voice ask, "Are you okay? Did someone die?"

Jack had been so wrapped up in his thoughts that he hadn't noticed his mother walking up behind the car. He glanced up at her, looking fresh and ready to take on the day even though the sun wasn't officially up yet.

She'd always been an early riser, so he wasn't surprised to see she was casually dressed beneath the wool coat that hung open despite the cold.

"What are you doing out here?"

She motioned a slender hand toward the street. "Just getting the recycling bin out before the collection. Your father forgot when he left this morning."

"Dad only forgets because he knows you'll do it for him."

She eyed him curiously. "We made a mistake by not trying harder to give you a sibling, didn't we? I figured if we were meant to have a bigger family, we would. When I didn't get pregnant, I just assumed it wasn't meant to be. Your father and I discussed the situation with the doctor a number of times, but we didn't have too many options back then. Not like now with fertility specialists and in vitro and surrogate—"

"Mom," Jack interrupted. He had to stop her. She was making his head spin and he hadn't gotten out of the car yet. "What are you talking about?"

She folded her arms across her chest and stared down at him with a look he knew intimately. Disapproval.

"Aren't you listening?"

"I'm listening, but you're not making any sense."

"I'm talking about the disservice your father and I did you when we left you an only child. We even discussed adoption."

"You're still not making any sense."

She took in a deep breath, part exasperation, part sigh, all disapproval that she had to explain herself. "If you'd have had a sibling, at least one, you might not think the sun spins around your little world. You might have some comprehension of what's involved in making a relationship work."

He motioned her back then got out of the car, so he could stare down at her and level the playing field. "This is about canceling on Jessica, isn't it?"

"No. This is about you and the fact that I don't want to see you wind up a lonely old man after I'm dead and buried. Look at your grandfather. Does he look like he's having much fun holed up in that house of his day in and day out?" She scowled. "You don't seem to have a clue that it takes two people working together to make a relationship work. Probably because you don't have many relationships that last long enough for you to figure that out."

He opened his mouth to reply, but she held up a hand to stop him. "And don't tell me that you're looking for the quote *perfect* woman. Your father already tried that."

"But I—"

"I did not raise an idiot, Jack. You know there is no such thing as perfect."

He wasn't going to touch that one. Not when she was tearing into him. His father had warned him, after all. Normally Jack would have kissed her, handed over the dog bones, claimed his meeting was earlier than it was, and made his getaway.

But today he actually had something to offer that might appease his mother. The truth was that he'd invited this rant. Not because he'd canceled on Jessica Mathis—that was his business and not subject to her approval no matter what his mother thought—but because he hadn't been making time for his family. His mother wouldn't come out and say that.

"How about perfect for me, then?" he asked. "I'm not interested in Jessica. But I met someone I am interested in."

Her eyes widened. Her mouth opened for the interrogation of who, what and when to start planning the wedding.

"Don't get too excited," he cautioned. "I haven't asked her on a date yet."

"But you're interested?"

He gave a decided nod. "I'm interested."

"And she's interested, too?"

"I think so. But the situation is a little complicated because of work, so I can't just ask her out."

His mother's expression positively lit up. And Jack couldn't help but smile with that pride he'd known his whole life to have such a beautiful mom, inside and out. Even when she was launching into him. Because she cared so much. And when Jack remembered his father's recent admonitions about making time to work out together, Jack decided that maybe, just maybe, he might have to give their concerns some thought.

He'd never made a choice to eliminate everything from his life in favor of work. Not consciously, anyway. But when he considered the past few years, he could see a trend. His job had always claimed the top slot in his priorities, but since becoming police chief, the job took more time.

Suddenly, her hand was on his sleeve and she was lifting up to kiss his cheek. "Come on in. Michaela's baking up a storm in there, and the coffee's fresh. I want to hear everything."

"Sure I'm not catching you at an inconvenient time? I should have called." Then Jack went for the kill. "But I heard Gus-Gus wasn't doing well, so I wanted to drop by."

His mother's expression collapsed. "My poor baby. I honestly don't know what life will be like without him."

Jack didn't ask how she'd notice one dog missing from that herd of hers. He just reached into the car for the bones and presented them as a peace offering.

"Oh, Jack. That's so sweet." A hug this time.

Jack couldn't help smiling as he followed her inside to pay his respects to the sick and clue his mother in on Frankie.

All was well.

But his feeling of well-being lasted only until he returned to the station.

"You always miss the fun around here," Randy informed him after Jack had walked the gauntlet through Communications to various greetings and updates about open investigations.

"What have you got?" he asked.

Randy motioned to a stack of computer printouts. "Someone's been having a field day with the Hickmans' good credit. Their daughter faxed me permission to access her parents' credit reports, and I hit the mother lode. Four new credit card accounts with high limits were opened between five and six months ago."

Not good. "Status on the accounts?"

"All delinquent. No surprise there." Randy gave a snort of disgust. "I'm sorry, but there's something seriously wrong with an industry that issues this much credit without oversight."

"No argument there." Credit card companies were in the business of making money, and the only way they could do that was by issuing credit and taking some risk. But Randy was dead-on about the oversight.

"These companies just sent the cards, which were maxed out almost immediately, and they're still sending late payment notices. I suppose eventually they'll turn the Hickmans over to a credit collection agency."

"Basically we're only investigating because Hickman filed the report about his missing wallet."

"Score one for *Dateline*." Randy frowned. "I don't know about you, but I'm pulling my credit reports from the Big Three pronto. Just to make sure someone isn't scamming on my dime."

Jack cocked a hip on the desk and thumbed through the reports. "Purchases in Texas and New Mexico?"

"And Arizona and Nevada," Randy added. "Four states—one for each card. How's that for systematic?"

Arizona. Damn it. That would feed the talk about Frankie even more.

"Says something about our perp. But how is this possible?" Jack asked, annoyed. "I can't even use credit at a gas pump out of state without my bank leaving twenty messages asking why my purchasing habits have changed."

"That's because you have purchasing habits. These were brand-new credit cards. The purchases were made in the same cities and states as the billing addresses on the accounts. No reason for red flags to start flying. Not yet, anyway. They like it when people max out their cards and have to pay all that interest."

Jack knew what this meant. "We're talking about identity theft."

He also knew of at least one person who would be happy with the news. Gary Trant, Bluestone's mayor. Now the BMPD wouldn't have to turn the investigation over to the U.S. Secret Service.

But Jack's precinct had just stumbled into a hornet's nest. "Our perp is methodical and organized. Shouldn't be too hard to nail him. How did you want to proceed?"

"We'll start with whoever has access to the Hickmans' personal information. That'll be family members—"

"And the Greywacke Lodge employees who found the wallet when Hickman lost it."

Randy nodded. "The most obvious suspects. We've got to look at every staff person who can walk inside the Hickmans' apartment and those who bill for services and insurance."

This brought this investigation around to the exact place Jack didn't want to be.

Greywacke Lodge administration.

And the woman he was interested in.

CHAPTER EIGHT

"I'LL TAKE IT FROM HERE, Otis," Francesca said. "Appreciate the help."

"Any time, Ms. Raffa."

She smiled at the lodge's maintenance supervisor and all-around handyman while hurrying past to open the apartment door. Otis wheeled the luggage carrier into the hallway and headed toward the service elevator.

Francesca shut the door. "There you go, Nonna. You and the china are reunited. Sorry it took so long."

"Not to worry." Nonna shuffled out of the kitchen, where she'd been keeping out of Otis's way. "Everything in its time. I know how busy you've been."

Concetta Cesarini might have come over from Italy as an excited young bride, but sixty some-odd years later, she'd matured into a little Italian granny. Barely brushing five feet, she was all soft edges and knowing smiles beneath a head of white curls. She didn't miss a trick, though, a quality Francesca couldn't believe *she'd* missed all those years ago.

The oblivion of youth.

Nonna had always been a laid-back, understanding sort, thankfully. Anyone less laid-back and understanding might have smothered her problematic granddaughter with a pillow during the turbulent teen years. A quality Francesca was trying hard to emulate with Gabrielle.

With a quick step, she reached out, wrapped her arms around Nonna's slight shoulders and pressed a kiss to the top of her head. "Have I told you lately how much I love you?"

"If memory serves, and it doesn't always, you've been telling me at least once a day since you came home."

Came home. Surprisingly, Francesca wouldn't argue that sentiment. She did feel as if she'd come home. Once she'd hated Bluestone Mountain so much she couldn't have left fast enough. But maybe that urgency had more to do with her feelings of not belonging than anything else. Certainly not with the love her grandmother had shown her while growing up.

"Your memory seems to be working fine. I'm trying to make up for all the days when I wasn't around to tell you."

"Think I'll live that long?"

"Nonna!"

"Don't *Nonna* me, Francesca Celeste Marie. You were gone a long time." Her expression brightened with humor. "But I'll hang on as long as I can. I like having you around. You've grown up to be a wonderful mother. I did my job."

And with that she headed toward the storage containers now propped in the middle of her living room. Swallowing a lump of emotion, Francesca watched Nonna take each small, careful step in embroidered silk slippers, her contentment obvious as she ran bony fingers along the edge of a container.

"Nothing chipped?" she asked.

"Not a thing," Francesca promised. "I can vouch for that personally, since I washed and wrapped each and every piece myself. Gabrielle helped with the bubble wrap. Hence the size of the storage containers. Will they still fit in your closet?"

"We'll make room."

No doubt. Nonna would get that china in the closet if she had to donate half her wardrobe to charity.

Nonna's one-bedroom apartment might be the smallest of the floor plans Greywacke Lodge offered, but it proved to have ample storage space. The containers easily fit in beside Nonna's shoe tree beneath the neatly stacked boxes of beads and sequins she hadn't been able to part with after leaving her workshop.

"How's this look?" Francesca asked as she backed out of the closet and straightened her jacket. "You'll still be able to move around them to get to your coats?"

"No worries." Nonna gave a sigh. "They'll be safe and sound until you find a nice man. I'll give the set to you for your wedding gift. The way I did your mama."

That was a loaded statement in so many different ways. "That's so sweet, Nonna. But I already told you. No men for me right now. I'm too busy being a mom and a director and a granddaughter. I'm quite content. And busy." Francesca eased shut the closet door then sat at the table to enjoy the coffee Nonna had brewed. "How about you? Is it feeling like home yet?"

"Still like a holiday."

"I'm really not surprised. You eat every meal with your friends and play bingo three times a week. It's a party around here." She grinned. "Don't you think you deserve some fun?"

"I do." Nonna smiled. "But you know what the best part is?"

Francesca shook her head.

"Spending time with you and Gabrielle. I'm glad you're back. I wouldn't have wanted to miss my chance to know my great-granddaughter. She's such a delight."

Nonna's big brown eyes grew misty, her smile moist around the edges. Every word was so heartfelt that Francesca grabbed Nonna's hand and gave it a gentle squeeze. There weren't really any words. Or if there were, she didn't have them.

Lifting Nonna's hand, Francesca pressed a kiss to her warm skin, to fingers that had seen so many years of hard work.

"You know." Her voice was a whisper that lingered between them even as she released Nonna's hand. "If you're having second thoughts about this move, you can change your mind. At the rate I'm packing… My offer stands. Live with me and Gab. We can sell the house if you're worried about all the work it needs and can find a place comfortable for all of us to live in."

Nonna met Francesca's gaze and said, "I know."

"Nothing's written in stone with the lodge. You know as well as I do there's a waiting list to get an apartment here, and we keep adding names. If you're not happy—"

"I'm not unhappy, dear." Nonna reached for her coffee cup and brought it to her lips, a slow-motion effort of co-ordination and strength.

"Does not unhappy translate into more happy and less unhappy or the other way around?"

Nonna shrugged. "Both, and neither."

"Is this some Italian dialect I never learned? Would you mind translating?"

"It means that at my age, I need to be practical."

Francesca braced herself, sensing the oncoming reality check and knowing she wasn't going to like it one bit. "You can be practical living with your family."

"I am. That's why I'm here. I came up with this brilliant idea, if you recall."

"The idea is only brilliant if you're happy," she pointed out. "I considered your idea, so I think you should return the favor. I didn't suggest moving in together because I knew you wouldn't take me up on the offer. I offered because I think it's a practical alternative to your brilliant idea."

Nonna raised her cup, whispered, *"Salute,"* before taking another sip. After a moment, she said, "I can't keep up with things the way I did. There's cooking, cleaning, laundry. The lodge takes care of all that now."

"I know, but Gabrielle and I take care of those things at home. You're one extra person. Hardly a lot more work."

"You have a busy job here. Remember that I see how hard you work up close now."

Francesca dismissed her observation with a wave of her hand. "This job is no different than my last job, or the one before that. Except now I run the Hilton for old people instead of a health care facility. Once I settle in, I'll manage my schedule better. Just going to take some time. Oh, and the weather is different, too." She cast a glance out of Nonna's living room window, the open drapes revealing the sloping expanse of snow-covered forest. "Did I mention how much I enjoy warm sunny days?"

But Nonna was on a roll. "The lodge has everything here. Transportation to get me to doctors' appointments and church and shopping. I take an elevator downstairs to the salon to have my hair done. If I lived with you, you'd have to take me everywhere. That would mean time away from Gabrielle and your job. Should I mention that you don't have any life besides your daughter and your job?"

"No."

"I never hear about you spending time with friends."

That would be because her friends were all in Phoenix. "I talk to them all the time. Kimberly's number three on my speed dial. Judith is number four. And Stephanie is number five."

"That's all well and good, but you need friends here."

"I'll make some. Until then, you and Gabrielle are my friends, and I'll do anything you need with pleasure. I've always gotten Gabrielle where she needs to go without any trouble." Or help from her ex. But she kept that thought to herself. "I've been parenting my daughter and running a house for a long time. I can multitask. That's one of the things that makes me good at my job. Besides, Nonna, you've got to remember that I've been caring for *my family* all these years. You'll simply be taking Nicky's place and not creating extra work."

And Nonna could never be as demanding as Nicky had been with his constant discontent that had everything to do with his own stubborn refusal to acknowledge he didn't want to be bothered with anyone's wants and needs but his own.

She didn't share that thought, either.

"Whether or not you're capable isn't the question, dolly. I know you are. But you deserve a life, too. You're young and beautiful. You should have a special man."

Francesca shook her head. "Not now. My daughter is even younger and more beautiful. She needs my attention."

"I won't argue that. Gabrielle deserves your time. I remember what it was like when you were that age. I was always working and missing out on too much of your life. Maybe if I'd been around more…" She let that thought trail off.

"Nonna, please don't go there," Francesca said softly.

The past would always be between them, and it didn't seem to matter what Francesca said. Nonna considered herself responsible. If only her husband hadn't died, then she wouldn't have had to work so much. If only her son and daughter-in-law hadn't died, then Francesca wouldn't have been left alone. If only Francesca had had more supervision, or a more normal family life, or more structure in school….

A lot of *if onlys.*

"Life happened the way it was meant to," Francesca said gently. "If I hadn't made the choices I did, I wouldn't have grown to be who I am. And you just said you like me."

Nonna considered that. "True. But it's also true I need help and I'm only going to need more help in time, not less."

Reality check.

As Francesca opened her mouth to reply, the radio at her waist crackled, a startling interruption that exactly illustrated Nonna's point about the divisions between work and family.

"I'm sorry." She reached for the radio.

"Without your job, dolly, none of us would have a place to live," Nonna shot back.

Francesca scowled. She'd lost this round. "Raffa here."

"Chief Sloan dropped by," Yvette said.

Exactly what she didn't need right now. Although Francesca couldn't decide if she meant revisiting the Case of the Reappearing Wallet or facing Jack. Not when she still hadn't cleared her head of their run-in this morning. What was it about Jack that made her rehash every word they'd said to one another? What was it about him that kept unraveling all her hard-won calm? On the upside, at least she looked and smelled better now.

"I've got to run." She set the demitasse cup back on its saucer. "Have fun reuniting with the china. You're going to have it all to yourself for a while."

"Chief Sloan is here about the captain's wallet?" Nonna asked.

Francesca shrugged. "Won't know until I get downstairs and find out what he wants. But I trust you're supporting my efforts to keep this place sane by not fanning the fires of curiosity."

"Francesca Celeste Marie! As if I would gossip."

Francesca knew this trick. "If you mention Jack, people will start wondering why he came by and speculate. The Hickmans don't need more drama. This situation is dragging on forever. I'm sure the captain would like it done and over, so he's not constantly reminded that he lost his wallet."

Out of that entire rant, Nonna latched on to only one word. *"Jack?"*

"Jack Sloan. The police chief." Francesca hoped this wasn't a symptom of Nonna's forgetfulness. "You've heard of him."

"Of course I've heard of him. Seen him, too. On the TV. He's very handsome."

Francesca wasn't going *there.* "I won't be able to make it for lunch today, I'm afraid. Love you."

Swinging around the wall that separated the kitchen area from the living room, she gave Nonna a kiss.

"Ever forward," she repeated Nonna's oft-spoken words as she walked out the door.

Shoulders back, chin up. Ever forward.

Good advice she intended to follow today because Francesca would have avoided Jack if she could have.

She'd been convinced her awareness of him was nothing but a throwback from years gone by. After all, while everyone in high school had been living the Jack Sloan mystique thing, she'd rebelled—no news there—and missed her chance to build any immunity against lethal charm.

She was a woman with a proven penchant for charming men, and she hadn't dated since high school. The charming rogue had probably scented her vulnerability like smoke on the wind. She was a new face in town, and he was single. It was entirely possible that her own past notoriety was making her seem a lot more interesting than she really was.

Made perfect sense.

But understanding wasn't giving her any control over her reactions to him. She should feel matter-of-fact. Even if she didn't—yet—Francesca knew that Bluestone's golden boy was taboo for a woman intent upon forging a new reputation and life for herself in a place where she had a history. There was nothing low-key about Jack. Whoever became involved with the chief of police would be all over the town's radar.

Nope, definitely not the place for her.

So, Francesca ignored the crazy flutter of excitement deep down inside, and hoped Jack had come to tell her that he'd solved the mystery. Bracing herself, she strode into the reception area of her office to face the man within.

He was still in uniform, only now he'd shed the outerwear and looked the impressive part of a police chief in his crisp blues with all the gold ornamentation. Stars at his throat. Bars on his chest. All that was missing was the flag flying in the background and the national anthem swelling in crescendo.

Francesca wanted to salute, but the impulse vanished as soon as she met Jack's gaze. One glimpse, and she knew he hadn't come to wrap up his investigation.

"I hope I didn't keep you waiting long." She didn't give him a chance to reply but motioned him toward her office. The best offense and all that. "Come in."

"You don't look so happy," she said without preamble once they were behind her closed office door.

"I'm not."

"Is it time to worry about my staff?"

He didn't miss a beat. "It's time to take a look, but with any luck I can spare you the worrying."

Nice of him to offer but Francesca was going to worry, thank you—for a number of reasons. "What can you tell me?"

Chin up. Shoulders back. Ever forward.

She could handle this.

When Jack slid an envelope across the desk, all thoughts evaporated. Francesca recognized the official-looking document before she even reached for it. "Oh, no."

"I need the personnel records of everyone with physical access to the Hickmans' apartment." He held the paper firmly in place when she would have pulled it away, forcing her to lift her gaze to meet his. "Don't worry, Francesca. Your employees aren't the only ones with access to the Hickmans' credit cards."

Staring into this man's face made thinking nearly impossible. "I'm so sorry for the Hickmans. I was really hoping for a speedy resolution."

Jack lifted his hand and let her take the document. "You keep right on hoping. I intend to make that happen."

"I appreciate that." She sought refuge from his gaze inside the subpoena, which appeared to be in order. Would she have expected any less from this man? "So, you want personnel records for everyone with physical access to the Hickmans' apartment. Since the captain's wallet went missing the first time?"

He nodded. "I assume you keep service logs."

"Yes."

"If they're on the property, I want to take them with me. If not, we'll need to make some arrangements."

"They're here." Francesca did not like the sound of this. Jack was well aware that his request would mean dropping everything to comply. She also knew he wouldn't have asked without good reason.

No, she didn't like the sound of this at all.

She pushed away from the desk. "With Yvette's help, we can probably pull everything together fairly quickly."

And she could send him on his way. Right out the door.

Goodbye, Mr. Too Handsome. See you after I've got my head screwed on straight again.

Then Jack gazed up at her, and from this vantage she could see his handsome face from an entirely new perspective. The striking cut of his jaw. The closely cropped hair that made the hard lines of his face almost severe. "Thank you, Francesca."

"Of course, Jack." And she almost sounded normal.

Hightailing it toward the door with Jack in her wake, she stepped out of her office to find… "Nonna?"

"Hello, dolly." Nonna tilted her cheek for a kiss, and Francesca automatically obliged.

"Is everything all right?"

But Nonna was staring at Jack, eyeing him from head to toe with interest.

"You're the police chief." Not a question. She extended her hand, and he brought it to his lips in a move designed to melt hearts. "You're even more handsome than on the news."

"Thank you. You're Francesca's grandmother."

Nonna beamed approval. "You can call me Etta. All my friends do."

"A pleasure then, Etta." Jack's smile had her eating out of the palm of his hand.

For a woman who'd claimed to be slowing down, Nonna had made it down to this office with impressive speed.

"Nonna, I just left you. Is everything okay?"

"No worries, dolly. I wanted to meet *Jack*."

Francesca wasn't sure how to respond to that. Turned out she didn't get a chance anyway because Nonna gave Jack a high-beam smile and told them, "I'll be on my way then. You kids get back to what you were doing."

"Hope to see you again, Etta," Jack said.

"Me, too, Jack. Me, too." Then, with a toss of her white curls, Nonna headed out of the reception area.

No worries? Francesca wished.

CHAPTER NINE

"WE'VE GOT NADA, JACK," Randy complained, shoving a hand through his hair.

Jack spun away from his makeshift desk in Randy's cubicle and met the detective's tired gaze. "Wrong. What we have has just brought us back around to where we started."

Randy snorted in disgust. "It's no wonder they made you chief. Damn diplomat. You're like a little ray of sunshine. *Nada,* Jack. *Nada.*" He scowled. "The Hickmans' family checked out. Both employees who found the wallet checked out. Emelina checked out. The other cleaning lady checked out. The maintenance man. The pest control guy and five different food service people. Say what you want. We've spent two days chasing our tails."

"We've eliminated all the obvious suspects."

"And wound up with *nada.*" Randy didn't bother trying to hide his frustration.

"You didn't think this would be easy, did you?" If this case were going to be easy, Jack wouldn't be working it. This meant he wouldn't have met the beautiful director of Greywacke Lodge. Funny how things worked out sometimes. Wasn't that what Frankie had said? "Look at these lists of purchases. I don't see service people jetting around the country buying high-ticket items then racing back to Bluestone to clock in."

"My money was on the family."

That got Jack thinking. "You know, Francesca mentioned Captain Hickman had been in the hospital recently. He also did a stint at the nursing center for rehab. We need to check out who had his wallet during those stays."

"Way ahead of you, chief." Randy's suddenly upbeat tone made Jack brace himself. "You're spending too much time parading around in those dress blues. Thought of that already. Had an answer within an hour."

"And," Jack prompted.

"Hickman's daughter took all her father's personal items when she met her parents in the emergency room. She brought everything home and locked it in her own fire-safety box. Only she and her husband have keys, and both of them checked out."

"Interesting that she didn't give those things to her mother."

"Her mother's loopier than her father." Randy looked pleased with himself. "The daughter's words, not mine."

Jack sank back into his chair and rubbed his temples, where a dull headache lurked. He definitely should have caught that sooner. But Randy was wrong about why Jack was so distracted.

The only reason he'd even remembered the captain's hospital stay and subsequent rehab was because Frankie had mentioned it and he'd been busy thinking about Frankie.

The way she'd looked the day she'd arrived to run interference for her residents with the police, all friendly professionalism and no-nonsense business.

The way her cheeks had flushed in embarrassed pleasure when she'd run into him at Wal-Mart.

The way her gray eyes had flashed when she'd thought he'd been accusing her residents of…what had she said that day? *Bonnie and Clyde.*

He almost smiled. He might have appreciated the humor more had his preoccupation with Frankie not had him missing the obvious. Jack was many things—single-minded and career focused among them—but he was not sloppy. Right now he needed to be on the top of his game because this investigation needed to be yesterday's news. He wanted to explore why one lovely woman was preoccupying him in a way he'd never been preoccupied before.

The first measures of the national anthem blared over the background noise of the station and into his thoughts. Jack glanced in the direction of the sound as Randy snatched his cell phone off his desk.

"My son," he said in explanation as he snapped the phone opened and asked, "Hey, what's up?"

Jack glanced back at the stacks of information covering the table that served as his workstation. Scanning the hard copies of collected data, he pulled the Greywacke Lodge resident list from the stack and tuned out the sound of Randy's conversation.

The time had come to refocus the investigation, and the place to start was with this list. Using his laptop, he pulled up Credit Alert, a national law-enforcement database with a feature that would grant him access to a view of a person's credit status, a handy tool for law-enforcement agencies, even if it didn't provide detailed information.

A superficial view was all Jack needed right now, just enough information to know whether or not he needed to worry about the one commonality of the names on the list.

Greywacke Lodge.

With any luck, clearing names off the residents' list would guide the investigation in the proper direction. Preferably *away* from the lodge and its staff.

Methodically, Jack keyed the names into the search function, starting on page one of the alphabetical list.

Lawrence Abbott of D-712.

No match found.

Ellen Acton of A-401.

No match found.

Rebekah Anderson of I-114

No match found.

Joseph Angelica of B-603.

No match found.

By the time Jack had gotten through the *C*s with no matches, he began to breathe easier. Then he hit the *D*s. The first two were okay then…

Richard Drew of F-327.

Delinquent.

One hit did not an identity theft make, but it did have Jack sitting up straighter in the chair, keying names in faster, exhaling a breath each and every time the words flashed on his screen: *No match found.*

Evangeline Humble of G-611

Delinquent.

Robert Garfield of F-707.

Delinquent.

Nicholas Montague of C-505.

Delinquent.

Sylvia Owen of I-532.

Delinquent.

Neil Patrick of A-204.

Delinquent.

Eleven in all and Judge Pierce among them. With a sick feeling, Jack pulled up the Clearinghouse Alert, a database that coordinated nationwide law-enforcement efforts about active investigations, and he was still staring dully at the monitor when Randy ended his call.

"Damn kid is being deployed to Afghanistan next week." Randy ran his hand through his hair, clearly rattled. "He's thrilled, Jack. Can you believe it? I didn't even know what to say. I suppose it was just a matter of time, but hell… His mother is going to melt down."

Jack dragged his attention from the computer, forced himself to face Randy and focus. "You okay?"

"No, I'm not okay. My kid's heading off to war. Who the hell knows if he'll make it back in one piece?" Randy exhaled sharply. "I'm not okay, but I am proud. He's twenty-one and planning to save the world. Do you even remember what it felt like to be on fire?"

Jack glanced back at the computer display. Not so long ago, cracking a case wide would have had him on fire.

Randy must have taken the continued silence as his answer because he gave a short laugh. "Hell. Me, either. Too damn long ago. What I want to know is how I'm supposed to sleep at night knowing he's over there dodging artillery?"

Jack stared at Randy, not exactly surprised that behind the competence and sarcasm was a father who loved his son. Randy didn't often share that glimpse of himself. He either felt comfortable around Jack in a way he didn't with most of his coworkers, or he was really rattled. Jack guessed the latter.

"If it's any help," he said, "I can give you something to take your mind off your troubles."

"What's that?"

He tossed down a sheath of papers in front of Randy. "How about eleven hits on the resident list?"

Randy's eyes widened. "No shit? We can wipe all the service people off the suspect list. That'll narrow things down a lot."

And point them in the direction of the people with access to the residents' personal information.

Greywacke Lodge administration.

CHAPTER TEN

"I CAN'T BELIEVE HOW TALENTED that daughter of yours is," Yvette said casually while striding through the office to place yet another folder on the precarious stack of paperwork that had taken root on the side of the desk.

Francesca glanced up from Susanna's proposal to change service providers and said automatically, "Thanks." Then she met Yvette's smiling gaze and dragged her thoughts out of the paperwork. "That was random."

Yvette laughed. "Not really. I just ran into her."

"Really? Where?"

"In the restaurant."

Obviously Yvette assumed that the elder generation Raffa had a bead on what was happening with the younger generation. Not so. Francesca glanced at the clock. Gabrielle should have been on the school bus headed home right now.

Yvette quickly figured out her announcement was coming as a surprise and, coward that she was, hightailed it out of the office with a hastily muttered, "Look at the time."

Francesca stared at the closing door with a frown. With a regretful gaze at the tottering stack of work, she deemed discovering what was going on with her daughter more important than making a dent in that never-ending pile.

Francesca left the office to find that Yvette wasn't even at her desk. Probably hiding in the copy room.

Clearly something was up with Gabrielle, that much was a given. Ashokan High was within biking distance of the lodge, but since Gabrielle hadn't brought her bike from Phoenix, she must have walked from school. Had she missed the bus?

That was a no-brainer.

If she'd missed the bus, she would need a ride home, which would have left her two choices—either calling Francesca for that ride or dealing with the situation on her own.

Getting a ride from school wasn't an issue as Gabrielle well knew. The fact that she'd already needed two rides this week…well, apparently she didn't want to deal with the questions that her actions would invite.

Something was up. Another mystery.

Strolling past the restaurant windows, Francesca glanced inside. The lodge hosted a monthly tea. The activities director occasionally hired professional entertainment, but more often than not, she encouraged residents to showcase their talents.

As a result the monthly tea was a well-attended event, so well attended that they'd established an arts and entertainment council whose sole function was seeking out the talent hiding in the lodge and keeping it from getting dusty.

Today, showcased on the small stage, was none other than…*her daughter.*

Gabrielle wasn't performing alone. Rather, she was seated beside Eddie Shaw, guitar player extraordinaire, who accompanied her on what Francesca believed to be a mandolin.

The audience sat in small clusters around tables decorated with fresh flowers and red and white tulle. They sipped coffee and tea, nibbled cookies and scones and enjoyed the music, an intricate piece that must have taken a good bit of rehearsing.

Likely the reason Gabrielle had been missing the bus.

Making her way to the restaurant's main entrance, Francesca hovered in the doorway to hear the performance better.

Gabrielle was very talented. She'd been playing the violin since second grade and had routinely earned superior status at solo and ensemble competitions. And every year she'd been invited to perform in All-County and All-State ensembles.

But guitar was her passion. She had her head filled with bands and concerts, not unlike her mother at that age, and to Francesca's sorrow, Gabrielle hadn't joined orchestra in high school because she'd wanted to use any free time left after schoolwork and social life to practice.

Of course, guitar had taken precedence to everything.

Francesca didn't enter the restaurant until the performance ended to appreciative applause and the guests began to chitchat among their groups. She spotted Nonna seated with Auntie Pippa and zigzagged through the tables to a chorus of polite greetings that announced her presence.

Gabrielle was primed and ready by the time Francesca reached the table. "Hello, Mother."

"Hello, dear. Miss the bus?"

Once upon a time, Gabrielle would have had the grace to look abashed when caught in the act. Now she gave an amused laugh. "Not exactly. Been practicing with Mr. Shaw."

She slanted her gaze toward the man who was now making his way to them, greeting his crowd of appreciative admirers. With bright blue eyes, a shock of thick white hair and a quick grin, Eddie Shaw looked the part of celebrity heartthrob. He was a charmer in every sense of the word given how often Francesca encountered him chatting with women in the hallways. Married and widowed alike.

As far as Francesca was concerned there were two types of charmers—charming gentlemen and charming rogues. Eddie Shaw was the latter. Just like her ex-husband had been. Completely engaging as long as no one expected anything more than wining and dining and romance. She didn't have any trouble imagining her ex-husband at Eddie's age, still the life of the party.

Jack, too.

Only Jack's future wasn't any of her business. If he wanted to spend his retirement charming the ladies, that was his prerogative. She wished him well.

Stubbornly fixing her attention on the room, Francesca pushed all thoughts of Jack from her head. Seemed like every thought circled to him.

"Isn't it awesome?" Gabrielle tilted the neck of the guitar from the case.

There was no missing that this guitar was in an entirely different league from the five-hundred dollar model Francesca had bought her daughter several years ago.

"It's lovely," she agreed.

"Custom-made for me by Señor Mendoza in Seville," Mr. Shaw said as if Francesca would understand what that meant.

Gabrielle obviously did because she gave an ecstatic sigh as Mr. Shaw launched into praise for Gabrielle's talent.

"Eddie has offered to give Gabrielle lessons since she hasn't found a new instructor yet," Nonna said. "Here, dolly. Sit down. You should try these pecan sandies. You look thin."

Not according to the scale. But she accepted the cookie anyway to avoid a debate. "That's a very generous offer, Mr. Shaw. Gabrielle and I can discuss it when we get home."

"Just let me know. Ladies." Mr. Shaw tipped his hat,

those blue eyes twinkling. "Now if you'll excuse me. I see Fanny flagging me down. Great job, Gabrielle. We'll work on some Count Basie next." With that he lifted her hand to his mouth in a gallant gesture before sauntering off with a jaunty, if somewhat slow-motion stride.

"Such a nice man," Nonna said.

"He's an old hound dog," Minnie Moorehead commented from a nearby table, obviously having overheard every word of the conversation. "I wouldn't leave my daughter alone with him."

Gabrielle slanted her chair so her back faced Minnie and stuck her finger in her mouth, as if the very idea of *that* sort of impropriety was enough to make her gag.

Francesca scowled. "I'll take it under advisement."

"You heed me well, girl. I don't want to tell you how he propositioned me in the elevator."

"Minnie," Nonna said, horrified. "He didn't?"

Gabrielle started up feigned twitching, and Francesca scowled harder.

"He did. Hound dog. Mind my words, all of you." Minnie shook her head, oblivious to Gabrielle's facial theatrics. "Now what about you, Francesca? How's it going with your new man?"

"I don't have time enough to clear my desk, let alone find time for a man," Francesca said.

"No wonder your grandmother is so worried about you."

Francesca turned her scowl on Nonna, who informed her, "He's a bachelor, dolly. I asked."

"Asked whom?"

"Why Dottie, of course," Mr. Butterfield announced from the table to the other side of them, proving that everyone within earshot was listening to this conversation. "She's the authority around here. Knows everything about everyone."

Dottie leaned around her husband and peered myopically from thick, large-rimmed glasses. "I'm well connected."

"I see," Francesca said, wishing she didn't.

"Into everyone's business, more's the like," Mr. Butterfield said under his breath. Unfortunately, as his hearing wasn't quite what it could have been, his whisper managed to carry a good ten feet in every direction.

"*Well connected,*" Dottie Butterfield repeated. "I've known Jack's family since long before his daddy was in knickers. In fact, Jack's granddaddy was sweet on me in our time." She fixed a glacial expression on her husband. "The life I might have had if I'd have stuck with him. Youth is wasted on the young."

Mr. Butterfield just grunted, clearly unwilling to tempt fate with a reply.

Dottie had the floor and ran with it. "Jack's a good boy from a good family. He's doing a lovely job running the police department, and from what I hear, the whole town's happy with him in charge. He's a man of his word like his daddy and granddaddy. The kind of boy you can bank on."

Nonna nodded approvingly. "And he's a bachelor."

"Sure is," Dottie said. "Never once been married."

"Not one of those homosexuals, is he?" Minnie asked in a voice loud enough to catch the attention of a few more tables. "Nice-looking boy like that. Pity."

"He is not homosexual, Minnie," Dottie stated emphatically. "He hasn't found the right girl to settle with yet. That's what his mama told me, anyway."

Nonna caught Francesca's gaze and winked. "A handsome bachelor."

"Who's not homosexual." Minnie nodded approvingly.

Gabrielle leaned forward and patted Francesca's hand. "Nonna's right, Mom. He sounds perfect. Not gay. No child support. He'll be able to afford me. Unless you want me to go back to Phoenix and live with Dad."

"Gabrielle Concetta Cecilia." Francesca glowered.

"There's more to life than work, dolly," Nonna said. "There should be more to *your* life."

"Exactly when would I have time for more *life* when my hands are full with you two?" The comedy team of grandmother who thought she knew everything and teenager who was sure she did.

"Read my lips, people. *Not interested.*" Francesca smiled so hard it hurt, reminding herself that they were worried about *her.* Since she was the one who usually did the worrying, she should be grateful. "So thank you all very much for your generous advice." *Very* generous. *Abundantly* generous. "Now I see folks are starting to leave. Nonna, why don't Gabrielle and I walk you back to your apartment?"

Gabrielle popped out of her seat as if she'd been ejected. "I've got to take the guitar back to Mr. Shaw's apartment."

"Fine, then straight back to Nonna's."

She muttered an agreement and packed Señor Mendoza's custom-made guitar back in its case while Nonna plucked a variety of cookies from a platter and wrapped them in a napkin.

"For coffee later."

Of course, she squirreled away enough cookies to serve half the fourth floor, but Francesca merely offered to carry them and steered Nonna in the direction of the door.

"You asked me not to start up speculation about the captain's wallet, dolly. And I didn't. I diverted people."

As far as plans went, this wasn't the best Francesca had ever heard. But she was impressed with Nonna's clarity of thought to point that out.

"I did mention Jack's a bachelor, didn't I?"

"You most definitely did."

So much for clarity of thought. Nonna's or her own. She was absolutely, positively not going to start thinking about Jack *the bachelor.* "I'll take it under advisement. That's the best I can do. I'm glad you care."

"Of course I care, dolly. I love you."

Francesca didn't say another word as the elevator whisked them up to the fourth floor and they walked the short distance down the hallway to Nonna's door, where she pressed the lumpy pile of cookies into her grandmother's hands.

"Gabrielle should be along any minute," she said. "I'm heading back to work so I won't run late tonight. I'll collect my daughter when it's time to go."

Nonna kissed her goodbye, and Francesca headed to the stairs, needing a few quiet minutes to collect herself.

She didn't question how much Nonna cared, but she had to figure out some way to reassure her grandmother that she was happiest as a single woman. If and when the time ever came for romance again, maybe after Gabrielle had gone off to college, Francesca would consider what sort of man she wanted.

But she would definitely steer clear of men like Jack, who could melt chocolate with a glance. Francesca wanted a man who wanted to be in a partnership, a man who understood that it took two people to weather life's ups and downs. She wanted someone who would have her back when she was feeling pounded on and someone she could care for without worrying that he'd take advantage.

She didn't buy Dottie Butterfield's explanation for Jack's bachelorhood. Not for a second. Charming, gorgeous man like him would have a world of possibilities to choose from. But Jack probably didn't have any interest in family life. Wouldn't be uncommon for such a charming man.

And if that was the case, then Francesca gave him credit

for living his life on his terms. There was no rule that said people had to get married and have kids. Family life was a gift she'd learned to appreciate after having a daughter of her own. Some men—and women for that matter—weren't interested in making those sorts of commitments to other people. Nothing wrong with that.

There was something wrong with people who tried to milk the best from both worlds. A family meant seeing to another's needs before one's own sometimes. Heck, a lot of the time. Men who weren't willing to do their share in the family only made life heartbreaking for everyone around them.

She knew that firsthand.

CHAPTER ELEVEN

"I'M AVAILABLE, YVETTE," Susanna said into the intercom. "Tell Francesca she can come now."

Susanna braced herself for the door to open. This unexpected visit must be about the changes she'd proposed to the property's service provider. If Frankie denied her proposal without any negotiation whatsoever, her reasoning would have to be personal. True, the property hadn't been hardwired all that long ago, but they stood to save considerably by making the switch. And those numbers would mean a great deal in this economy.

Hopefully Frankie wouldn't get in the way of Susanna doing her job, but she honestly wouldn't be surprised. She'd been waiting for the other shoe to drop ever since walking through the door of Northstar Corporate to meet her newest director.

Maybe Frankie was pissed off because she'd been ostracized all those years ago. She could have been biding her time to establish her credibility before using her position to make Susanna's life miserable as payback for past sins.

Kids could be so brutal. Even worse when they were in groups, especially with Karan as the ringleader. But the ugliness had worked both ways. Frankie had made herself an easy target with her attitude. She'd never once backed down to any of them, which had invited a lot more animosity. An unhealthy circle that had fed the enmity on both sides.

Everyone involved had a responsibility in those situations. She'd tried to explain that to her son, Brandon, after his latest run-in with Trevor McGraw, the boy who'd been bullying him on the baseball field since T-ball. Sometimes Brandon stood up for himself. Sometimes not. Either way, the situation always took a tremendous amount of emotional energy for both Susanna and her son.

Yeah, kids could definitely be brutal.

When a knock sounded, Susanna called, "Come in."

Frankie appeared, her professional demeanor cranked up to high. She stood just inside the doorway, and Susanna didn't bother inviting her to sit down.

"I'm calling a staff meeting," Frankie said. "I have some news, and since it involves some of your people, I didn't want you to be sandbagged when I make the announcement."

Not about her proposal then. Susanna wasn't sure what to make of that. "What's up?"

"I got a call from the police, and it seems they've eliminated the suspects with physical access to the captain's wallet. They're narrowing their investigation to people with access to our residents' personal information."

"Why?"

"They've discovered suspicious charges on a number of our other residents' cards and suspect an identity theft scam."

Susanna could only stare. "How many residents?"

"Twelve so far."

Her mouth dropped open in surprise, and she blurted, "You have got to be kidding me?"

"I wish."

"The police think someone here is responsible?"

Frankie inclined her head, expression grim. "I guess so. We're the most obvious connection, anyway."

That's when it clicked, and the pieces all fell into place. Frankie had said she had news about Susanna's people in accounting. And her heartbeat stuttered in her chest.

"My department is the most obvious connection." Her voice was a strangled whisper.

Frankie held up her hand. "They're looking at everyone here with access. That includes your department, but you know as well as I do there are others. Not only here in senior living but the nursing center. They'll be looking at everyone."

Frankie included, Susanna realized. As director of operations, she had oversight on everything that happened around here. Yet she didn't make a move to leave, probably wanted to give Susanna a chance for this bombshell to sink in.

Susanna forced herself to take a breath. Then another. "Do you know what kind of numbers we're talking about?"

"No clue with the newest victims," Frankie said softly. "I do know the theft on the Hickmans credit was reaching into the high six digits."

Susanna's breath caught in her chest. "Oh, heaven forbid."

Frankie nodded and the silence fell heavily between them, filled with implications that were staggering.

Reputations. Careers. Futures.

Susanna still couldn't get her brain around it all, not while meeting Frankie's grim gaze, and that weird, somehow companionable silence growing between them as if they were watching an avalanche descend toward them.

She had the craziest impulse to say something that would cross the carefully erected boundaries of professionalism, to commiserate about a turn of events that impacted them both on so many levels. Whatever else she and Frankie had been in the past, in the present they were united for their residents.

"Did Jack tell you about this?"

Frankie nodded.

The first tiny bit of relief began to penetrate Susanna's shock. The detective on the case, the one who wasn't from around here, wouldn't have a clue. He knew she would never turn a blind eye to any wrongdoing in her department. He knew she would never jeopardize the job that supported her family.

"What do I need to do?" she asked automatically. "Let me know. I'll help however I can."

"Chief Sloan asked to be at the meeting. I'm sure he or Detective Tanner will let us know what they need. We'll go from there and hope for the best." She glanced at her watch. "Twenty minutes in the conference room."

Her gaze trailed across the photos propped on the desk beside the computer display—Brooke and Brandon posing in front of the Christmas tree barely two months ago. Susanna thought Frankie might comment, but she seemed to think better of it and turned to leave. "See you there."

Frankie was halfway through the door before Susanna finally snapped out of her daze.

"Frankie," she said, "I appreciate the heads-up."

If Frankie noticed the unintentional use of that long-ago nickname, she made no indication and simply nodded. The door closed. Minutes passed before Susanna realized she was still staring at the door.

Then she reached for her cell phone.

She wasn't sure why. Maybe she needed to hear a familiar voice. Maybe she needed to talk to help her process this news. Then again, maybe Susanna just needed Karan to reassure her that Jack would never suspect her of *stealing*.

After depressing Karan's speed dial number, Susanna paced her breathing while the call connected. It rang, and rang, and when she expected to hear a voice mail message, she heard Karan pick up.

"Hello?" the groggy voice asked.

Susanna glanced at her watch. Only Karan. "It's worth waking up for. Trust me."

"Dish." Not a hint of grogginess left.

Susanna could imagine Karan sitting bolt upright in bed, wide-awake, ready for the scoop. For as much as Karan tried to act above it all, she was predictable. She'd deny it, but she still thrived on drama. Too much free time on her hands, Susanna decided, then quickly explained.

"So, Frankie's a suspect." Karan didn't sound remotely surprised.

"So am I." How could Karan miss the point of this call? "The first place Jack will look is at my department. Everything runs through accounting. *Everything.*"

Billable services. Accounts receivable. Direct deposits. Her department ran credit checks for residents who applied to the lodge. They were the accounting department, for goodness sake. That's all they dealt with. Money, money and more money.

"Oh, Suze, be real," Karan scoffed. "There's no way Jack will think you had anything to do with fleecing the old folks. Even if Frankie wasn't around."

Karan, in her roundabout way, had come through, and that anxiety deep inside Susanna quieted. She'd had nothing to do with theft in any way, shape or form, but life didn't always play fair. She'd been learning that the hard way the past few years. She and Skip had followed the rules.

They hadn't waited to live their dream—family life. A house with a white picket fence. Little League and Girl Scouts. Life had graciously obliged—up to a point.

She sighed heavily. "It's my department, Karan. It won't

matter if I'm innocent. If one of my people are caught breaking the law, then I'm guilty because I let it happen on my watch. My reputation is on the line here."

"You're not talking petty theft," Karan pointed out. "And you're not stupid. You'd have suspected something if someone was running a scam right under your nose."

Would she? She'd been so busy keeping up with her work. After all, along with the title of chief financial officer had come not only a substantial salary increase but a lot of new challenges. She'd been enjoying those challenges for the most part, but add to the new job, her solo parenting gig, money stresses, an active family and her in-laws.

Skip's parents had been devastated by their only son's death. They could be tremendously helpful by showing up to root for Brandon at ball games and taking Brooke on daylong shopping expeditions to the mall.

But there was also a shadow side to their involvement. They called at least once a day to check in and see what was going on with the kids. They showed up on the weekends unexpectedly for dinner or to attend church service or to watch movies. Susanna understood how important that connection was to all of them, but those phone calls and visits added more responsibility in her already jam-packed days.

Stupid? No, she wasn't. Distracted? Yes. Would she have noticed a problem? Or would she have missed it completely in the frenzy of her days when her attention was scattered in a hundred different directions?

"Suze, listen to me," Karan admonished over the connection, pulling Susanna from the downward spiral of her thoughts. "Stop dwelling on worst-case scenario. I know you. I know exactly what you're doing."

Karan's firm tone came like a mental slap in the face. "You're right. *You're right,*" Susanna said more firmly.

"That's exactly what I'm doing. I know I'm not involved in any identity theft scam, and I don't think any of my people are, either."

"There you go. No worries then. You have enough to worry about without adding this to the list. Stop stressing."

"You're right."

"Of course I am" came the fast reply.

Susanna smiled. She did have a lot on her plate. Rearing her family alone. No college or retirement money left to fall back on. She was barely scraping together the mortgage each month even with this salary increase. Was it any wonder she was near the point of hyperventilation? She wouldn't sleep well until Jack found out who had been *fleecing the old folks*.

"Thanks," she whispered into the phone, and meant it.

Karan laughed. "Don't mention it. You're in good hands with Jack. I shouldn't have to remind you. But I'm thinking… Maybe I should swing by and visit you at work one of these days. Sounds like you need a little moral support. And I wouldn't mind seeing what Frankie the Felon looks like all grown up. I mean, before I can pull up her mug shot on the Internet. Those photos are always so unflattering."

"Karan!" Susanna's feeling of relief evaporated as quickly as it had appeared.

Moral support? More likely taking advantage of another chance to bash Frankie. Honestly, Karan was a dog with a bone.

Susanna found herself annoyed. Maybe because Frankie had made the effort not to sandbag her at the meeting. Susanna wasn't sure. She only knew that she didn't like the drama of high school bleeding into her professional world any more than she liked feeling disloyal to her friend.

CHAPTER TWELVE

WHEN FRANCESCA OPENED HER eyes to glance at the alarm clock, she knew this day wasn't off to the best of starts. Not only had she slept through any hope of a morning run, she would barely have time to shower and dress for work.

Bolting out of bed, she winced when her bare feet hit the cold floor. She shouldn't be surprised she'd overslept. Ever since Jack had informed the lodge's administration that most of them were suspects in an identity theft case, she hadn't been able to think of much else.

Even when she should be sleeping. She tossed and turned and when she wasn't obsessing about being a suspect, she was obsessing about being the suspect of the man running the investigation, a man whose handsome face she could see when she closed her eyes no matter how hard she tried to block it out.

And while she wasn't surprised about oversleeping—anything was preferable to the reality of what she would face in the office—she was surprised that Gabrielle hadn't awakened her. She should have been getting ready for school by now.

Francesca found her daughter burrowed warmly beneath the covers in her room, the cell phone she used for an alarm buried with her. Only her hair peeked out from the pillows and blankets. Francesca couldn't help but smile.

"Move over, toasty girl," she whispered, sliding into the warm cocoon.

Gabrielle only sighed and rolled to her side, one of the rare times she didn't protest a display of affection. She'd never protest "spoons," anyway, a beloved tradition from childhood she hadn't given up yet, along with green blankie, the handmade baby quilt that had weathered childhood with her.

Francesca smoothed the threadbare blanket where it had balled up in a makeshift pillow, unable to resist stroking the wispy curls at her daughter's temple.

"Sleeping through school today?" she whispered. "We're running late."

Gabrielle gave a semiconscious groan. "Don't care."

"Me, either." Letting her eyes drift shut, Francesca gave into the lure of the warmth, unable to face another day of turning over data to the police to assist the investigation.

If the extra workload didn't kill off her staff, the extra emotions would. The reactions had been running the gamut from disbelief to fear. And while everyone, Francesca was proud to note, interacted professionally with the police, behind the scenes was another story. The administrative offices had turned into a pressure cooker of tension. They couldn't discuss the case. Not with each other. Not with the residents—the *victims*. "Let's both skip today," she suggested.

That got Gabrielle's approval. Nestling closer she reached up to pull Francesca's arm around her in a familiar move that melted Francesca's heart.

How many more times would she get to spoon with her beautiful, growing-up-so-fast daughter before college and adulthood got in the way?

Gabrielle had never liked sleeping alone as an infant. Not in her crib. Not in her toddler bed. Not in her Disney princess bedroom. Francesca had never minded, and the years since had been filled with spoons. In Gabrielle's bed or Francesca's, didn't matter which, during childhood illnesses and upsets, or whenever Francesca simply needed time with her daughter after exhausting days filled with work and school and familial responsibilities.

Now she snuggled closer, fighting a battle to stay awake. She wasn't about to miss a second of this moment, an unexpected gift. Or a moment spent wrapped in the comfy arms of denial. When was the last time they'd spooned?

"We can watch *Lord of the Rings*. All three" came the sleepy suggestion just as Francesca was dangerously close to drifting off. "And eat ice cream."

"That sounds so good." Francesca heaved a resigned sigh. "I wish I could."

"You can." Gabrielle snuggled back until Francesca's face was buried in the silky curls. "Don't go. Stay with me. We'll have fun."

Barely functioning sanity wasn't much help here. Not when Gabrielle was right. Spending time together blowing off the world would be fun. *So much more* fun than facing what awaited her in the office today.

"I can't abandon the ship." No matter how much she wanted to. "I'm totally ready for a *Lord of the Rings* marathon, though. This weekend? We'll hole up and blow off the world."

"Well, I'm not going to school." Gabrielle sounded prickly.

"Why not?"

"Head hurts."

Francesca slipped her hand over Gabrielle's forehead, tried to gauge her temperature, which was entirely impossible when they were burrowed in this cocoon.

Gabrielle pulled away, and the heavenly moment was over. Reality intruded. Her daughter was fifteen again.

"I'm not sick, Mom. I just don't feel good."

"Do you feel like you're coming down with something?" Now that Francesca thought about it, Gabrielle had gone to bed unusually early last night.

Gabrielle shrugged.

"What about school?"

"No problem. I'll get the notes online."

Francesca didn't resist. She'd give Gabrielle a chance to sleep off whatever the problem was and hope she fought it off. And if her daughter simply needed a mental health day…well, she'd been working hard to keep her grades up. She knew better than anyone whether or not her schedule could handle an absence. And the consequences if it couldn't.

"Okay, pup. Sleep. I'll lock you in and turn on the security. I want you to text me when you wake up, okay. I want to know how you're feeling."

Gabrielle nodded. "Call school. I won't be able to exempt if I have an unexcused absence."

At this stage of the game, life was all about keeping up attendance for the clever incentive of exempting exams of choice. Usually anything math or science related.

"I'll call." With a sigh of profound regret, Francesca kissed Gabrielle's cheek and slipped out of bed, smiling when she saw the tiny smile on her daughter's face.

Life could be so, *so* good.

She was sailing out the door in record time, nursing her first sips of black coffee as she drove to the lodge. There'd been snow during the night, which had made a mess of the roads. The plows never made it up the mountain until later in the day, after they'd cleared the town proper. But without the trip to the school, she made it to work barely noticeably late, where Yvette greeted her with some unexpectedly pleasant news.

"Your grandmother called. She made lasagna for last night's pinochle tournament. She saved some for you, so don't eat lunch in the restaurant."

Francesca skidded to a stop in the doorway. "You go, Nonna. Something to look forward to today."

"You're going to share, aren't you?" Yvette asked. "This place has been like working in the seventh circle of hell since Chief Sloan brought the good news. Rachel's already been in this morning with an invitation to a staff tea. It's at three in the break room. Be there or miss the cookies."

"Really? I don't remember hearing about any tea."

"That's because she just added to the calendar about 8:01 this morning." Yvette shrugged. "She wants to raise morale."

"That's a good thing," Francesca said. "Exactly what an activities director should be doing."

"Yeah, right. Easy for her to be all chipper. She's not on the suspect list." Yvette looked as surly as she sounded. "So I do get some lasagna, right?"

"I'm thinking about it. I might need every one of those carbs to keep me awake."

"I know what you mean." Yvette collapsed back in her chair in a clearly feigned display of weakness. "I'm relapsing with that horrible flu. I might have to take a personal day and leave you alone to deal with the phones."

Apparently Francesca wasn't the only one who thought work sounded about as fun as an infectious disease today. Despite the tea. "Wench."

"I might be able to make it to five if I can look forward to a yummy lunch. Y'know, something homemade and delicious that'll fuel me through the long afternoon until I can sugar up at Rachel's tea."

"You win, then." There was no battle to fight here. Not when it meant answering the phones.

Yvette smiled slyly. "Your grandmother makes the best."

"Medicinal, too," she said drily. Not only for Yvette, but for herself. Leave it to Nonna to provide something to look forward to. Not only with the promise of lunch, but with the interest and effort cooking had entailed. Lasagna translated into a lot of work with all the care and skill Nonna gave it. And she hadn't forgotten to turn the stove off, since the lodge was still standing.

The telephone beeped an electronic greeting, and with that sly smile still on her lips, Yvette reached for the handset.

Francesca headed into her office, telling herself to look on the bright side. Sharing lasagna meant also sharing the four pounds she would have gained from eating all those carbs. That thought appeased her a little.

Diving into a stack of paperwork, she started on the reports that needed to be in Northstar's corporate office by the end of the week and didn't resurface until Yvette put a call through from Ashokan High School.

"Damn." Francesca depressed the flashing button that connected her to the call. "Hello, this is Ms. Raffa."

"Beth Fairweather, Gabrielle's AP Euro teacher."

"Oh, no." Francesca groaned. "I forgot to call in."

And if an unexcused absence jeopardized Gabrielle's ability to exempt exams, Francesca was in deep trouble.

"So you do know she's not at school today?" Beth said.

"I do. She wasn't feeling well this morning."

"I'm not surprised. I suggested she talk to you about what happened yesterday, but when she didn't show up for class and wasn't listed as excused…well, I thought I'd call. I'm relieved she didn't skip."

Every flag on Francesca's parental flagpole started flapping. "No. I gave her permission to stay home. But she didn't say anything about yesterday. What happened?"

"Kids, I'm afraid." There was a sigh on the other end of

the line. "Apparently a few students shared some news with the rest of the class and got everyone talking about Gabrielle."

"News about what?"

"A police investigation happening where you work. I walked in when they were telling everyone you were the main suspect in the case. Not in quite those exact words, I'm afraid."

Francesca closed her eyes against a sudden wave of nausea. "How did you handle it?"

"I didn't write referrals. Unfortunately, school policy doesn't consider gossip a prosecutable offense. But I did pull the two instigators from class and gave them an earful about gossip and unkindness. I let them know what will happen if they pull anything like this in my class again. I wish I could say they'll take my words to heart, but considering the source...I think Gabrielle might have been more upset than she let on."

Francesca forced herself to breathe deeply, to dispel the sick feeling that accompanied a creepy sense of déjà vu. She remembered exactly what it felt like to be the target of ugliness in a classroom, to be a target for kids who wanted to belittle, demean and amuse themselves at her expense.

No wonder Gabrielle hadn't felt well today.

"I'm so glad you called." Francesca had to force the words out. "I had no clue there was any trouble. Gab and I do need to discuss this. Not only what happened in class yesterday, but the investigation. I understood the police were keeping everything low-key, so it didn't occur to me she'd hear about it." She fought the urge to defend herself, hated that she felt this way when she'd done nothing wrong.

"Life in a small town." Beth sounded resigned. "I'm sure everything will work out. But if you wouldn't mind letting Gabrielle know I won't allow another repeat performance in my classroom, I'd appreciate it."

"I certainly will."

"Oh, and please tell her we'll be having a surprise quiz on chapter seventeen tomorrow. She doesn't want to miss it if she plans on keeping the first desk."

The high point of the first semester at Ashokan had been Ms. Fairweather's incentive program. The highest grades in the class commandeered the first row of desks, and Gabrielle had been excited and proud every time she managed to keep a place in that coveted row. This much Francesca did know even if she'd missed everything else.

"Beth, may I ask you a question?"

"Of course."

"Has Gabrielle been having trouble with the students in your class before this? To my knowledge this is one of her favorite classes."

"I'm glad to hear that. I certainly enjoy her. She's a breath of fresh air. Intelligent. Motivated. Funny." There was a smile in her voice. "I haven't noticed any trouble, but she doesn't seem to be making friends easily. She sticks to herself. Is that typical for her?"

"Not really. I wouldn't call her a social butterfly, but she had her fair share of friends in Phoenix." A few of whom Francesca wasn't sorry to leave behind.

"This is a tough crowd. She's in with a group that has been together a long time."

No surprises there. "I'll talk with her and see what she has to say. I really do appreciate you calling."

"No problem," Beth said. "Go ahead and call the attendance line. I'll let the assistant principal know what happened, so the absence will be excused."

By the time Francesca disconnected the call, she had a good bead on why Gabrielle liked her AP Euro class so well.

She stared out the ice-paned window. Fresh snow blanketed the forest sweeping down into the valley. Thick gray clouds hid the sky. So different from Phoenix.

It didn't matter that Gabrielle had grown up accusing Francesca of depriving her of the snow. At fifteen, she couldn't have foreseen the reality of a cross-country move, of what it would take to start up a new life.

They'd needed a fresh start. No question. Francesca still believed that. Gabrielle's long-time friends were all growing up and heading down different roads, a few of those roads leading to places Francesca didn't want to see her daughter go. And Phoenix had been filled with memories, but even the good memories reminded them of how their family had broken apart. Even worse, how their family had never really been.

And here Francesca was, so busy settling into her new job, packing up Nonna's house and filling her days with the fourteen hundred other things that came up between work and home…she hadn't been accessible to her daughter.

She didn't think for a second that Gabrielle would have willingly shared news of the incident, but had Francesca been paying closer attention, she might have noticed something was up and figured out a way to get her daughter talking.

The very first time she'd stared into Gabrielle's sweet newborn face, Francesca had promised to treat every moment they had together as precious. She'd learned first-hand that life didn't come with guarantees. One moment she'd been a girl, perfecting her part as the Little Red Snake in the school play. She'd wanted to shine because her parents would be in the audience. The next moment she was sitting in the principal's office while Nonna tearfully explained how a traffic accident had changed their lives forever.

That promise to be a good mother had prompted so many

positive changes in Francesca's life. But not since returning to Bluestone. If she'd stuck to her promise as carefully as she had through the years, through financial obstacles, night school and marital difficulties, she wouldn't be in this office while Gabrielle was alone in a big empty house, likely replaying yesterday's unpleasant incident over and over again.

But Francesca's promise had gotten buried somewhere beneath the piles of paperwork that had become her life. Beneath the need to prove herself completely different from the girl who'd left Bluestone years earlier.

And her time with Gabrielle had become a casualty.

No more. She wasn't going to sacrifice quality of life—Gabrielle's or her own—for anyone or anything. Not a job. Not a town. And especially not for people who were going to judge her on long-ago history.

She could feel the old resentment flare to life, but Francesca was no longer the teenager with the lousy, rebellious attitude. She'd come to understand that her attitude had been her way of trying to convince herself their opinions didn't matter. When they really had. *All too much.*

A self-destructive defense mechanism.

Perhaps she'd been foolish to think she could get a fresh start in a place where there was so much baggage, to think folks would be able to leave the past in the past and get to know her for the woman she was today. But Francesca didn't accept that. She'd known it would take time, but sixteen years was a long time. A lifetime, in fact.

Yet someone had decided that she was the likeliest suspect in this investigation, and now Gabrielle was hurting.

With a sigh, Francesca picked up her cell and text messaged her daughter. If she stood any chance at all of getting Gabrielle to talk at this stage of the game, she'd have to do it the roundabout way.

You awake yet?

In seconds, the reply came.

Yep.
How are you feeling?
Crappy.

Francesca stared helplessly at the one word, heart aching.
Once upon a time, she could make everything better for Gabrielle with a hug, but now the hurts weren't so easily fixed.

Need to go to the doctor?
No.
Want to talk about it?

When no immediate reply came, Francesca knew she'd
gotten her daughter's attention. Finally the display lit up.

How broke are we?

There it was. Had the teacher not called, Francesca
might have dismissed that random question. She might
have thought Gabrielle was angling for a new pair of
seventy-dollar sneakers or the hardcover version of Stephe-
nie Meyer's latest book.

Not broke enough to risk my job and reputation by
stealing.

The response came quickly, bristling with attitude.

You, steal?! Be real, Mother.

Francesca couldn't help but smile at that, but the response did go a long way toward easing her anxiety.

Lots going on around here. I'll tell you more about it when I get home. You getting lonely? Want me to send someone to pick you up and bring you back here to hang with Nonna? She made lasagna.
Nope. I'm reading *New Moon*. You could bring me Hägen-Dazs Mango Sorbet or Ben & Jerry's Coffee Heath Bar Crunch on your way home.

Francesca smiled. Food, naturally. Gabrielle's cure-all. Resisting the urge to tell her daughter to check on the school Web site for the work she was missing today, she typed instead:

You got it. I won't be late. Call if you need me. BTW, you're having a surprise quiz on chapter 17 in AP Euro tomorrow.
You didn't forget to call me in?!
OF COURSE NOT!!!!
Kk;-)

The smiley face eased even more of Francesca's anxiety. She might actually make it through this day, after all.

But concentrating on her reports proved impossible. Francesca might have been away from Bluestone a long time, but she knew how things worked around here. And rumor of her guilt had infiltrated Gabrielle's world.

Her mind raced with thoughts of who might accuse her

of identity theft. Had the gossip started as a matter of unkind speculation or did someone simply dislike her enough to start spreading lies?

Either way, had Beth Fairweather not arrived in class when she had, Gabrielle would have probably come out swinging with that mouth of hers.

Like mother, like daughter.

It had taken years for Francesca to learn that fighting back wasn't the only way to defend herself against feeling hurt. Such a hard-won lesson. A lesson she wished her daughter could learn without so much pain or so many bridges burned. Had Francesca had someone in her life who had recognized that her defense mechanism was so incredibly self-defeating, she might have learned new coping skills a lot sooner.

Nonna had tried, bless her heart, but she'd had her hands full working to support their family alone, at a time when most folks were kicking back and relaxing in life, and all on a job with no perks like health benefits or life insurance. She'd only gotten paid for the garments she beaded. Period.

Francesca couldn't be sure she'd have listened to anyone as a teenager, but she knew that someone reaching out to her at that age would have gone a long way to making her feel accepted.

She needed to be that person for her daughter.

And she damn sure wasn't going to let her daughter suffer for her mother's old sins. That wasn't acceptable or fair. Just the way it wasn't fair for anyone to label her a suspect because of her past. Even way back in the throes of her absolute worst rebellion, she'd never stolen anything.

Well, except for Mr. Hazzard's tractor, but that actually hadn't been theft since she'd had his permission to drive it. More like *borrowing* the John Deere tractor without prior notice.

Had anyone bothered to look at her résumé, they'd plainly see that her work history was above suspicion.

Reaching for the telephone, she depressed the intercom and said, "Yvette, please get Chief Sloan on the phone for me."

Within minutes, she heard the click of the transferring line then Jack's smooth-silk voice.

"Francesca." The pleasure in his throaty voice was so undeniable that she felt a physical ripple of awareness.

"This is a surprise," he continued. "What can I do for you?"

Shoot her. Right now, please.

"Hello, Jack." She forced her voice to sound coolly professional. "You mentioned once that you were having a tough time keeping people from talking on your end. I need to speak with you about that. Do you have a minute?"

There was a beat of silence then he replied, "I've got a break in my schedule later this afternoon. I can be there a little before five. How will that work for you?"

"You don't have to make a trip out here," she said quickly. Jack Sloan in the flesh was exactly what she didn't need. Not when she was annoyed and worried and ridiculously dull-witted from exhaustion. "If you have a few moments now, we can—"

"I wouldn't miss a chance to see you, Francesca."

That husky admission came at her sideways. All she could do was stare at the phone for a stunned beat. Was the man flirting with her?

"And Susanna said she should have the bank statements by today, anyway. I'd like to get them to work on over the weekend."

Francesca had the ridiculous urge to plug her fingers into her ears and chant, "La-la-la-la-la," so she couldn't hear him. A favorite trick of Gabrielle's. Unfortunately, she wasn't fifteen, so she would pretend she hadn't heard him. Every ounce of her sanity warned to steer clear of this man, especially now, but she couldn't impede his investigation. Not when she needed him to get to the bottom of this mystery *yesterday.*

"That'll be fine then, Jack. I appreciate if you'll give me a few minutes of your time while you're here then."

His low chuckle filtered over the phone, a throaty sound of pleasure that galvanized her. "You'll be my first order of business, Francesca. Trust me."

La-la-la-la-la.

Not for her life would she trust this man. Not when she couldn't trust herself around him. People in town were talking loudly enough for her child to be impacted, for heaven's sake. For all she knew Jack could have turned on his high-beam charm to win her over so he could use her as his entry point to the inner workings of the lodge. He'd certainly jumped at the chance to visit. *Again.*

And that thought bothered her *way* more than it should. She wanted Jack to wrap up this investigation as quickly as possible for a variety of reasons. Her daughter's sake. The residents'. Not to mention her own. She was new to Northstar Management and didn't like criminal activity happening on her watch.

But Francesca couldn't deny that she really didn't like the thought of Jack wielding his charm for any other reason than to charm her.

Damn it. Damn it. *Damn it.*

She couldn't deny that, even though she wanted to with every fiber of her being.

Only by sheer stubbornness did Francesca shove aside all thoughts of Jack Sloan to plow her way through the last of the reports. And by the time she deposited them on Yvette's desk to be couriered to the corporate office, she'd managed to find some semblance of her equilibrium again.

She would need it to face Jack in the flesh.

"What's the ETA on lunch?" Yvette asked. "I'm starving."

Lunch had completely slipped Francesca's mind. No small wonder. She'd lost her appetite long ago.

Glancing at her watch, she was surprised to note the time. "It's after two."

"I know." Yvette patted her stomach suggestively. "When is your grandmother coming?"

"You're sure she said lunch?"

Yvette nodded.

"Then I would have expected her before noon." Francesca motioned to the phone. "Dial her room, please."

Yvette did the honors and handed the receiver to Francesca, who listened to the line ring a number of times before rolling over to voice mail. "Hey, Nonna, it's Francesca. Not important. Just calling to get an ETA on the lasagna."

"What do you mean, not important?" Yvette demanded, taking the phone and returning it to the cradle. "Lunch is already over in the restaurant."

Francesca eyed Yvette's slight figure with a frown. Lunch might be over, but dietary had already started prepping dinner. Short of a food delivery strike or a siege on the lodge, no one would ever starve around here. "I need to get out of this office for a bit. I'll go see what's up."

Yvette settled back at her desk, appeased for the moment, so Francesca beat a hasty retreat.

Francesca's knocks went unanswered so she used her key to discover that Nonna wasn't in her apartment.

Had she forgotten her promise to bring lunch?

Francesca checked inside the refrigerator. No traces of lasagna or the plastic container and carrier combo that she usually used to transport food. Nonna and the lasagna had made it out the door.

Francesca locked up the apartment again, considering her options. Arriving back in the office to tell Yvette that lunch was MIA wasn't one of them.

The most logical next step would be to check with Nonna's friends, but Francesca didn't want to cause unnecessary worry. Especially with the way news spread around this place.

No, Francesca's only sane option was the back door approach. So she checked the activities calendar at the reception desk. Bingo. Water aerobics in the pool. Rosary in the chapel. The only off-site trips scheduled today were to the mall in Saugerties and the monthly trip to Atlantic City.

Nonna wasn't listed on either of those rosters, nor had she scheduled private transportation for a medical appointment. She hadn't mentioned anything to Francesca, but with those memory lapses of hers, Francesca wanted to double-check.

The most likely places to find Nonna were the chapel and bingo. Since the game had already started, Francesca started there. No Nonna but lots of excitement when Mrs. Svenson called bingo on B-8, which afforded Francesca the perfect opportunity to ask Fanny Brent if she'd seen Nonna.

"No, dear, I haven't. You make sure she knows I held her seat for as long as I could. She always sits with me, but there was no telling Eileen that," she added conspiratorially with a sidelong glance at her perfectly coiffed neighbor.

"I'll tell her," Francesca whispered and motioned to the bevy of paper cards on the table. Too many to count at quick glance. "Good luck next round."

Francesca headed to the chapel next, where she found a traffic jam of walkers and motorized scooters parked outside the door. She tried to gauge where they were in the prayer to time her interruption, but her shadow must have been visible through the shade on the glass insert because the next thing she knew, a figure within was shuffling toward the door.

So much for casual questions. Plastering a smile on her face, she greeted Mrs. Weissing when the door opened.

Still no Nonna.

By the time she reached the pool, which was about the last place Francesca would have expected to find her grandmother, who didn't swim, Francesca was starting to worry. True, Nonna might have been visiting in one of her friends' apartments, but short of making an announcement over the PA system, there was no way to find out. She had to be here somewhere.

Hopefully not collapsed in some unnoticed corner of this very large property. It would take an hour alone to search the public restrooms on each of the eight floors in all four wings.

Francesca finally decided to ask the staff to conduct discreet walk-throughs in all the common areas in their sections when Evelyn Jonas revealed the first clue. "Concetta left this morning. I said goodbye to her on my way to breakfast."

"She was leaving the lodge?"

Mrs. Jonas shrugged. "She was wearing her coat."

There was the par course, outdoor activities field and the garden area, all of which were buried under four feet of snow. Nonna wouldn't be outside. Unless… She might have ventured a visit to John, the retiree who worked the gatehouse during the dayshift. He was the husband of a long-time family friend, who'd taken the job after his wife had passed away. He and Nonna had been known to swap books, as his not-so-demanding job left him plenty of time to read.

Francesca couldn't see her grandmother making her way even that short distance in this weather. But if Nonna had gotten it into her head that John was outside freezing, she might very well have brewed him an espresso and taken it out to him.

Then another thought struck—the nursing center. Henry Benson had just moved over there permanently because of growing dementia. His wife, Margaret, had made the difficult decision to give up their apartment in senior living so they could be together. Margaret had been one of the reasons Nonna had wanted to move to the lodge. Had she decided to bring lasagna to her friend? If so, why hadn't she asked for transport? Staff members shuttled residents back and forth in golf carts all day long.

Had Nonna forgotten and decided to walk herself?

Francesca glanced through the steamy windows at the pristine scene outside. It was winter, and dusk came early. By five it would be dark, the temperature would start dropping, and if Nonna were out there, in trouble…

Out of options, Francesca headed back to her office for her coat, memory fresh of the last time she'd gone outside without it. Yvette wasn't at her desk, so Francesca slipped in and out of her office, fighting back the worry niggling away her calm.

The Mystery of the Missing Grandmother.

This would not officially become a case.

CHAPTER THIRTEEN

JACK LOOKED FORWARD TO seeing Frankie this afternoon. She'd sounded too matter-of-fact on the phone, leaving him guessing that she'd had a run-in with the grinding rumor mill.

With the hopes of bringing her some good news, he'd spent the afternoon going through the last of the victims' statements. He wasn't sure why he'd expected a place with the name of Greywacke Lodge to be normal, but after reading the statements, he'd come to the conclusion that most of the folks living here were both gray and wacked.

Eddie Shaw, for example. This computer-savvy old man had given his personal information via e-mail to a company that promised to help him meet women online. After back-stopping his online activities, Jack's tech guy uncovered a phishing scam the FBI had recently shut down.

And luckily before they'd done more damage than charging online fees for Web hosting services, which totaled less than four hundred dollars. The extravagant credit lines established with Shaw's identity eliminated everyone at the lodge with less than supervisory access to his personal information.

The Connells insisted the clerk at a local music store had stolen their credit information when they'd purchased a gift card for their great-granddaughter at Christmas. According to them he was the likeliest suspect because of his blue spiky hair and variety of piercings.

The clerk, however, despite his unconventional appearance, hadn't run through anything but the approved total of the Connells' purchase. And fortunately for Jack, a bank camera had caught an image on video of an unidentified woman making a cash withdrawal on the Connells' fraudulent credit line in Tucson. Jack notified the FBI to discover the woman's identity.

It wasn't Frankie or Susanna. That much Jack knew. Both had been ensconced in their offices with an impressive number of witnesses to corroborate their whereabouts. And even if they hadn't, Jack knew better. He might not see much of Susanna since Skip's death, but he cared about her. And Frankie…his gut told him she wasn't a criminal, either.

However, since a prosecutor could argue that either could have been working with an accomplice, Jack needed a positive ID on that female.

Another unexpected development came because Bridget Minahan's purse had been stolen out of her shopping cart during one of the lodge's Wal-Mart outings. By the time she'd arrived at the checkout and noticed the theft, the thieves had already hit up two office supply stores for computer equipment. Those thieves were still at large, but Bridget's daughter-in-law had closed her accounts and had the banks issue new cards.

The timing of this incident and the change in Bridget Minahan's personal information meant that, like Eddie Shaw, not all members of Greywacke Lodge's accounting department had access to the new information used to open the credit lines, which enabled him to narrow the suspect list even more.

As far as Jack was concerned, this progress was coming as a mixed bag. On one hand, he was both pleased and impressed with Randy and the chosen few detectives they'd assigned to work this case. On the other, their skilled handling had whittled suspects down to exactly the two women Jack wanted off the list.

Susanna, an old friend, and the woman who oversaw her work. Frankie. The woman he was interested in.

Jack suspected Frankie would find this development a mixed bag, too. She'd be relieved her staff was honest, even if it meant taking a turn at the top of his list. Susanna would freak. No question. She'd had a rough couple of years, and Jack didn't like that he was about to make things even rougher.

He parked in a visitor space and made his way inside the front lobby. "I'm here to see Ms. Raffa," he told the smiling receptionist. "Is she available?"

The woman's smile didn't budge, and when she hopped up from her seat, Jack knew instantly something was up.

"Chief Sloan, if you'll wait here please."

Jack waited. She quickly returned and escorted him to the reception area of the administrative offices, where Frankie's administrative assistant greeted him.

"Chief Sloan," Yvette said. "I know Ms. Raffa was expecting you, but I'm afraid she's not here right now."

"Not a problem. I'm early. I'll wait."

Yvette hesitated too long, looking suspiciously stumped for an answer, so Jack asked, "Is something wrong?"

"I'm not exactly sure where she is or when she'll be back," she admitted with a sheepish shrug. "She's not answering the radio or her cell."

"But she's on the property?"

"I assume. She went upstairs to find Nonna over an hour ago. Nonna's not picking up her phone, either."

"Ms. Raffa's grandmother, right?"

Yvette nodded. "We misplaced her and her lasagna."

Okay. Jack thought he understood. "Ms. Raffa went out looking for her grandmother?"

"Now she's MIA, too."

The Case of the Missing Lasagna.

That's what Frankie might have called it. The thought made him feel like smiling. He didn't. Yvette looked really worried, so Jack asked, "What have you done to find her?"

"I keep calling her cell and trying to contact her over the radio. I called around to the different department heads to ask if anyone had seen her, but I didn't want to make a big deal and get the whole place in an uproar."

"No one's seen her."

Yvette shook her head.

"Is her car still here?"

"Oh, I hadn't thought to check."

"Let's start there then. Does she have an assigned space?"

Yvette was already circling her desk with a quick step, looking relieved to have an action plan. "We can call John at the gatehouse. He'll tell us if she left the property."

Jack waited while she placed the call.

"No, she hasn't left."

"Has she disappeared like this before?"

"Never," Yvette said decidedly.

"Okay. Then we need to figure out if she's inside or outside."

Yvette was up and on her way again. This time toward Frankie's office. "Let me see if her purse and coat are here."

Jack followed.

"Her coat is gone, but her purse is still here," Yvette informed him when she reappeared.

"Okay, so she went outside but didn't plan to leave the property."

That eased some stress from Yvette's expression. "Sounds as though we're in an episode of *Law & Order.*"

Jack didn't point out that television crime shows usually

featured bodies, and bodies weren't on the docket today. "Would she have gone outside to meet her grandmother?"

"I can't imagine why. We expected Nonna with lunch a long time ago. Should I call the nursing center?" Yvette asked. "I can ask the receptionist if she's seen her. I didn't think about it before, but it's right across the road, and Nonna does have friends there. I don't think she'd have walked in this weather, though. Most residents have one of the staff members drive them over on the golf carts. It might not seem like a long way, but it really is for someone having trouble getting around."

"Wouldn't John have seen her leave the property?"

"Only if she went through the front gate. There's a pedestrian path with access. That's usually the way the golf carts go to avoid cars."

"Give them a call. If no one's seen them, I'll take a walk."

Yvette did as he suggested and, within minutes, Jack was ready to take that walk.

"I won't be long," he said. "Call me if either shows up."

"You got it, Chief."

Jack headed out of the reception area, wondering where Frankie and her grandmother might have gone.

The temperature had dropped noticeably in the short time he'd been indoors. They were probably looking at more snow tonight. Following the path around the building, he abandoned any hope of heading back to town before his desk sergeant got off shift. Friday night traffic in Bluestone Mountain wasn't anything to write home about but, still, even if he located his missing persons quickly, by the time he talked with Susanna… He'd check in at the station after Brogan came on duty.

Jack wound his way along the path carefully. While all the walkways around the lodge had been meticulously shoveled and salted, and tall ornamental lamps ensured the paths would remain well lit, there was no way to mask the terrain itself, the steep slopes that descended into the valley.

Despite the dimming light, his well-trained gaze caught a disturbance in the snow ahead, a place where the path wound a final descent to the gate. Ice had formed more thickly here beneath the cover of firs that blocked the gray sky overhead. He moved carefully beneath that shadowy overhang, his dress shoes offering no traction on the ice.

Training had kept Jack from speculating about Frankie's and her grandmother's disappearances. Discipline had kept him thinking clearly and dealing with the facts, so he was surprised by a pang of real fear when he took in the scene before him.

Deep gouges in the snow might have been caused by a fall, by someone slipping and shattering the brittle surface… Tree limbs twisted and broken as if someone had grasped vainly for purchase… Jack sank to his knees on the icy path, bracing himself as he peered down the dark slope.

Even from a distance he instantly recognized that wild tumble of caramel hair, the slight shoulders so unnaturally still.

Frankie.

She'd slid a good dozen feet down the slope before coming to rest in the lap of an old oak that had loosed a mound of snow on top of her.

"Francesca!" he yelled out, breath catching in his throat, adrenaline forcing him to reach out and steady himself against the trunk of an alder. "Francesca."

Silence.

Jack's heart throbbed hard in his chest, the only sound to fill his hearing as he stared down at her still form. He had no way of knowing how long she'd been down there, but he knew the cold would readily claim her life if she hadn't killed herself on the way down already.

Slipping his cell from his pocket, he speed dialed 9-1-1 and detailed the situation to the dispatcher.

Jack faced a choice. Help was on the way, but he couldn't wait. The late afternoon sun, already well hidden behind the blanket of cloudy gray sky, was setting. It would be dark soon.

Grabbing ahold of a low-hanging branch overhead, he braced himself for the descent. He couldn't lose his footing and come crashing down on top of her.

Each warily placed step brought another surge of adrenaline, another wave of unfamiliar helplessness as doubts crashed in on him. How badly was she hurt? How long had she been down here? Was she even alive?

Be alive. Be alive. Be alive.

The litany played over and over again in his head as he descended, trying not to misstep, cursing when he almost lost his grip and sent another shower of snow on top of her.

He fought to catch himself as the boughs of an evergreen bowed beneath his weight, sending more snow tumbling down and tearing apart his hand as twigs broke beneath his palm.

He grasped for the familiar calm that gave him a clear head and made him effective in crises, but today it wasn't there. It simply wasn't there.

Be alive. Be alive. Be alive.

He was so close he could have stretched out his foot and touched her. But balance was crucial. He couldn't trust his grip on the branch, the limb bowed so violently it could easily break. He levered himself alongside of her, finally released his grip, came to a sliding stop with his feet bracing against the trunk of that sturdy oak.

"Francesca." He reached for her, assessed the damage. Was she breathing?

Be alive. Be alive. Be alive.

He felt for the pulse at the base of her throat, plunging his hand beneath her collar, dismayed when he was forced to brush aside hard snow that had wedged itself inside her woolen coat. Her skin icy beneath his fingertips, *too cold...* there it was, the steady flutter of her pulse, low, but there. Hypothermia might be on the way, but hadn't gotten there yet.

Had she broken her neck? Damaged her spine? *Anything* that might prohibit him from moving her?

There was no visible blood, and he breathed a little easier.

"Francesca." Sliding the scarf from the collar of his coat, he lifted her head gently and maneuvered the scarf around her head and neck balaclava-style to curtail heat loss.

The hem of her wool coat barely fell past her knees, leaving her legs clad only in sheer hose. He spotted one of her shoes farther up the slope, but didn't see the other.

Kicking away his own, he stripped off his socks and pulled them onto her feet. It would help keep the cold at bay. Then he slid his feet back into his own wet shoes. They only had to make it until the emergency snow rescue arrived.

She wore knit gloves more suited for a walk to the car than winter protection. Better than nothing.

Gathering her against him, he pitted the possibility of permanent injury against the reality of exposure. She was cold, but not wet, which meant she hadn't been down here long. Gathering her against him, he drew her inside the folds of his coat. He twined his legs through hers, anchoring her close and using his body to shield her.

He guessed that she'd hit her head and been knocked unconscious in the fall. She might not have awakened as the cold robbed her body of heat. It wouldn't have taken long for her to freeze to death.

What stroke of fate had brought him here at this exact moment? Jack didn't know, only that he was very, very grateful.

Trapping her hands between his, he massaged her slim fingers, chanted her name. Still she didn't awaken.

Fear finally prompted him to grip her chin and ease her face from side to side. Her face was flushed, her cheek bitten by the snow.

"Francesca, wake up." Then more forcefully. "Francesca."

Her eyelashes fluttered. She exhaled a shuddering breath.

Jack's heart started beating again.

"Francesca." Her name sounded like a prayer in the quiet, a sound so wholly unfamiliar, the sound of relief.

It took halting moments for her to awaken, to stare up at him, dazed. He lowered his face to the top of her head, breathed in her icy smell, let the aching minutes pass as she came back to herself. He crushed her against him, until her every curve molded against his, anchored close as if his own life, not hers, depended on it.

"Help's on the way." His voice was a whisper in the shuddering silence. "Just hang on."

"N-no." Her hand fluttered against his chest as if trying to find the strength to brush him away. "I'm f-fine."

Her voice was tremulous but coherent, not slurred, another sign of hypothermia. Laughter escaped from him, an absurd emotional reaction to the relief he felt, so strong he couldn't make sense of the feeling beyond surprise he felt so deeply.

He hadn't known, had no way to know, not until seeing her, the hair wisping out from his hastily wrapped scarf to frame her pale face, that something had been happening ever since they'd met. Attraction, no question, but *this* was different, more.

This, whatever *this* was, had made coming to Greywacke Lodge today about more than dealing with the gossip mill, about more than the investigation, about more than even wanting to see Frankie again and understand why she kept shying away from him.

This made holding her close, her body molded against his as if she'd been designed to fit, a feeling as natural and right as any he'd ever known.

"Forgive me," he whispered, resting his cheek on the top of her head, staggered by the awareness he felt. "I don't think you're fine."

No more than he was fine to learn *this* had changed everything.

"I am." She tried to suppress her shivering. "What— what happened?"

Just hearing her voice was so welcome, the relief extreme. "I assume you slipped and fell."

He glanced down into her face, watched as she visibly tried to make sense of the facts, her struggle so evident.

"Nonna," she gasped aloud.

"Don't worry. Yvette's in your office tracking her down as we speak. She'll be back by the time we get you out of here."

Jack hoped. He didn't want to be proven a liar. But there was nothing either of them could do at the moment. He'd alerted emergency services of a second missing person, so they'd be on the lookout, too. It was the best he could do.

Frankie frowned again. She glanced over his shoulder.

"Let me go. I can stand."

He brushed strands of hair beneath the scarf, enjoyed the

simple freedom of touching her. "We'd literally have to crawl up that slope hanging on to tree branches, Francesca."

She strained to see into the twilight. "You're sure?"

"This ground is solid ice."

"That much I know," she said drily.

Again Jack was struck by that overwhelming sense of relief. Her humor was making an appearance, a sign that she was exactly what she said—fine.

"I don't believe this." She exhaled a shuddering breath. "I am s-so stupid."

"I'll buy worried. Or accident prone. Clumsy even. But not stupid, Francesca. Never stupid."

She let out a weak laugh. "*Stupid.* And too tired to think straight. I—I should n-never have tackled this path in heels."

He traced her foot with the toe of his shoe. "I passed one on the way down."

She groaned. "I don't need this right now. Northstar's going to see this report and think they hired an idiot."

"They'll be grateful you discovered the possibility of liability before a resident did."

She gave a weak laugh. "No resident would be stupid enough to be out here in this weather."

He didn't need to remind her that a resident might not recognize the danger of heading down this snowy path.

The silence swelled between them, filled with awareness of their closeness. Frankie trembled against him, her lithe form fitting in a way that was so much more than shared body heat.

But silence wasn't allowed, not when her eyes drifted shut again.

"Francesca," he said, sharper than he'd intended. "What's this about missing lasagna?"

She groaned. "I'm freezing."

Rolling onto his side, Jack unbuttoned her coat, shoving it open. Then he sank onto his back and lifted her on top of him, readjusting his coat until it became a cocoon and nothing more than their street clothing marked where he ended and she began.

"Better?" He needed to keep her talking, not only to distract her from slipping back into the lure of that slumber but also to divert him from the feel of her lush curves molded so close.

"My head is throbbing."

Resting his cheek on the top of her head, he tucked her face against his throat to stop her teeth from chattering, the way he might have held her in bed, body pressed close, legs twined together, only with a lot more skin. "You might have hit your head when you fell. Help will be here soon. They know exactly where we are, so just hang on."

Jack was relieved not to be proven a liar on this one score when the sound of an engine suddenly rent the quiet forest. "What did I tell you?"

"Bravo."

He chuckled, the sound bursting as white mist over her head. Her arms tightened around him, a small, simple gesture, but one he felt straight through him with awareness entirely inappropriate to the situation. "My pleasure, Francesca."

The engine humming on the path above them suddenly whirred to a low purr and a male voice called out urgently, "Ms. Raffa? Chief Sloan? You down there?"

"Otis," she said.

"We're here, Otis," Jack called back.

"Emergency Services called," came the reply. "They're almost here. I brought blankets. I'm going to toss them down."

Jack lifted his head and peered into the dimming light.

A head appeared, a black face crowned by cropped gray-ing hair.

"Be careful," Jack cautioned.

"Will do, Chief," Otis shot back. "You okay, Ms. Raffa?"

"Glad to see you," she said, her lips brushed his throat, a chill whisper that managed to spark heat inside him.

Getting a blanket down to them wasn't as simple as tossing one down the mountain, not with winter-bare trees and low-lying limbs barring the path. Otis finally succeeded by working one down with the handle of a rake he carried on the golf cart.

Jack was forced to release Frankie and stretch the re-maining distance to catch the blanket. Then he tucked it tightly around her bare legs. "Better?"

"Much." He could feel her smile, feel the way her cold lips curved against his skin. "Thanks."

He heard more than gratitude for a blanket in that one word. She was grateful he was here.

"Can't think of anything I'd rather do." He meant it.

The Snow Rescue Task Force consisted of volunteers trained exclusively in emergency winter rescue. These dedi-cated folks often assisted emergency service personnel in Bluestone and neighboring hamlets in locating the occa-sional tourist who strayed from a ski run or ran into snow-mobile trouble on the trails.

Jack could hear their approach long before their arrival, wasn't surprised when they came to a stop in front of the pedestrian gate. The sirens quieted, but Jack could see the lights flashing in the twilight.

"We've got company," he said.

"Sounds like the whole town."

He heard the dread in her voice and didn't mention that he'd dispatched emergency services, the fire department and the Snow Rescue Task Force. She'd find out soon enough.

Voices began shouting directions then heads were peering over the side of the slope.

"Well, hey, Jack," Bob Wilkins, a battalion chief with Bluestone Fire Department, yelled down. "Good to see you."

"You, too." Jack smiled when Frankie buried her face in his neck as if she could hide.

Bob detailed the plan, and within minutes snow rescue patrols were harnessed and heading down the slope toward them. With the help of the patrols and harnesses, both Jack and Frankie made their way back up the mountain, where she was wrapped in thermal blankets. He refused medical attention but accepted a warm parka to replace his coat.

Emergency vehicles weren't an unusual sight at Grey-wacke Lodge, but vehicles blocking the road in front of the pedestrian gate were. Since the gate opened in full view of the nursing center, avoiding notice wasn't possible.

"Oh, God." Frankie groaned when faced with the crowd they'd drawn. "This is a nightmare."

Jack actually thought Emergency Services had done a good job at keeping onlookers away. He spotted Yvette in the small crowd, Susanna, too, and knew Frankie's staff would show up to make sure she was okay. Not to mention the eight floors of residents who had the time to come lend support. And from the looks of it, those who could manage the trip did. The faces in the crowd were curious, and concerned.

Several called Frankie's name through the gate and shouted encouragements as she was hoisted onto the path.

"I can walk," she insisted, but the patrol, to his credit, didn't budge in the face of her scowl. Instead he waited until she finally allowed him to guide her to the nearby stretcher.

"I'm fine. I can walk." She glanced at Jack for help, but he pointed to her feet and said, "No shoes."

She sat down heavily, but refused to lie back, and her

annoyed scowl melted as they emerged from the gate to face the waiting crowd.

"You okay, Ms. Raffa?" someone called out, starting a barrage of questions firing from every direction.

"What happened?"

"Did you break anything?"

"Are you going to be all right?"

Frankie faced the crowd with a wry smile. "I'm fine. But be careful. It's slippery out there."

Laughter erupted, and Jack could practically feel the relief that rippled through the crowd.

"You should have let me freeze to death," she whispered, smile stubbornly fixed as the rescue patrol freed her from the harness beneath the watchful eyes of the crowd. "Less painful."

Jack chuckled, waving off the patrol and releasing his own harness. "You didn't die on a frozen mountain, so I don't think a little embarrassment is going to kill you."

"Like you'd know. You're hero to my damsel in distress."

Jack liked being her hero. And he liked that so many folks obviously cared, which said a lot about his damsel.

Just then he heard some commotion. Moving away from the stretcher, he peered between emergency vehicles to see a Greywacke Lodge bus in the roadblock of vehicles. The doors were wide-open and someone was arguing with the bus driver.

Jack glanced at Frankie, who said, "That would be the bus returning from Atlantic City."

"I can get them to clear the road—"

"Oh, thank God." She cut him off, and Jack followed her gaze to see a woman being helped off the bus by the driver.

Jack recognized the small woman with a head of white curls. The driver assisted her around the fire truck and Yvette emerged from the crowd, linking an arm through

Concetta's and making some comment that brought a relieved expression to her face.

"Dolly, what happened?" Concetta asked as they approached.

"I slipped and fell on the ice, Nonna. No worries. They're checking me out as a precaution." Frankie's eyes glinted with tears. "You went to Atlantic City? But you weren't signed up with the group."

"I didn't plan to go, dolly, but I saw the bus…" She let her voice trail off, gave a shrug and a sheepish grin. "You can have lasagna for dinner."

She held up a plastic bag from a local grocery with what appeared to be a food container inside. Jack noticed Yvette cast Frankie a sidelong glance, but Frankie just eyed the bag, and said, "It'll be delicious."

She made a move to hop off the stretcher, but the paramedic stopped her.

"Please stay seated until we get you inside, ma'am."

Frankie stared as if he had three heads. "I'm not going in the ambulance. I'm fine. These people need to get inside."

"Standard procedure, ma'am." He looked to Jack for backup, but Jack didn't get a chance to weigh in when Concetta said to the paramedic, "She'll go. You'll let me go with her?"

"Okay, okay," Frankie said. "I'll go peacefully. But, Nonna, I'd rather you didn't come. I need your help with Gabrielle. She's at the house alone, and I'm not sure what time I'll be home. Would you mind if I send a car and have someone bring her here? She can spend the night with you, and you can keep her from worrying."

"Of course, dolly."

Frankie leaned forward and kissed the top of her grandmother's head. "Thanks, Nonna. You don't worry, either. I'm fine. I'll call as soon as they spring me." She turned to

Jack. "You said you can get this road cleared. Would you mind? These people really do need to get inside."

"Done," he said then extended his arm to Concetta. "I'll see you back to the bus."

Concetta took his outstretched arm and said, "I'll wait for your call, dolly. Don't worry about Gabrielle."

"May I?" He reached for the bag Concetta carried. She relinquished it, and Jack led her away, whispering to the paramedic, "Get her in, then wait for me. I'll make the trip."

Concetta didn't miss the exchange. "You'll take good care of her, Jack?"

"You have my word."

"She'll fight you every step of the way. She's used to doing all the caring."

That said a lot about Frankie. "Appreciate the heads-up."

"Appreciate you rescuing my granddaughter."

"My pleasure."

"Make her return your socks before your toes freeze," she said as he handed her over to the driver for help into the bus.

Jack laughed. "I will."

He didn't know the details of the missing lasagna or the unexpected trip to Atlantic City, but whatever else was going on with this little lady, she was sharp about her granddaughter.

Jack made his way back to Bob, who immediately began directing traffic to clear the road. The small crowd of onlookers started to disperse, some of the lodge staff lingering to make sure their residents made it down the sidewalk and through the entrance. Susanna was one of them. He caught her gaze and waved, reconciling himself to wait a little longer to tell her that she and Frankie were the last two names on his suspect list. Maybe, with any luck, the entire investigation could turn and he wouldn't have to have the conversation at all.

Hopping into the back of the ambulance, Jack rapped his palm against the hood and told the paramedics, "Let's go."

The paramedics had wrapped Frankie warmly in blankets, and while she still sat on the gurney, she looked nominally more resigned. She suffered through the paramedic's ministrations as they checked for signs of exposure and concussion, answered questions politely, and appeared more tired than anything else.

When the paramedic finally made his way into the front seat beside the driver and strapped himself in, she turned to Jack, "Did your cell phone survive?"

"I assume yours didn't."

"Must be with my shoes. The radio had made it, though, minus the battery pack. I must have fallen on it." She gingerly touched her side where the radio had once hung and winced. "May I borrow your phone?"

Jack handed it to her and watched as she began keying in a number, scowling in frustration when her thawing fingers didn't cooperate and she was forced to redial.

He guessed he was better off not offering to help.

"Hey, pup, it's Mom."

Jack could hear the murmur of a voice on the other end of the line.

"I know," Frankie said. "I've misplaced mine. This is…a friend's."

She shot a glance at Jack in her periphery, and he just held her gaze. Friend was a place to start.

And Jack wanted to start.

"Listen, pup. I slipped on the ice and bumped my head. No, no. I'm completely fine. I promise. But since I fell at work, I have to go to the hospital and get checked out. Nonna's upset, though, so I need you to come here and spend the night so she's not alone. Okay?"

Her daughter must have agreed because Frankie went on

to say, "I appreciate it, and I need you to do something else for me. Do not eat the lasagna and don't let Nonna eat it, either. It spent the day at the Shore unrefridgerated."

Frankie laughed. "Definitely gross. Think you can distract her long enough to confiscate it and get it to the incinerator? Great. I know I can trust you, puppy."

Jack slid off his coat and repositioned himself on the hard plastic stool that served as his seat.

"I promise I'll call as soon as I see the doctor," Frankie said. "I'll have John drive over to get you. Be ready. Make sure everything's off and locked up. And, remember, we've got a date for a *Lord of the Rings* marathon this weekend. Love you."

She disconnected the call and placed another to the lodge, making arrangements to transport her daughter. When she finished, she handed the phone back to Jack. "Thanks."

"My pleasure." He slipped the cell back into his pocket. "Everyone taken care of?"

"I hope so."

Jack did, too, reminded of what Concetta had said about Frankie caring for everyone else. He liked that about her, had seen hints of her nurturing with Greywacke Lodge's residents. He liked her family, too, how they looked out for each other.

He wasn't sure what had happened between him and Francesca, when things had changed and he'd started to care, but as he watched her sitting on the gurney, submitting to an examination though she clearly would rather be anywhere else in the world, Jack was very sure of one thing.

He wanted to be the one caring for her tonight.

CHAPTER FOURTEEN

FRANCESCA HAD BEEN TRANSPORTED by ambulance and gurney, evaluated in triage, examined in the emergency room while answering questions like: "What year is it?" and "Who is the president?" only to be pronounced in the exact state she'd claimed to be four hours ago: *fine*.

"You're not fine," Jack argued. "The doctor would discharge you if you were. He wants you observed. Didn't you hear him?"

"I heard. *Almost* fine then," she conceded. "I'm not concussed. Trust me."

There was a vast difference between concussed and humiliated in Francesca's book. Vast. And she was gearing up to explain the differences to the doctor as soon as he returned. She would not spend the night in this hospital. Period.

"So why are you here, Jack?"

He flashed a grin that reminded her of exactly what his arms had felt like around her. "I want my socks back."

She was not going there with Mr. Charming. She simply didn't have the energy to talk herself out of each and every reaction to him when she could vividly remember the feel of his hard body imprinted against hers. She was disappointed because she needed to be with her daughter tonight, and instead she was yakking around in the emergency room. "I know you came to the lodge so we could talk, but it'll keep until another day. You've done your bit rescuing the damsel in distress."

Folding his arms over his chest, he drew her gaze to the subtle suggestion of muscle beneath what was once a pristinely tailored shirt. A shirt he'd completely trashed in his rescue efforts, along with his coat, jacket, pants and shoes. She'd taken care of the socks for him.

"I had some business to discuss myself," he said.

"Then hit me. I need something to think about besides what a mess I've made of my night. Yours, too." She shot a glance at the door. "And how ready I am for that doctor to return."

"You couldn't have known the lasagna would make an unscheduled trip to the Shore."

"Sad but true. I never could outthink Nonna. Thank God she's okay, but now I've got to look at policy and procedure. She should never have been able to get on that bus unnoticed. Fred—he's the driver—was about to have a heart attack."

"Good employee?"

"Very. If I was to guess, I'll bet Nonna slipped on after he checked his roster. Since he's taken her on most of the Atlantic City outings since the lodge opened, he just didn't put two and two together."

"You've pinpointed another problem for your management company without any devastating consequences."

Except for the gray hairs she'd sprouted worrying about Nonna. "Are you always so cheery?"

"A side effect of law enforcement. Too much time with the underbelly of society." He shrugged. "Can't get depressed."

How refreshing for a man to be proactive about his attitude and mental health. Okay, unfair, she chided herself, *so* not fair to compare him to her ex-husband.

And why was she thinking about Jack as a man again?

"Makes sense," she said. "So, what's the latest update on the case?"

"Later," he said, and as though he'd orchestrated the moment, the doctor stepped into the room so she couldn't question Jack further.

Francesca quickly prepared a list of objections in case he wanted her to stay overnight. Not that she thought she'd get to use them. She likely wouldn't get a word in edgewise since the doctor and Jack were good friends and her initial exam had been peppered with discussion about the merits of Arctic Cat versus Rupp.

Men and their snowmobiles. Honestly.

"Everything looks good on the X-ray, Francesca." Dr. Reese flipped up a film of her skull and gave it a cursory glance in the overhead light. "You need to be monitored. If you don't demonstrate any symptoms tonight, I'll discharge you in the morning and your family can keep an eye on you through the weekend. Sound good?"

"No. I want to go home...to convalesce." She threw in the last part so he'd know she took his diagnosis seriously.

With a frown, he slipped the X-ray film into the projector before reaching for her chart. Francesca knew what was coming next and mentally reviewed that list of objections.

"Now, Francesca—" the doctor began.

"Jay," Jack cut him off. "If I promise to monitor her through the night, will you sign her out?"

Dr. Reese didn't even blink. "Done. I'll send the nurse with discharge instructions." He made a few notations on the chart then met Francesca's gaze. "No working out. No housework. No shopping. Take it easy over the weekend and you should be able to go to work Monday morning. Don't give Jack a hard time."

That statement didn't deserve a reply.

Jack, on the other hand, couldn't be ignored.

He was still beside her even after she'd returned his socks, replacing them with hospital booties. In his rumpled and water-stained shirt and pants, he looked suspiciously as though he meant to keep his promise of monitoring her through the night.

Francesca hadn't decided what to do about that yet. This whole experience had been new to her. On the one hand, his concern was very thoughtful, more charming gentleman than charming rogue. He knew how much she didn't want to spend the night here and had stepped in to rescue her again.

On the other hand, she found being poked, prodded and forced to reveal some very personal details in front of him downright unsettling.

She would have expected the gritty intimacy of this night to send him fleeing in the opposite direction. Emergency rooms were not good places to charm women, but here he was, still beside her, such a confusing mix of gentleman and rogue.

Francesca couldn't let the fact that he'd charged in to save the day undermine her good sense. She knew better than that, had lived entirely too long stringing from one gallant moment to the next. The wild highs of romantic interludes didn't carry her through the loneliness of the reality in between. Gallant moments were all fine and dandy, but they didn't translate into the real world.

If and when she ever decided to get involved in a relationship again, she wanted a real man who wanted a real life complete with all the good and bad that might entail. Period.

The nurse appeared with discharge orders, giving Jack a complete rundown of what symptoms to look for in his patient, before finally calling transport. Francesca took one look at the wheelchair and swallowed back another argument. Jack had already gone to bat for her. She wouldn't push her luck. At least until she got out the door. So she sat with the nurse in the exit while waiting for him to bring around his car, which he'd had a patrol officer drive over from the lodge.

And the second they were driving away, she said, "Jack, I really appreciate all you've done tonight, but I'd like you to drop me off at the lodge. Gabrielle and Nonna can babysit me. I don't want to be any more trouble."

"You're no trouble, Francesca."

His voice was low and smooth between them, his profile lit by the warm glow of the display panel. Every morsel of common sense inside her screamed, "No, no, no! Thank him politely and send him home." That was the only safe thing to do, the *sane* thing to do.

The very last thing in the world she needed was to cross the boundaries between professional and personal with this man any more. She simply couldn't afford to get sucked in, not with the feel of his embrace fresh in her head. Not when all these gallant moments touched her in places that were too vulnerable.

Not when he'd been flirting with her. Besides, she reasoned *sanely,* what did she expect the chief of police to do—leave her to die on a snowy mountain? Not hardly.

"I appreciate that, Jack, but I insist. You've lost your whole night because of me. Take me to the lodge."

He brought the car to a stop at a traffic light and slanted a level gaze her way. "I promised."

She pressed a finger to her lips. "I won't say a word."

He released the steering wheel and spread his hand in entreaty. "I promised."

His word must be solid gold, apparently.

The light turned green, but he didn't accelerate. "Your place or back to the hospital, Francesca. Your call."

She glanced over her shoulder to find the street empty, no promise of a horn-blaring driver to force Jack into motion. She scowled. "Cut me a break here."

"Honestly, Francesca. Do you expect me to pass up the chance to spend the night with you?"

"Jack Sloan."

His warm chuckle only underscored their nearness. A smile twitched around his mouth. He was enjoying the upper hand far too much to back down.

Arrogant, stubborn man. "Not the hospital."

He didn't say a word. He didn't need to. His smile said everything as he adjusted the rearview mirror and hit the gas.

To distract herself from the dark quiet and their proximity, she snatched his cell phone from the console and checked in with Gabrielle, needing a very real reminder that the attraction between them was no-win no matter how she cut it.

Jack was an unmarried man. She was a divorced mother with a daughter who needed her, an impressionable daughter.

"Everyone okay?" Jack asked after she disconnected. "I'm surprised you called. It's pretty late."

Spoken like a man who'd never lived with a teen. "Barely after midnight on Friday night. Of course my daughter is awake."

"Your grandmother?"

"Sound asleep on the couch. She had a long, eventful day. Turns out she won two-hundred dollars on the Lucky Seven slot."

"Then she wouldn't have wanted to miss the trip. What about the lasagna?"

"Safely disposed of, I'm happy to report. Gabrielle told Nonna she was starving and ate every last bite."

Jack chuckled. "Slick kid."

"*Too* slick. She can be downright scary."

What was even scarier was how easy Francesca found it to chitchat about her life with this man even when she knew she was playing with fire.

And the instant she opened her front door, she discovered that Jack, a pounding headache, exhaustion and an assortment of bruises weren't the only problems to contend with tonight.

"Do you normally keep the house this cold?" he asked, sidestepping her to hold the door open.

"Gabrielle would have lowered the thermostat before she left but only to sixty-eight."

"Feels a little colder than that."

Francesca swallowed back a groan while flipping on the lights between the foyer and the basement door. "I'm not going to catch a break today, am I?"

"I'll see what I can do."

"My hero."

Jack flashed a pleased grin that made her heart thump hard for a few beats before she willed herself back under tight control. Leading him into a basement as cold as a meat locker, she maneuvered a path through moving boxes packed with all Nonna's worldly possessions to reach the furnace closet.

"Damn it. It's stone cold." She let out a groan that made her head ache dully. Her vast sum of experience ran the gamut of central heat and air.

Jack waved her aside.

"Be my guest," she said, a little surprised at how relieved she felt to pass on the responsibility. The feeling took her off guard. Proved nice even. He did his man thing, turned a few knobs, pressed some buttons she would have been too scared to press lest she blow up the house. Then he seconded her opinion. "Damn it."

"I have no heat?"

"You have no heat," he repeated with a grim expression. "I hate to admit defeat, but there's nothing I can do tonight. This unit is on its last leg. You're better off giving Harvey Stockton a call in the morning. He's the only one I know who might be able to coax some life out."

A game plan. How refreshing. She was more than happy to accept his solution to the problem. Well, tomorrow's problem, anyway. "Looks like you'll have to take me to the lodge, Jack. I've had my fill of freezing today. Haven't you?"

"Nice try." He smiled jovially. "Got a fireplace?"

Oh, God, this day just kept getting better and better. "If you take me to the lodge, you can go home to your nice warm house…or wherever you live."

"Apartment," he supplied. "I live in the square."

"Really?" She pictured Bluestone's quaint town square with the canopied shop fronts and picturesque balconies.

"Can't beat the commute to work."

"No kidding." He could roll out of bed and be in the police station, or courthouse or mayor's office in a heartbeat. The epitome of a bachelor pad. "Seriously, Jack. Please let's go. Just accept this isn't meant to be."

He gazed at her, and even the dim light didn't hide how his expression softened, how his gaze caressed her.

"You're wrong, Francesca. It is meant to be."

His voice was a throaty whisper between them, intimate, and she was galvanized by the sound, by the promise. Because he was referring to more than babysitting her tonight. A lot more.

"Will you take me to the fireplace or should I find it myself?"

She stared into those black eyes. He stared back, and she saw a battle she wouldn't win even if she had the energy to fight. She didn't.

"Family room."

His smile flashed. "Then you'll be warm soon."

She was warm enough, thank you. Proximity, imagination and the intensity of his gaze all combined to chase off the chill in a big way. Time to flee. She started toward the stairs.

"Is this one of those situations you're determined to find good in?" she asked, effectively rerouting their conversation to a safer topic, to place a barrier between them, even something as insubstantial as her voice.

He didn't answer right away, just followed in her wake up the uneven stone stairs, much too close, especially when he placed a hand on her hip to steady her at the top.

She practically jumped in response to his touch, too jumpy. And his smile proved that he was aware of the effect he had on her.

What else had she expected? He was Jack Sloan. Of course he knew. Pleasure was all over his face as he pushed the door wide. She slipped through, so completely aware of the moment their bodies almost touched as she passed.

"If you hadn't fallen and wound up at the hospital," he finally said, "your daughter would be in this freezing house instead of at the lodge with your grandmother. She'd have tried to kick-start that antiquated furnace and would have probably blown up the whole house."

She gave an outraged laugh. "That's not funny."

"Then why are you laughing?"

"Because you're not normal, and that's very funny."

"You find me amusing?"

There was something in his voice, something serious, and she turned to face him, to find an intensity in his face that made her breath flutter hard.

"Not amusing." There was nothing whatsoever amusing about the effect this man was having on her.

"Good. Because I was going more for interested, Francesca. Interested in me enough to want to get to know me."

Every cell in her body melted. She just stood there, drowning in the earnestness she saw in his eyes.

He reached out and brushed the hair off her cheek with his fingertips, a simple gesture that made her heartbeat stall in her chest. "I want to know you better."

This man was fire, *fire.*

Reality check.

"I'm involved in your investigation. What about conflict?"

"You're different."

She shook her head, denial winning over curiosity. "I'm not."

"You are, because I know you're not guilty. Just a matter of proving it."

"Jack, please—"

"I need to clear up this case fast. It's in the way of us getting to know each other better. I'd hope you feel the same."

Breathe, Francesca. Breathe.

But a deep breath only cleared her head enough to realize she was behaving ridiculously. Her heart pounded. Her knees felt weak. Her every brain cell had stubbornly wrapped around the fact that this man wanted to get to know her better, wanted her to want to know him.

And with his dark gaze caressing her, his expression inviting, Francesca couldn't think of anything she wanted more.

She must be concussed. She had to be. Why else would she be reacting to Jack in this purely physical way, a way that melted all the years of sanity that had proven this fluttery, wildly attracted feeling wasn't real. Couldn't possibly be real. And even if it was, it would only last an instant before life got in the way and reality blotted out any and all hint of romance.

She literally had to bite back a smile that would only encourage him. She could practically hear the fifteen-year-old wisdom pouring from Gabrielle's mouth.

Snap out of it, crazy woman.

Jack, though, looked very content with her response. Of course he'd be used to women getting stupid around him. He'd know all the telltale signs.

That energized her.

"Jack, I—" She what? She had to stop this right now. *Before* she got sucked in. "I have a teenage daughter. I can't get involved in a casual relationship. I just can't."

For a moment he only stared. Then all the *pleased* faded.

"You think I'm looking for casual." It wasn't a question, and something about him seemed so surprised.

Why, oh, why was he putting this between them? Why couldn't they keep dancing around their chemistry? They were so much safer that way.

"I have no clue, Jack. I do know that we're in two different places in life. Add this investigation, the fact that I'm who I am and you are who you are. Since you're being so honest with me, I want to be honest with you back."

Not really. She wanted denial.

"I won't deny that I find you very attractive."

He'd know she was lying if she denied that.

"I like you. And I completely appreciate all your help. Not only with the investigation but tonight."

"But?" he asked, and she couldn't read his reaction. His law-enforcement face was on big-time.

"But I'm a mother. You're a single man, a serially single man from all accounts. Not that there's anything wrong with being single. There isn't. But I have a lot of responsibilities and not a whole lot of time to juggle them. My daughter. My grandmother. And my job that supports all of us."

"You don't think I understand your responsibilities?"

"No, that's not it. Well, yes. I guess it is. The family part, anyway." She exhaled heavily. "You're the police chief, Jack. I know you understand responsibilities and what it's like to be busy. But my life is my family. I'm living on borrowed time with my daughter and my grandmother. I can't fit anything else on my plate right now. I just can't." She was babbling and she knew it, so she shut her mouth and waited.

"Okay, Francesca" was all he said, so anticlimatic. "You've been honest and I appreciate that."

Then he flipped the collar of her coat beneath her chin and said, "So where's the wood? Or do I have to take down that tree in your front yard?"

"No, no. I'll show you." Francesca beat a hasty retreat, coward that she was. Heading into the mudroom, she made a move to grab a log, but Jack stopped her.

"I got it. Just show me where to go."

She retraced her steps to the family room. He glanced at the fireplace then turned to her. She met his gaze, tried not to look expectant, knew she did.

Then just a hint of a smile. "You sit right there on that couch. I mean it. You're supposed to be resting."

She sank onto the sofa, unwilling to admit that she was utterly exhausted. Physically *and* emotionally. Wrapping an afghan around her, she tucked her knees close and wriggled into the cushions to collect herself, which might be impossible with this absolutely handsome, completely forbidden man waiting on her.

This was all Nonna's fault. If she hadn't started up all the craziness about Jack being a *bachelor,* she wouldn't have gotten Francesca thinking about him as a man. She might have been fascinated by how attractive he was with the tongue-tied sort of fascination she should have exorcised in high school.

She wouldn't be here short of breath, remembering how it felt to be wrapped all around him, listening to his deep breathing, feeling his heart pound. She wouldn't still be imagining his strong arms cradling her, and wondering how his mouth might feel on hers.

That was Nonna's fault, too.

CHAPTER FIFTEEN

FRANCESCA REFUSED TO OPEN her mouth again until her wayward emotions were under control. She forced her attention off Jack, who moved with efficient movements as he got a fire blazing. The television sat in the corner, along with Gabrielle's boom box. But the room's focal point was the fireplace, so the warmth radiated through the seating area quickly.

That heat radiated through her, too. Suddenly she could feel the physical effects of the day and a few sleepless nights bearing down on her as adrenaline ebbed.

"You'll need to stay down here close to the fire." Jack stood and turned to her. "Pillows and blankets?"

"I'll get—"

"You'll stay right where you are."

"Closet in the hallway beside the basement door. If you get to the bathroom, you've gone too far." She simply didn't have the energy to argue.

Jack disappeared and reappeared again with an armful of blankets. He made up a serviceable bed on the other sofa that created a comfortable conversation pit before the fireplace.

Then he came to stare down at her. "I need to make a bed where you are, and you need to get out of those frozen clothes."

No argument there. Her clothes had dried long ago, but

they were still stiff and chilly beneath her equally trashed coat. "I'm too comfortable."

"You'll be even more comfortable after you change and I bundle you up. I can even make you something hot to drink. Whatever you have—tea? Cocoa?"

"Coffee."

He shook his head, and the firelight cast copper glints in his hair. "No coffee. You need to rest."

"I had no idea you were such a bully." She gave a huff. "You've always been so polite when you came by the lodge."

"Official visits."

She tried to sit up, but even the effort of lifting her head proved too much. The sofa was much too warm and comfortable. She closed her eyes instead, tried to absorb the heat from the fireplace. "I shouldn't have sat down."

"Okay, let's try this. Tell me what you need, and I'll bring it to you."

"No, no, that's silly. I'm fine."

"Do you realize how often you say that? Are you trying to convince me or yourself?"

That got her attention, and she opened her eyes to find him smiling down at her.

"I'll help get you settled."

All this help. Who knew that lots of help could be as annoying as no help at all? But the thought of him poking around in her pajama drawer proved too much. Pajamas made her think of sleep. Sleep made her think of beds....

Throwing off the afghan, she forced herself to her feet, didn't resist when he took her elbow to help her. "You should change, too. Nonna won't have anything to fit you."

"Don't worry about me. I keep a change of clothes in the car. Never know when I'll be pulling an all-nighter."

She supposed she shouldn't be surprised. He was foresighted and prepared, unwilling to let little obstacles get in the way of his work. She could appreciate that.

She could also appreciate how attentive he was, slipping the coat from her shoulders and casually resting a hand on her waist to steer toward the stairs. His hand was light, guiding, but she could feel his touch through her blouse, was so intensely aware of such a small touch.

Of course Jack probably thought she'd fall on her face without his help, and as much as it pained her to admit it, she couldn't blame him. She was a sight after the night's travails, and not a pleasant one.

"It's freezing up here." The cold air blasted her when she stepped onto the second-floor landing.

"Be quick then. I'll wait here."

What Francesca really wanted was a steaming hot shower to thaw her out. But the very thought of being naked anywhere close to that man gave her palpitations. And as tired as she was, she'd probably drown, and invite another gallant rescue…

Snap out of it, crazy woman!

"I won't be long." She glanced at him, smiled to let him know how much she appreciated his help. The expression of a mature, responsible woman who could easily handle an innocent night spent with an attractive man.

"I'll be right here. Tell me if you need anything."

She kept on smiling as she escaped into her bedroom, where she changed into warm sweats then washed her face, brushed her teeth and grabbed the comforter and pillow off her bed. She reappeared on the landing in five minutes flat.

"Impressive." Jack took the comforter before stepping aside to let her precede him on the stairs.

"The lure of that fire."

"Still feeling okay?" he asked. "How's your head?"

"Pounding. But I'm okay. I'm tired."

Then he was settling her on the sofa, puffing the pillow behind her head, pulling the comforter beneath her chin. The warmth of this room stole through her immediately, and she nestled into her toasty nest with a sigh, feeling cared for in a way she couldn't ever remember feeling before.

"Thanks," she said, her voice a whisper above the crackle of the burning logs. "I really do appreciate you saving my life and rescuing me from the hospital."

"Wish I saved you from the broken furnace, too."

"You did. Maybe not like you wanted."

He only chuckled. Francesca could barely keep her eyes open, but didn't have the energy to resist the drowsy, delicious feeling he inspired.

"Make yourself at home." She forced the words out thickly, and the last thing she heard was the sound of his laughter.

The next time she opened her eyes, the house was filled with the heavy quiet of the late night. The wood snapped and popped in the fireplace, and she blinked her eyes to focus to find out what had awakened her.

Jack.

He was crouched before the fire, adjusting the logs with a poker, dressed in jeans and a flannel shirt, so different from the man who looked so stylish in his suits or so very impressive in his uniform. Through heavy eyes, Francesca watched him.

He moved with an economy of motion, smooth and physical. She'd have known he was athletic even if she hadn't been aware of his stint as a football jock. The firelight burnished his hair, formed a halo around those shoulders so straight and broad. How could he seem to be everything she would choose in a man if she were choosing—gorgeous, driven, capable, thoughtful—as well as everything she wouldn't choose?

Was he just a charming rogue who could easily read what would impress her? Had he guessed she was a woman who'd spent too many years with a husband who hadn't paid attention to her, didn't value her because he didn't want to be burdened with the realities of marriage good, bad or otherwise?

Or was this just Jack, not a charming rogue, but a charming gentleman? A man who paid attention to what she had to say because he was interested. A man who was easy to be around because he valued the ups and downs of life rather than viewing every single thing as a stress or a pressure.

Francesca wasn't sure when Jack knew she'd awakened, but when he turned, he said, "It's snowing again."

His voice was a husky murmur in the quiet, a sound that shouldn't sound quite so delicious, but did.

She had no reply, still hadn't relinquished slumber, so she watched as he stretched out on the other sofa and pulled a blanket to his waist. She faced him across the expanse of Nonna's coffee table.

"Feeling any better?" he asked.

"Mmm-hmm." She tested the sound in her throat.

"You should go back to sleep. It's almost morning."

She'd known, and not because she could see the clock on the mantle. She could hear the lateness in the quiet, feel it in the sleepiness of her muscles.

"Do you need anything?" he asked.

Francesca considered him a moment longer, wondered if he'd slept at all. "Will you tell me about the updates on the case?"

He didn't reply for so long she thought he'd sidestep her question about "business" again.

"Anything good at all?" she prompted.

"I cleared most of your staff."

"That is good." Francesca let her eyes drift shut and exhaled a contented sigh. She should ask the most obvious question, and she would. But not too quickly. Not when she was so content to sit here, sleepy in the warm darkness, with Jack and the fire and the quiet.

"Most, but not all?" she finally asked, still avoiding the illustrious question.

"Afraid not."

She steeled herself and, knowing she wouldn't like the answer, asked the illustrious question. "Who didn't make the cut?"

"You and Susanna." He sounded resigned and regretful, not at all like the chief of police. Or maybe that was because he occupied a sofa in her living room, an attractive display of long legs and sleep-tousled hair.

Which was precisely why she wouldn't open her eyes. "Great. The town good girl versus the town bad girl. And I'm already down in the polls."

"Francesca—"

"You have some work to do then, Jack." She finally faced him. "Because I don't think Susanna's a thief. And I know I'm not."

His gaze held hers steadily, but there was something in his expression, she wasn't sure exactly what, but that something convinced her he took what she said seriously.

"I'll find out what's going on. I have a vested interest in both of you."

She wasn't exactly reassured. Susanna was a friend of Jack's from way back. If only two of them were left on the suspect list, would he be forced to choose?

Francesca didn't think so. Maybe she was way off base. Maybe tonight had been nothing more than Jack keeping an eye on his suspect. Maybe he was using his charm and their attraction to keep her close and off balance, hoping to shake loose more clues when she let her guard down.

Charming gentleman or charming rogue?

She had a choice before her. Jack had told her why he was here. He also claimed to believe her innocent.

Bottom line: she believed him.

"I do appreciate all you're doing," she said softly. "Maybe you can help me out with a problem I'm having. Sort of a side effect of the investigation."

"Is this what you wanted to talk about today?"

She nodded. "People are gossiping. I don't have much control on my end. I have residents who have been victimized. They're going to talk. With family. With friends. And they should. This whole situation is upsetting to everyone concerned. But to my knowledge, no one is talking about how I'm number one on your suspect list. Your department has been careful not to discuss specifics with my residents, so I'm not sure where this sort of stuff is originating. I was hoping you might help me figure it out."

"Exactly what have you heard?"

"Not me. My daughter."

"Someone said something to her." Not a question. That law-enforcement expression settled over his face in barely the blink of an eye, and Francesca found she liked when he got all to-protect-and-to-serve about her daughter.

"Another one of yesterday's traumas." She exhaled softly. "Have I mentioned how glad I am yesterday's over?"

"Tell me what happened."

She gave him the PowerPoint version of her conversation with Beth Fairweather then found herself talking, just talking.

"This move seemed like the perfect solution. Nonna needed me here, and Gabrielle was struggling so hard to deal with her father. Now she's dealing with fallout from another crazy parent. Only she doesn't even have any friends. Well, I take that back," Francesca amended drily. "I wasn't exactly happy with some of the friends she was making in Phoenix."

"You're not stealing your residents' identities, so how are you responsible for this?"

"Bluestone's a small town, Jack. People are going to talk. That's a given. If not for my past, I might have gotten the benefit of the doubt. I can't imagine anyone seriously considers Susanna guilty." She didn't wait for his reply. "Of course not. Put me and her in a room together, and everyone's going to look my way when the diamond bracelet goes missing."

"Francesca—"

"Don't get me wrong. I don't blame Susanna. I've never had any reason to question her honesty. Since I don't want anyone holding my teenage choices against me, I'm certainly not going to hold them against Susanna. Not when we've established a working relationship. It's not friendly by any stretch, but it is working."

"Francesca—"

"I didn't steal anyone's identity, Jack. I gladly accept responsibility for my past. But no one should be spreading rumors that my daughter has to deal with. Gossip is unkind. Plain and simple."

Her rant had everything to do with exhaustion, the lateness of the hour and weirdness of the situation. But she couldn't stop. She'd decided to take action with the problem, and Jack was the logical place to start. Now they'd established how things stood between them, she didn't have to hold back.

"That's what I wanted to know about, Jack. The people you have working on the case. Anyone I would know?

Anyone who might pass along details to fan the flames? Anyone—"

"*Francesca!*"

Her name rang out like a command, so unexpected that it brought her rant to a startled halt. She blinked.

"I'm sorry that your daughter had to hear about the case at school," he said. "My men know they're not at liberty to discuss this case. I'll talk with them and see—"

"I appreciate that, but will you do me another favor and be really careful when you do. I'd hate for anyone to think you were playing favorites. Susanna's a personal friend of yours. The only thing I have going for me is that no one in their right mind would ever expect you to play favorites in my direction. I realize it's not much, but it's about the only thing I have going for me right now."

That made him scowl. "There's no reason for anyone to question my actions."

"They might think you feel sorry for me or that you've somehow fallen under my spell."

"They'd be right then." His gaze captured hers, his eyes reflecting the firelight still so stern, so somber. "Well, not about the feeling sorry part."

Francesca's heart stopped beating, just plain stopped right in her chest. She stared at him, the jumble of emotions inside tying her tongue into a knot. She had no reply, nothing but that swelling feeling in her chest, a feeling of such excitement that she had to consciously remember to breathe.

"Francesca," Jack said in a voice that told her he had absolutely no intention of playing by her rules. "Just because I'm under your spell doesn't mean I won't do my job. Please, trust me. I'll talk with my men, but the best way to stop the gossip in this fishbowl of a town will be to solve this case."

Then he laughed softly, a sound that filtered through her like the warmth from the fire. "For the record, I respect how you feel about your family. But that doesn't mean I'm not going to try and convince you to make room for me on your plate."

Francesca knew right then and there that she was in trouble. Deep, deep trouble.

CHAPTER SIXTEEN

JACK OPENED THE CAR DOOR then extended his hand to
Frankie. She slipped her cool fingers within his, and he
savored the contact, enjoyed the show as she emerged in a
jaw-dropping display of long sleek legs. She looked so
much better this morning after a night of rest.

He, on the other hand, had barely slept. He'd been too
focused on figuring out what he wanted from this woman and
how he was going to convince her to give him what he
wanted.

A chance.

"Harvey said he'll be working on that furnace all day,"
Jack said. "With any luck he'll be able to find the right
parts, and you can go home to a warm house tonight."

Her hand lingered in his for a moment before she lifted
her gaze to his. "Thank you so much for all your help,
Jack."

"My pleasure. I mean that."

Her gray eyes, usually so expressive, were guarded this
morning, so careful not to reveal anything that might encourage him in his pursuit of her. "I hope you can salvage
something of your day."

He glanced at his watch. "It's still early. Got the whole
day ahead of me."

She smiled at that. "I'm glad. I know you've got a lot of
work to clear your suspects."

"Wish me luck."

"You know I do."

He had to resist the urge to stroke a stray curl from her cheek. Instead, he slipped a hand under her elbow and motioned toward the front doors. "I'll see you upstairs."

To his surprise, she didn't argue, just walked along at his side, unbuttoning her peacoat as they headed inside the lobby.

"Good morning, June," she said to the woman behind the receptionist desk.

"Good morning, Ms. Raffa. Glad you're okay."

"Right as rain. Today's a new day, and as far as I'm concerned yesterday never happened."

June laughed. "Good luck with that. I've already had a half-dozen residents show up wanting to know where to send the cards and flowers."

"How thoughtful." Frankie ground out the words from between gritted teeth.

Jack laughed. Then they were on their way to the fourth floor, where they found Etta waiting for them in the hallway outside her door when they emerged from the elevator.

"Dolly, how do you feel?"

Frankie hurried forward and kissed her grandmother's cheek. "Perfectly perfect as you can see. Now that I'm someplace with working heat. Who knew how cold that big house could get?"

"I could have told you that." Etta stepped inside her apartment. "The repairman may have trouble fixing the furnace, though. Your grandfather put it in such a long time ago."

"Hello again, Etta," Jack said, following Frankie into the small foyer. "I called Harvey Stockton. He said it might take some doing, but he thought he could get it working again."

"You are a good boy, Jack. Thank you for taking such good care of my granddaughter."

"The pleasure was all mine."

Etta gazed at him with sparkling eyes. "Did you get your socks back?"

He chuckled. "I did."

Frankie rolled her eyes and stepped into the living room, shrugging off her coat. "Is Gabrielle still asleep? Oh, there you are, pup."

Then she strode toward the bedroom, where a young girl, tall and slim like her mother and a few inches taller, stood in the doorway.

"My poor puppy," Frankie said, stroking her hair. "I abandoned you yesterday. I'm so sorry."

Gabrielle was a beautiful girl, with the same expressive features as her mother. Jack thought she looked relieved when she hugged Frankie with no hint of self-consciousness. With her cheek resting on her mother's shoulder, she eyed him curiously.

"Gabrielle, this is Chief Sloan," Etta said. "The one I told you about. Remember?"

"I remember, Nonna. The bachelor," Gabrielle said, deadpan.

That got a response from Frankie, who disentangled herself from her daughter's arms with a frown. "Knock it off, you two." She met his gaze. "Jack, my daughter, Gabrielle."

Jack was too busy trying not to smile. He was glad to know he had at least one member of this family in his corner, because admittedly, he didn't have much experience with teenagers. Except for the delinquent variety. So he chose a straightforward approach, crossing the distance and extending his hand.

"Pleased to meet you, Gabrielle. Your mother has told me a lot about you. All good."

She took his stock in a glance, her expression noncommittal, but Jack was a cop at heart and knew she didn't miss a thing about him. She was reserving her opinion.

"*All* good?"

Jack inclined his head.

Gabrielle just smiled.

And Jack realized right then that not only did he have to convince the mom to take a chance on him, but her daughter, too.

Apparently, Etta already knew that because she popped her head through the cutaway leading into a tiny kitchen and asked, "Jack, you'll stay for coffee, won't you?"

"Yes, Etta," he said with enthusiasm. "I'd love to."

SUSANNA TOPPED OFF HER MUG with the last of the coffee then automatically went to rinse the carafe. Unfortunately, there was no getting in the sink. Not with last night's dinner dishes piled high.

"Brooke, damn it." Couldn't her daughter have loaded the dishwasher? Was that really so hard to do?

Wait a sec…today was Saturday, which meant yesterday was Friday. *Her* day for the dishes. Except that she hadn't left work until late after Frankie's escapades. Come on, who traipsed around the property after a snowstorm? She was lucky she didn't fall down the mountain and break her neck.

By the time Susanna had left the lodge, she'd had to go straight to the school to pick up Brandon from practice, which meant she hadn't cooked dinner until after they'd gotten home. That full sink of dishes hadn't even computed in her tired brain. After dinner, she'd curled into a ball on the couch with a blanket and pillow and subjected herself to the tail end of some completely forgettable made-for-television movie.

If you'd have been here, Skip, you'd have rescued me from these dishes. My knight in shining armor.

Okay. So she'd bump last night's dinner dishes into the first slot on today's to-do list. Not a tragedy. Setting down the carafe, she sipped her coffee and waited for the caffeine to kick in, not hopeful as this was already her fourth cup.

"Mom." Brooke sailed into the kitchen with purpose.

"Yes, dear?"

"I want to go to a show tonight. That okay with you? I'm giving you plenty of notice since I know how much you hate last-minute plans."

Brooke was being cooperative? The hairs on the back of Susanna's neck stood on end. "What kind of show? And where?"

"Transitions. It's a venue in Saugerties."

"What's a venue?"

Brooke rolled her eyes and started digging through the pantry, presumably for breakfast. "A place that has shows."

"I shopped on Thursday. There's oatmeal, cereal and bagels. Or if you want, you can make eggs."

Each suggestion earned a disgusted grimace. "No Pop-Tarts?"

"Ah, real food, please."

Another grimace.

"Okay, no eggs then." Susanna wasn't at all surprised, but talking about breakfast bought her some time to collect her thoughts about this proposition.

Brooke still wore her pajamas, sweatlike pants made out of some clingy fabric and a muscle shirt that left too much of her tummy bare. And she was barefoot on the tile floor.

"Aren't you cold?" Susanna asked.

"No." Brooke quit the pantry and moved on to the refrigerator.

"Okay, so a venue is a place that has shows," Susanna said. "What kind of shows?"

"Bands."

"You want to go see a band?"

Susanna must have sounded as surprised as she felt because Brooke wheeled around from the refrigerator, armed with a bag of bagels and tub of cream cheese, ready for battle.

"Yes, a band, Mom. My friends are playing."

"You have friends in a band."

Brooke didn't even dignify that with a reply as she deposited her breakfast on the baker's rack beside the toaster and rummaged through the silverware drawer.

"What friends?"

"Justin's in Frantica. Matt and Ethan are in Tranz PM."

"So more than one band is playing."

"Yeah. Four or five, I think."

"Any girls going to this show?"

Brooke sawed apart a bagel, not seeming to notice the crumbs sprinkling onto the floor. "Mmm-hmm. Tyler'll be there, and Kaley, too."

Kaley was a longtime friend, so no problem there. Susanna hadn't ever actually met Tyler, but knew from Brooke that Tyler dated Matt. Both were sophomores, if memory served. "Anyone going to be there with a car?"

"I don't know. But I won't get in anyone's car if that's what you're asking."

It was. At this age, these kids were a terrifying mix of those who could drive and those who couldn't. At fifteen, Brooke wasn't going to be driving in anyone's car. "That was the right answer. So who hangs out at this kind of venue?"

"Kids, Mom. It's by the skate park."

"You mean a teen club?"

"A *venue*. It costs seven bucks to get in, but they don't serve alcohol or anything. So you don't have to worry."

Oh, Susanna was worried all right. "Let me get this

straight. You want to go clubbing tonight in Saugerties to see your friends play in a band?"

"It's not clubbing," Brooke insisted. "I told you there's no alcohol."

Inside the club, maybe. But it was clubbing all the same, which meant Brooke would be primed and ready for the bars as soon as she could legally drink.

Susanna stifled the impulse to laugh and say, "No way." No, she was going to handle this rationally no matter how much it hurt. That was the only way she could expect Brooke to communicate rationally. "I appreciate the advance notice, so let me give it some thought. Why don't you get me some more information about this…venue." *Club.*

"What kind of information?"

Setting her mug on the counter, Susanna reached into the cabinet for a plate before Brooke took out any more of the floor with her mess. "Surely they have a Web site or a MySpace page?"

Brooke nodded.

"That'll be good enough. E-mail me the URL and I'll go check it out as soon as I finish cleaning up in here."

"Will do." Brooke withdrew the bagel from the toaster and placed it on the plate. Then she sauntered off to the table with the tub of cream cheese. That was it. No argument.

Susanna almost smiled. Rational had won the moment and they hadn't degenerated into an argument that invariably would wind up with Brooke accusing Susanna of treating her like a child.

Unless, of course, Susanna discovered this *venue* was inappropriate for a fifteen-year-old, in which case the argument would start as soon as Brooke was told she wouldn't be going.

But Susanna wasn't going to borrow trouble. She'd savor the triumph of the moment—

"Aunt Karan's here," Brandon yelled from the living room.

Glancing out the window above the sink, Susanna did a double take as the low-slung Jaguar wheeled to a sharp stop in her driveway. Glancing at the clock above the baker's rack, she wiped her hands on the dish towel and started for the door.

For Karan to get up and out before noon on a Saturday... Susanna pulled open the door to find Karan already out of the car and heading up the walkway with long, graceful strides.

"What on earth is going on?" Susanna asked.

One look at Karan's expression answered several questions instantly. Karan was positively in a state. Her bright blue eyes were flashing, and her well-maintained mouth was compressed into a tight line that would have had her plastic surgeon scowling.

"You are simply not going to believe it," she said, sweeping past Susanna.

Susanna shut the door and would have offered to take Karan's coat, but she was already slipping the fur-lined wool off her shoulders and tossing it onto the antique bench.

"Let's go into the sunroom, where we can talk." Susanna inclined her head toward the living room where Brandon was on the floor in front of the couch, hands clutching the remote controller to his video game.

"Hey, kiddo," Karan called out, and Susanna was pleased when he glanced away from his game long enough to smile.

"Hey, Aunt Karan."

Any further interaction was cut off when Brooke sailed

into the room and let out a squeal, before launching herself at Karan for an enthusiastic greeting, complete with air kisses.

"Aunt Karan!"

"Hello, gorgeous." Karan was momentarily distracted from the drama at hand. "Look at you. Mom can't keep those boys away, I'll bet. You remember what I told you?"

"Only the rich handsome ones who have their eyes on the future," Brooke quoted.

"Good girl."

There was no mystery why Brooke was so enamored with Karan. What young girl wouldn't be fascinated by a beautiful woman who wore wealth and style as comfortably as Susanna wore Skip's old flannel robe? She was tall, blonde and always dressed impeccably, whether bundled up against the snow, on her way to a show in the city or heading to the club for a kickboxing class.

She was the one who brought extravagant gifts— Broadway show tickets for Brooke's birthday and an autographed baseball for Brandon at Christmas.

Aunt Karan was like the gorgeous Fairy Godmother.

"Convince Mom to let me go to a show tonight, will you, please?" Brooke begged.

Karan wrapped an arm around her shoulder and squeezed. "See what I can do. A girl's got to have a social life."

"Don't shoot yourself in the foot, young lady." Susanna ended the debate before it began. "I said I'd think about it."

"Oh, let her go, Suze," Karan said with a wink at Brooke. "She's got to get out into the world and be seasoned. Or else how is she going to attract all those rich handsome men with their eyes on the future?"

Susanna simply smiled in reply then shooed Brooke away. "Go get that information for me. I'm sure Aunt Karan didn't drop by this early to run interference for you."

After another enthusiastic hug, Brooke headed into the kitchen while Susanna led Karan out to the sunroom where they could talk in private.

Even with gray skies swelling in preparation for another snowstorm, the sunroom was Susanna's favorite space in the house. Once the kids' rooms had held that distinction, but now they were older, and Skip was gone, the sunroom was the one place where she could go that wasn't overcome with bittersweet memories, a place she could be alone with her thoughts.

The room, mostly windows, stretched into the conservation lot that was her backyard and had initially sold her on the house. Come spring it would awaken with greenery and bright flowers. But right now it was tiered in snow, winter-bare trees reaching spindly fingers into that gray sky. A scene that felt a lot like her mood.

The door had barely shut behind them before Karan said, "You are never going to guess who Charles saw at the hospital last night."

Charles had been Karan's first husband and one of the hospital's surgeons, so the answer could have been anyone. Why Karan had been talking to her ex was a mystery in itself, but Susanna wasn't about to ask.

"No clue," she said, even though she had a good idea. "Who did Charles see?"

"Frankie. She was in the emergency room."

This much Susanna knew, but that wouldn't have brought Karan around this early. "And…?"

"Jack." Karan dropped into a chair…well, dropped wasn't exactly the right description. More like melted, a fluid motion that spoke more eloquently than any words about what she thought of Jack being with Frankie last night. "Did you know?"

Hmm, how to avoid getting blasted because she hadn't

picked up the phone and called Karan with this news? "I saw him take off in the ambulance with her, but I assumed the paramedics wanted to check him out, too."

Karan looked unimpressed. "I can believe the klutz almost killed herself. I can believe Jack rode in to save the day like her bloody knight in shining armor. But I can't believe you didn't call me."

Susanna knew Karan must be willing to let the slight go otherwise she wouldn't be here. Sinking onto the couch opposite Karan, she curled up in the big cushions. "I was going to call. But I expected you to be off doing something special on a Friday night. And you *never* pick up the phone before noon."

"Who slept last night, anyway?" She gave a dismissive wave with a perfectly manicured hand. "And I do hope you appreciate how I'm looking out for you when you can't even bother to pick up the phone until it's convenient for you."

Susanna was guilty as charged, so there was no point arguing. "What did Charles say?"

For a moment, Karan looked as if she might keep the news to herself to keep Susanna in suspense, but that lasted all of a heartbeat. "Charles said that Jay wanted to keep Frankie overnight for observation. But apparently she didn't want to cooperate—big surprise there, I'm sure—so Jack had him release Frankie into his care."

Susanna frowned. She knew where this was going. "Frankie has a daughter the same age as Brooke. Jack probably dropped Frankie off at home and let her daughter babysit. Or he might have taken her back to the lodge to stay with her grandmother."

Karan sat upright and folded her arms across her chest. "You think? So why was his car at her house all night?"

"You're kidding?"

Karan shook her head, a smug smile in place.

"How do you know that? Are you sure?"

"I drove by and saw for myself. At midnight. And two. And five." Her mouth twisted in a distasteful moue. "He didn't leave until after eight this morning."

"You drove by Frankie's house last night?" Like a real, live stalker, only Susanna kept that to herself. "All right, you got me. I am surprised. I completely didn't see this coming. You don't think something's going on between them, do you?"

"That's what I'm worried about."

"Even if there is, Karan, why do you care?"

"I thought *you'd* have been worried. That's why I gave up my entire night to find out what was going on."

"I have no interest whatsoever in Frankie's personal life. Or Jack's for that matter."

Karan smiled that slightly exasperated, very smug smile. "I would have thought that since you and Frankie are the only ones left on Jack's suspect list, you might be worried she was trying to throw the investigation in her favor."

That stopped Susanna short, and for a moment she could only stare. "I'm still on the suspect list?" she finally sputtered. "Me and Frankie? That's it? Where did you hear that?"

"The grapevine, honey. That's why I'm here. If Frankie's sleeping with Jack while he's investigating…"

"Jack would never fall for that."

"Don't be so sure. What wouldn't a man do for sex?"

Susanna didn't have an answer for that. She'd never slept with Jack. Admittedly Karan's relationship with Jack had ended long ago, but she still had more of a clue about what might go on in Jack's bed than Susanna did.

The thought made her shiver, and the goose bumps that rose on her arms had nothing to do with the temperature. She heard the muted sound of the phone ringing somewhere, but it was only a stutter in thoughts that had already bolted from the gate.

Would Frankie actually sleep with Jack to distract him? Was Jack even capable of being distracted?

Every fiber of Susanna's being rejected the notion that Jack would play favorites. She'd known him most of her life. He played fair. But what if Frankie didn't? What if she managed to hold something over his head?

"Jack wouldn't stoop so low for sex, would he?"

"Oh, come on, Suze. He's a man. A man who hasn't been involved in quite some time. He's getting it somewhere. Trust me on this. I *knew* him, remember."

Fair enough. And Skip had always said Jack had married his job and only had time for flings. Susanna had never questioned that. But maybe there was more there than either of them had known. Maybe Jack only liked wild women.

Not that Frankie struck her as wild. Maybe in high school, but certainly not anymore. Then again, what if these past six months of acting professional had been a ruse to throw everyone off the trail? In high school she'd been mouthy and confrontational. Could someone really change so completely?

Of course, Karan had been on the warpath back then, too. And her friends—Susanna included—had always jumped on the bandwagon with the unkind taunts and propensity for high drama. From an adult perspective, Susanna knew Frankie hadn't had too many choices to cope. Not so surprising that she'd chosen to fight back with nastiness and rebellion.

In the corner of her eye, she caught sight of Brooke approaching the sunroom door. When she opened it, Susanna waved her off. "Please, Brooke, I'm busy. Deal with that. Take a message or whatever—"

"It's *your* work," Brooke snapped sounding irritated as she pressed the portable handset against her stomach to mute the sound. "Someone from Northstar Corporate."

The home office? On a Saturday morning?

Karan clearly understood the significance of such a call. "Do you need a good lawyer, Suze? I know quite a few."

Brooke's eyes widened, and Susanna stifled the urge to tell Karan to use her head before opening her mouth. Now she'd have to explain the situation and hope Brooke understood the meaning of discretion otherwise this news would be making the rounds via MySpace and Facebook within minutes.

With a sigh of entreaty, Susanna motioned for Brooke to bring her the phone, where she found Gerald Mayne, the president of finance and her immediate supervisor at Northstar, on the other end of the line.

"Gerald, this is a surprise. How are you and Betty?"

"Good, Susanna. Betty's great, too. Nagging me to retire, as usual." He gave a gruff chuckle. "Hate to bother you on a weekend, but we received the latest update on the investigation of your property. The board's convening to discuss the situation."

"That doesn't sound good. What can I do?"

"Hop on the next flight to Chicago. Corporate wants a chance to talk with you before the board convenes Monday."

"Me, Gerald? I understood the director has been in constant contact with the corporate office about the proceedings."

"She has. That's why the board wants to meet. Now that you and the director are the prime suspects in the investigation, we need to look at whether or not it's appropriate to appoint temporary replacements until the situation is resolved."

For a moment all Susanna could do was stare at the phone. Was she the only person who didn't know she was occupying a top slot on Jack's suspect list? "The director told you that she and I were the prime suspects?"

"President of Operations got a call from her."

"I see. Then I'll make the arrangements and get to town as soon as possible."

"Call me back when you know the flight times, Susanna. I'll come get you."

"Thanks, Gerald." She barely got the phone away from her ear when she met her daughter's shocked gaze.

"You're not for real, are you, Mom?"

"Brooke, what's wrong?" Susanna hadn't had enough time to process the bomb that just dropped on her head, but the look on her daughter's face brought her back to reality fast.

"You're the one ripping off the old people?"

"Of course not. Why on earth would you think that?"

Brooke's expression collapsed. "It's all over school. I just thought it was that stupid Tara O'Neill making up crap to torture Gabrielle. But it's really real? One of the managers is ripping off those cute little old people?"

"So Jack told Frankie and not you," Karan said. "There's a surprise." Then, helpful as ever, she held up her cell phone. "Need that lawyer's number now?"

CHAPTER SEVENTEEN

AFTER ENJOYING A GOOD CUP of coffee and even better company with Frankie's family, Jack headed to the precinct. He'd barely pulled past the Greywacke Lodge's security gate when his cell rang. After checking the display, he flipped open the phone and said, "Susanna, the exact person I need to talk with."

"Oh, really?"

"I've got an update on the investigation. But let me preface by saying that everything is fine—"

"Everything is not fine, Jack." Susanna shot the contradiction back, and he heard the distress in her voice, the anger. "You told Frankie that she and I were the only suspects left in your investigation. Didn't you think I'd be interested?"

"Susanna, listen to me. I apologize it's taken me so long to get ahold of you, but I can explain—"

"You didn't get ahold of me, Jack. I got ahold of you. Let's for one minute forget we're friends. That you've been a guest at every important event in my life since high school. You were a groomsman in my wedding. At both my kids' baptisms. A pallbearer at my husband's funeral. Let's pretend none of that matters. But you're the police chief. You're supposed to play fair not pick favorites."

"Frankie is my contact person on this case, Susanna. You know that," Jack reminded her calmly. "And I apologize about not calling you sooner. I went to the lodge yesterday to let you both know that we'd cleared all the other names off the list. You know what happened after I got there. By the time the emergency room released her, it was too late to call. It has nothing to do with favorites."

He wasn't sure where *that* had come from as he drove down the winding road that led into the valley. But his hand gripped the steering wheel a little more tightly.

"What am I supposed to think? You don't tell me something this important. You leave me to hear the gory details from Karan and my *supervisor* from corporate. I was completely unprepared." She exhaled sharply, a sound of profound disbelief. "This is my job we're talking about here, Jack. The job that feeds my kids and keeps a roof above their heads. Do you understand that?"

Karan. That explained a lot. Susanna had every right to be angry that he hadn't explained the situation to her personally—as he'd intended—but the agitation and accusations of favoritism would undoubtedly be a result of dealing with Karan, who had the unique ability to escalate emotions in any situation. Add an extreme dislike of Frankie and the two would be a lethal combination.

But Jack was completely at fault here, no matter how unintentionally. He could have easily telephoned with the news yesterday. Instead, he'd seized the chance to meet with Frankie in person, and he hadn't been able to break the news to Susanna until after speaking with Frankie. "I am sorry, Susanna. I would never deliberately leave you hanging out to dry with something like this. I wanted to deliver the news in person. I hope you'll take me at my word."

Silence greeted him on the other end of the line.

"Susanna, please forgive me."

"I've got to go, Jack," she said shortly. "I've got to make arrangements to get on a flight to Chicago today."

The connection ended and Jack clutched the phone in his fist and whispered, "Good luck."

The absolute last thing he'd wanted to do was give Susanna more grief. Yet that was exactly what he'd done. And damn Karan's insatiable need for dramatics. He had nothing to do with the woman and hadn't for years. The only time he ever saw her was when they attended the same functions or special occasions of mutual friends. But she could still manage to impact his life—like a damned ball-peen hammer.

He slammed his palm against the steering wheel. Damn it. And Susanna should know better than to let Karan wind her up that way. Susanna usually did know better, which told Jack everything he needed to know. She was feeling the pressure of this investigation, as he'd known she would.

As he wove in with the traffic, he tried to think of some way to help. The best he could come up with was to wrap up the investigation. For all their sakes. Which got him to thinking. If Susanna had been called into Northstar Corporate…

When he got to the traffic light on the corner of Spruce Street and Main, Jack scrolled through his contacts and depressed the send button.

"Good morning, Greywacke Lodge. June speaking. How may I direct your call?"

"Concetta Cesarini's room, please."

"Thank you for calling Greywacke Lodge. Connecting."

A series of clicks sounded in his ear, then the line rang through. Frankie answered on the second ring.

"You're supposed to be resting," he said.

Her laughter filtered through him in a way that calmed the edges of his frustration. "Are you checking up on me?"

"Yes. How are you feeling?"

"Rushed. I've got a command performance in Chicago. Got to hop on the next flight out."

"You feeling up to the trip?"

"Not really, but I'll be okay. I'll sleep on the plane. I'm just inconvenienced, that's all. I'm supposed to spend the day watching movies with Gabrielle."

"I'm sorry."

Silence. "For what?"

"For not being able to end the investigation before this."

"You're trying, Jack. That's all any of us can do."

She sounded so practical, so unruffled. She'd learned to roll gracefully with the punches. He liked that about her. He also liked that talking with her came so easily. Although she'd flat-out told him that he didn't stand a chance with her, Jack knew better. She was on the other end of this satellite signal, making him feel better with her reassurances and graciously allowing him to check up on her.

It was a start.

"Anything I can do to help you with corporate?" he asked.

"I wish. Solve the mystery. That's all I can think of."

All he could think of, too. Unfortunately. "What about a ride to the airport?"

"That's nice of you to offer, but I'm good, thanks. I'm not sure when I'll be back, so I need my car parked there. The board doesn't convene until Monday morning." She hesitated. "They may choose to install an interim director until this situation is resolved."

"I'm heading into the precinct as we speak. I'll figure this out, Francesca. You have my word."

"I know," she said softly. "I'm counting on it."

He savored her admission. Not so much the words, but the trust in her tone, the belief he would do what he said.

"Have you heard from Harvey?" he asked.

"Not yet. Sounded like it was going to take some time to find the right parts. And a miracle."

Jack laughed. "Have a safe trip then. Good luck with your bosses. I'll try to have some answers for you before they decide to temporarily replace you. Okay?"

"That works for me. Good luck, Jack."

"Good luck to you, too, Francesca. I'll stay in touch."

The sound of her voice lingered as he pulled into the precinct parking lot.

Jack checked in with the desk sergeant. Then made his way through the station, dismissing any thought of heading home to clean up until he shook loose some break in the case.

Randy wasn't in his cubicle, but Jack spotted him when he emerged from the document room.

"Randy."

He glanced up from the document he was holding, eyes widening. "You're timing is downright freaky, Chief."

"What have you got?"

"Hot off the press." Randy waved a fax transmission. "Want the good news or the bad news."

Jack scanned the information quickly. "Good news and bad news is right. Damn it."

"Didn't think you were going to be happy with that."

Jack hadn't realized until then that he was holding his breath. He'd wanted a break in the case. He'd gotten it. But he'd also wanted a miracle that would exonerate both Frankie and Susanna. He hadn't gotten that.

This document eliminated his last clue and targeted his alleged perp. After playing the process of elimination game, these two sheets of paper, including cover letter, verified that Greywacke Lodge's Director of Operations didn't have authorization to transfer resident funds, which limited access of pertinent information to the CFO.

"I don't think Susanna's a thief." Frankie's voice replayed in his memory. *"And I know I'm not."*

She'd been right on one score.

But he couldn't accept that Susanna was responsible for these thefts. The broad scope of these crimes…the level of knowledge and manipulation and intent….

No. Not Susanna.

But evidence didn't lie, and now he had a real problem. He'd run out of suspects.

"Let's go," he told Randy.

"Where?"

"To work. We're going to revisit every piece of evidence. I need another suspect."

Randy clamped a hand on Jack's back. Hard. "Listen, man. I know you aren't happy right now, but deal. We've got our perp."

"We don't."

Clutching the documents, he headed to Randy's cubicle, determined to go over absolutely everything they had from every source to see what they had missed.

Randy stomped along behind him, clearly pissed. "We're done here, Jack. We're ready to start building our case. We've got everything we need."

Jack shook his head. "No. We don't have the right perp."

Randy snatched up a disposable coffee cup from his desk. "Now's not the time to get personal. I know you know these people but—"

"You're right. I do know these people. Susanna isn't responsible. She'd have to be working with someone to pull off—" He shook his head emphatically. "We still don't have an identity on the mystery woman making the withdrawal. The FBI is working on that surveillance tape. In the meantime, we're not proceeding until we double-check every available fact."

Randy practically growled his frustration, but Gary Trant's arrival cut off his reply.

"Jack, Randy," Gary said in greeting, smiling as if he had every reason in the world to feel good which, as far as Jack was concerned, he didn't. "I was coming through the building, so I thought I'd check in and see how you're coming along with the old-age home. Pierce was running his mouth at the council meeting yesterday and getting everyone riled up. I was hoping you had some good news."

"Hate to disappoint you," Jack said.

At the same time Randy said, "We're ready to start building our case."

Gary shifted a narrowed gaze between them. "Which is it?"

"Our alleged perp isn't our alleged perp," Jack said. "We're not ready to make a move."

Gary wasn't stupid and he guessed quickly what was going on because he asked, "Who?"

"The CFO," Randy supplied. "Susanna Adams."

Gary frowned. "You're sure? To be honest, I find that difficult to swallow."

Randy rolled his eyes, took another swig of coffee to dismiss them.

"My thoughts exactly," Jack said.

"Then again…" Gary let his statement trail off. "Marietta said Susanna has been having a rough time getting back on her feet after Skip's death. He was sick a long time. I'm sure that had to cost a chunk of change."

"Could she be struggling to keep afloat financially?" Randy asked. "I don't know the lady, but I do know when it comes to my kids, I might get creative if things were bad enough."

"She might be struggling, but if she were in over her head, she'd go to Skip's parents. They'd help out. No question."

"I suppose it's something to know it isn't Frankie. Might

shut a few people up, at least." Gary folded his arms over his chest and leaned back against the desk, clearly intending to become part of the resolution process. "So what comes next?"

"We bring her in for questioning," Randy said.

"Bringing her in isn't a bad idea. At least we'll exonerate Frankie and look like we're doing something here."

"I am not bringing in an innocent woman as damage control," Jack said simply. "I'm on this case for exactly that reason."

"Some job you're doing, too. The whole damn town is talking, so let's not go there," Gary said.

Jack agreed with that, at least. The news had even trickled down into the high school.

"That's the real problem, though." Randy half sat on his desk. "We've got no good reason *not* to bring the CFO in for questioning. Nada, but Jack's opinion of her character. The evidence points to her. If we don't bring her in for questioning, then we leave ourselves open to obstruction. Don't know about you gents, but I don't want to defend myself for interfering in due process."

Gary winced. "Pierce will wipe the floor with us."

"We're still waiting on the FBI for an ID."

Randy snorted. "What? You think the Feds are working through the weekend to get you that evidence?"

Gary met Jack's gaze. "At least cover your ass while you wait. Bring her in for questioning. They know you and Skip were good friends. You don't want people spreading around how you cut the widow a break."

And that gave Jack an idea. Not a great idea, but a good way to buy some time. "I think you may be right."

"Bloody hallelujah." Randy lifted his cup in salute.

"Susanna is already on her way to Chicago to address the board of Northstar Management." At least Jack *hoped* she was on her way to the airport otherwise *he'd* just committed a crime. "I'll fly there to escort her back."

"Sounds like a plan." Gary sounded relieved. "Keep me updated with what's going on. I won't be into the office until Monday so call my cell. I'll be waiting to hear from you."

Jack nodded then charged Randy with a glance. "Get going on that."

"You still want me to go through everything?"

Jack nodded. "Get another *con leche*. You're going to need it. I'll be in touch."

Then he turned his back on Gary and Randy and headed out of the office. He had a flight to catch. He had no clue how yet, but he was going to fix this situation. Jack wasn't about to let down two people he cared for any more than he already had.

CHAPTER EIGHTEEN

FRANCESCA WASN'T SURPRISED to find Susanna, looking tired and anxious, in the reception area of Northstar's corporate headquarters. Francesca had arrived in Chicago last evening and assumed Susanna had done the same. Because it was still the crack of dawn and she'd already spent two hours answering questions from her supervisors in all Northstar's departments: Operations, Financial, Human Resources, Marketing, Planning and Development Services.

Her nerves were still jangling. Yet not a one of the executive had left her feeling interrogated. Neither had anyone implied that she'd fallen short in her duties anywhere along the way.

That was a plus. So was the fact that she hadn't been sitting in the reception area waiting like Susanna. Her title had counted for something.

She was glad, too. Facing the firing squad was a lot better than worrying about facing the firing squad, and Susanna's expression suggested that wait hadn't been pleasant.

"They're ready for you now, Susanna." She forced a smile. "Good luck."

There was really nothing else to say. She would have offered to wait and offer moral support. They might have commiserated together while awaiting their repeat performance with the board of directors tomorrow morning.

But Francesca knew Susanna wouldn't have welcomed

the offer. Or any reminder of the events that had brought them together in such an unlikely way.

The last two names on the suspect list.

Who could have guessed they'd have such rotten luck?

Not in her wildest imagination, so she offered another smile as Susanna got to her feet, smoothing imaginary wrinkles from her skirt and headed off to face the firing squad.

"Good luck," Francesca said again then made her way down the long hallway to the exit.

She flagged a taxi and was soon in the warm, if not plush, interior watching the city pass by through steamy windows.

Hopefully Jack was doing exactly what he promised to do right now—figuring out who the real thief was. Before she and Susanna were replaced.

Francesca wouldn't have minded commiserating right now. She'd never missed her friends in Phoenix more.

Kimberly would have suggested running together to exercise away her stress.

Judith would have let her rant and rant and rant then offered some profoundly practical advice.

Stephanie would have told her to stop worrying and meet her after work for a beer.

Just the thought made her smile. She was so making time to call all her friends as soon as she finished the interrogation with the board. She'd been so buried at work that she'd been letting all the important things in life slide. Quality time with family. With friends. She needed a good dose of familiar right now to ground her in reality. Identity theft and Jack Sloan were *not* reality.

She sent Gabrielle a text message to find out how she was holding up after her slumber party at Nonna's.

Resting her head against the seat, Francesca closed her

eyes. Why couldn't she get Jack out of her head? She'd already made this decision, the *right* decision.

She shouldn't be obsessing about Jack. Again.

So what if he made her remember there was a whole part of her that had gotten buried a long time ago beneath a failing marriage. The part of her that wasn't a mother, or a career person, or a granddaughter, or a student, or one of the many other roles she'd played through the years.

So what if he made her notice that she was a woman? A woman who'd once known what it felt like to be desired by a man.

That didn't change the fact that she should be huddled up on the sofa with Gabrielle right now, wrapping up a twelve-hour marathon of extended version *Lord of the Rings* movies.

Maybe this trip to Chicago was a blessing in disguise: A little time away from the scene of the crime—no pun intended—would help her rein in her wayward thoughts.

And they were seriously wayward.

This was all Nonna's fault, too. Darn her. If not for Nonna and her relentless desire to pass on the china, Francesca could have kept ignoring the fact that she was a living, breathing woman with needs and desires, no matter how buried.

SUSANNA ENTERED THE CONFERENCE room knowing one thing and one thing only—she had to keep her job. She'd invested too many years with this company, had established a reputation as an honest employee with a strong work ethic. Even in the face of Skip's illness, she'd done her job. She was the sole breadwinner in the Adams family and her children depended on her.

"Susanna, come on in." Gerald rose and circled the table to greet her. "Thanks for making the trip."

She exchanged pleasantries with the others around the

table and caught up on family news about spouses and children growing up too quickly. An assistant served coffee. They chatted about how the residents were settling into the new facility and how Bluestone's community had embraced the lodge. By the time Gerald said, "Now let's talk about this nasty business with the police." Susanna's anxiety had nearly melted away and the knot in her stomach had almost disappeared.

She explained events as she understood them from the trouble with Captain Hickman's wallet to Jack's handling of the investigation. She answered questions thoroughly and gave honest opinions and played the personal card for all it was worth.

"Susanna, you've been with the company a long time," Gerald said. "You're familiar with our standards and how we run the Northstar properties. So we'd appreciate knowing a little more about the work environment at Greywacke Lodge."

Susanna knew exactly what Gerald was looking for— information about the only variable in this equation.

Frankie.

Squelching an uneasy feeling, Susanna reminded herself that it was her against Frankie. And she wasn't going to feel guilty for protecting her job and reputation. Susanna wasn't stupid. She'd known Karan had been caught up in the drama about Frankie—as usual—but Karan was also right about one thing.

Could Susanna afford to ignore the facts?

She would never have thought Jack would play favorites, but something was clearly going on between him and Frankie.

Frankie had a head start at convincing everyone in this room of her innocence.

Taking a deep breath, Susanna told the bosses about the

professional and capable work environment under Frankie's direction, adding that people had been pleasantly surprised when Frankie had returned to town as Greywacke Lodge's director.

She didn't hang Frankie out to dry. That would have been unfair since Frankie did run a tight ship. But Susanna did present the unique aspects of the situation, offered the personal history and hoped her loyalty to the company would count for something.

One crime. Two suspects.

She wasn't guilty, which meant Frankie must be.

CHAPTER NINETEEN

JACK PAUSED OUTSIDE THE DOOR and inhaled deeply to collect himself. His course of action had already been decided when he'd left the station house yesterday. He'd had all night to consider his plan, so he wasn't sure why his heart raced now. He'd waited to take the red-eye out of New York, buying himself an entire night to realize he wasn't going to accomplish what he wanted unless he took a few risks.

He knocked and waited.

"Who is it?" came the familiar voice.

"Jack."

A pause before the door flung wide.

"Jack?" Frankie stared at him, as if she couldn't quite believe what she was seeing. Her eyes went from surprised to sparkling with pleasure before she asked, "What are you doing here?"

Jack couldn't get over how his entire body seemed to exhale the unaccustomed tension at the sight of her. How much he wanted to pull her into his arms and kiss her in greeting. He had to question whether he'd been motivated to this particular course of action because he'd wanted to see her, to convince her to take a few risks of her own.

"Hello, Francesca," he said. "Officially, I've come to bring Susanna in for questioning. Unofficially, I'm buying time, and I need your help."

Emotions played across her beautiful face. Relief. Surprise. Disapproval, too, he thought. Because he'd followed her to Chicago or because of his news about Susanna?

"If you're telling me Susanna is guilty, Jack, I still have trouble believing it."

"Why?"

She shook her head, expression set. *Definitely* disapproval. "I know it sounds crazy, but I don't feel it. Susanna's a strong employee. Competent. Resourceful. Admittedly, she's not particularly friendly—to me, anyway—but her people work hard for her. I've been in management a long time, and I can't believe she'd inspire that sort of loyalty without good reason."

"Not crazy," he said softly. "But if criminals were easy to spot, I'd be able to take more vacations."

"I'm not wrong about this."

He understood gut feelings, and he also knew her history with Susanna. And was impressed by Frankie's sense of fair play. She didn't let the past cloud her present. Her conviction and concern were such integral parts of the woman he was getting to know—a woman who cared.

"You don't have to sell me." He glanced over her shoulder into the room beyond. "Mind if I come in? I'd like to talk."

She swung away from the door in a fluid stride, motioning him in. Dressed in business clothes sans the jacket, she looked so beautiful. "I'm sorry. I shouldn't have kept you standing in the hallway. I'm just surprised to see you."

And pleased, too. She might be resisting for all she was worth, but she was definitely pleased.

"What do you need?" she asked. "I'll help however I can."

He knew she would. Simple. No nonsense. He liked that about her, too.

"Want something to drink? Coffee, maybe?"

"No, thanks."

He watched with appreciation as she toed off her pumps, sank onto the couch and curled her legs beneath her. Shrugging out of his coat, he sat in a chair across from her, not needing proximity to distract him when he was already so preoccupied with the fact she was no longer his suspect, and he could ethically begin the campaign to overcome her objections.

"We're ready to start building our case," he began. "I bought some time by coming here. But I can't interfere with due process, either, which means I've got to come up with another suspect before we head home."

So leaning forward, arms over his knees, he closed the distance between them. "We've cleared everyone on your property, but there's got to be someone else. I'm missing something. What can you tell me about Susanna's work? Specifics."

"She's internal control. She handles all the training and monitoring of our community-level accounting staff. Like I said, her people work hard for her. I haven't had a complaint. No drama. No aggravation. Not in the six months since the lodge opened. She runs a tight ship."

"Walk me through her day-to-day duties."

"She handles month-end control and all the financial reporting for the board of directors. She's responsible for the annual budget and tax preparation. She looks for ways to maintain and cut expenditures."

Massaging his temples, Jack racked his brain for details in the seemingly never-ending stream of data he'd reviewed since the start of the investigation. "Northstar must have someone who reviews the financial statements from their properties."

"Of course they do." She frowned. "But they're oversight.

They don't deal with the specifics that cross Susanna's desk. She's the financial officer for one property. Northstar's financial department oversees the reporting on all the properties they manage. We're talking about annual project costs of about two billion dollars annually. I researched this company thoroughly before making my move, and know for a fact they tailor services to more than senior-living communities. They manage hospitals, universities…they're the industry leaders in management services. The financial department makes sure numbers from all those interests add up."

"So you're telling me it's not likely that anyone in their financial department would have the sort of information they'd need about your residents to establish fraudulent credit card accounts and bank loans?"

"I don't see how. Susanna and her department bill for twelve hundred units at Greywacke Lodge. Northstar's financial department must oversee…ohmigosh, I don't have a clue. But it would have to be at least thirty thousand units for their senior-living division alone. And that number would be from over a year ago when I did my research. They've probably acquired more properties since."

She met his gaze steadily. "Northstar's financial department is the top of the food chain. And unless I'm really off base, I don't see how it would be possible to handle the personal information about residents on so many properties. I know from my own reports, Northstar has me filter out the minutiae. I only send the bottom line."

Jack thrust a hand through his hair, considering what she said. "Then Northstar is another dead end—"

"Wait a minute," Frankie said suddenly. "Do you know who might have access to the details Susanna has?"

He shook his head.

"Our investment banking firm. Rockport."

"What do they do?"

"They're a fiduciary for retirement funds." She met his gaze, growing more animated as the idea gained speed. "Some of their divisions deal exclusively with corporate investors for the project costs, but other divisions focus on private investments for individual retirement funds. They're the ones who make it possible to liquidate assets and buy into communities like Greywacke Lodge. I dealt with them to get Nonna's financial affairs in order since we hadn't sold her house yet."

"Rockport Investment Banking." He was already reaching into his pocket for his cell. "Perfect. It's a place to start. Excuse me. Let me make a call."

She watched curiously as he flipped open his cell and speed dialed Randy, who picked up on the second ring. "Yo. What's up?"

"Randy, I want you to start running Rockport Investment Banking. I want to know who in their financial department has access to the personal data for Greywacke Lodge. And while you're at it, check out the other properties they deal with. I also want to know if anyone else is having similar troubles. Pull in whoever you need to help. I'll start inquiries here."

"Damn it, Jack." Randy's annoyance blasted over the line loud and clear. "I thought you were bringing our girl in."

"Not if the case is a lot bigger than we suspected. You wouldn't want to miss a golden opportunity, would you?"

Silence on the other end. Then a heavy sigh. "Where are you starting?"

"Clearinghouse Alert and Auto Query." These features would put Jack in contact with law-enforcement agencies nationwide and eliminate the need for repeat searches. "We need answers fast."

CHAPTER TWENTY

FRANCESCA LOOKED UP FROM HER computer display, bleary-eyed and exhausted, to find Jack pacing before the window. He held the cell phone against his ear—where it had been for so many hours he'd had to plug the phone charger into the wall.

He'd long ago discarded his suit jacket, tie and shoes, and now paced in his socks, looking rumpled but determined as he ran his investigation from her hotel room. He had to be as tired as she was, but the man was a maniac. Nearly two in the morning and he didn't show any signs of slowing down.

She and her laptop had been recruited onto Jack's team. She'd been getting a crash course in law enforcement ever since.

Once they confirmed that Rockport Investment Banking had access to the personal information needed to perpetrate the crimes committed at the lodge, they set about to discover if crimes had been committed at any other properties.

His detectives ran credit checks in Bluestone, and every hit added a new name to her list. Then Francesca matched up the dates and locations of specific purchases to discover that in most cases high-ticket items and cash withdrawals had been made in places far from their homes.

Just like with the Hickmans.

Jack periodically checked her progress and added more names to the list, and as the hours progressed, it became obvious that he and his detectives had blown open an identity theft ring operating on a scale much larger than any of them had imagined.

Jack narrowed down specific employees with access to the growing list of victims—the precise process that had led them to Susanna. But he assured Francesca that now they knew what to look for it was simply a matter of finding it.

Unfortunately, no luck yet, and Francesca couldn't keep her eyes open another second. The Northstar board would be convening in a few short hours, and she was expected to be there. She needed some sleep. Now seemed like a good time. The effects of the room service meal she'd eaten earlier had worn off, and even caffeine wasn't doing the trick any more.

She must have nodded off because she jolted awake to find Jack kneeling beside her.

"Go lay down," he whispered, so close she could make out individual features instead of his face as a whole. The chiseled jaw and square chin. That strong mouth. Those dark eyes that melted every rational objection to keeping her distance.

For one wild, crazy moment, she wondered what would happen if she leaned forward and pressed her mouth to his.

"You're falling asleep," he pointed out.

"I'm tired."

He arched an eyebrow. "Really?"

"I'll take a break."

Even as exhausted as she was, Francesca knew sleeping simply wasn't possible. Not when she knew Jack would be pacing in the adjoining room, working his case down to its conclusion. No, she'd lie down only to find herself staring at the ceiling, obsessing over what it would be like to kiss him. She already knew what it would feel like to lie in his arms, pressed against his hard body. What it felt like to be warmed by his body heat, enveloped in his arms. Their closeness and her drowsiness such a potent combination.

"I'll shower," she said, trying not to drown in his dark gaze. "That'll wake me up."

"You should rest. You're supposed to be convalescing this weekend."

She shook her head, and he acquiesced with a wry expression, stood and extended his hand.

Slipping her fingers in his, she rose in a sleepy glide, so close she could inhale his familiar masculine scent. Their proximity dragged an earthy response from her and, again, she felt a wild urge to press forward and kiss him, such a strong impulse she actually felt a tremor low in her belly.

She really did need a shower. A cold one.

"I won't be long." Making her way into the bedroom, she hoped the distance would clear her head of all these crazy reactions to this completely irresistible man.

Jack Sloan, maniacal investigator, was chipping away at her good sense, at her determination to resist. She'd seen him soft-edged from sleep. She'd seen him professional and by the book. Now she'd seen his sense of fair play in action, making him intense and determined as he'd run a full-scale investigation from a place as unlikely as her hotel suite.

She'd seen him compassionate and attentive on a snowy mountain. She'd seen him bend the rules, worried about Susanna, a woman he cared about. He worked as hard to prove her innocence as he'd worked to prove Francesca's.

Jack Sloan—more charming gentleman than charming rogue.

Tonight only proved it.

There was no denying the way she felt right now, so she

fled into the bathroom. The steamy water washed away some of the drowsiness and calmed a lot of her conflict. Her feelings for Jack weren't a deadline she had to meet or a report she had to tackle. She didn't have to figure out everything tonight. The *only* thing she had to do right now was stop fighting the way she felt and accept that she felt this way. That was the first step.

Francesca couldn't control everything. Sometimes it was best to let life unfold the way it was meant to and stop bucking the inevitable and accept.

She'd learned that firsthand.

Which meant she would answer her questions about Jack when she was ready and not a moment sooner. She must content herself with that. Let it be enough.

Another question was miraculously answered when she stepped from the bathroom dressed in a robe. She'd never seen a more attractive sight than Jack lying stretched out on her bed, eyes closed, so perfect he literally took her breath away.

She paused in the doorway, willing to stand there forever in her bare feet with her wet hair wrapped in a towel. She didn't want to disturb him, or this moment. The moment she came face-to-face with proof that after so many empty years, she could still feel like a woman.

And she *felt*. Profound appreciation for this wildly handsome man. For the fire sparking her insides to awareness.

She felt completely, undeniably alive.

Jack had awakened this inside her, made her dare to hope that maybe, just maybe, there might be something more for her than being a mom, a granddaughter, a hardworking director.

She wasn't sure how long she stood there. She was too blown away by the anticipation stealing her breath as surely as the sight of the gorgeous man stretched out on the bed.

Then he cracked open an eyelid.

Suddenly, he rolled onto his side, appreciation softening his expression as he took in the sight of her.

"We got it," he said softly, and Francesca was still in such a daze that it took a minute for his words to register.

"You did?"

He smiled. "Not everything we need, but a good, solid connection to start building a case. Susanna's off the hook."

Francesca sighed. "I knew it."

"You were right."

"You believed me even though I didn't have anything more than a gut feeling to go on."

"I had my own gut feeling, and it told me that your gut feeling was right."

She chuckled, and Jack patted the bed beside him. "Come, sit. I didn't mean to steal your bed. There was no place else to stretch out, and I suddenly felt how tired I am."

She shouldn't get close to this man, not with his voice all low and tempting and all these realizations bouncing around in her head. She should wait and take one step at a time, first accepting she had feelings and identifying what they were then working through the problems one by one, each in its own time.

"I don't want casual, Francesca. I understand why you might think that, but I don't want casual with you."

She was rooted to the spot unable to reply, barely able to breathe. She held his gaze, saw the earnestness there, and realized she wasn't the only one with all sorts of crazy reactions happening right now.

"I don't know what I want with you," he said, the throaty intensity in his voice making her ache, "but I want a chance to find out."

Five seconds or five years might have passed as she drowned in that determined gaze. She needed to respond, but for the life of her, couldn't force out a word, had no clue what to say even if she could.

One step. That's all he was asking for.

A chance.

"I think you should give it to me," he said.

And when her reply finally came, it was one she could never have expected.

"Oh, you do, do you?" The words were suddenly there, bubbling out on laughter that expelled all the pent-up emotion, prompted by that easy camaraderie they shared, such a gift.

"Yes. I do." He frowned, all seriousness. "I understand you're a mother and will respect that completely."

Her laughter faded but the smile remained. "Just a chance, Jack? Really?"

"Really. Now come sit and I'll tell you what broke the case. Give me that chance, Francesca." Then he was Jack again, that smile splitting his handsome face as he patted the bed beside him. "I'll behave."

A chance. That was only one step.

Climbing onto the bed, she leaned back against the head-board.

Jack stretched out again. "We can let Susanna know she's off the hook first thing in the morning. Northstar, too. I hope that'll solve some problems for both of you."

"It should," she said, relieved. "We're scheduled to meet with the board at eight. I can't think of a better time to share the good news. So who is responsible? Can you tell me?"

"No, but I'll tell you anyway." Jack propped a pillow behind his head, settling in comfortably.

Francesca gazed down at him, tried to breathe evenly when her pulse was rushing and her heart was beating too quickly.

"A financial analyst. The one responsible for Grey-wacke Lodge."

"Daniel Magee?"

Jack nodded. "He's the man you dealt with for your grandmother?"

"He was really helpful, too. I'm glad we haven't run into trouble with Nonna's credit. I'll pull her reports as soon as I get home to be sure."

"Good idea. And don't forget we'll still be running things on our end to build the case. From what I can assess so far, Magee has been at this a lot longer than Greywacke Lodge has been around. He's been picking and choosing victims from properties around the country, spreading the wealth to avoid raising flags. He'd probably still be at it if not for the Mystery of the Reappearing Wallet."

"The *Case* of the Reappearing Wallet."

He chuckled.

Unwinding the towel, she fingered her damp hair and tried not to think about how she looked with no makeup and her hair solidifying into a mass of frizz. With any luck, she'd frighten him enough to keep his distance. She didn't need any temptation right now. "Well, the captain will definitely be glad to hear that he blew open the case for you."

"Give him something to talk about at lunch."

"You know it."

"Don't worry about your grandmother. The bureau will step in now. They're picking up Magee for questioning as we speak. But we'll keep digging until we dredge up everything."

"So what was your solid connection?"

"Identifying Magee's girlfriend on a security feed from a bank in Arizona. Didn't even have to wait for the FBI. Randy recognized her from a picture on Facebook."

"Wow. Who knew social networking could be so productive? I'll be sure not to tell my daughter." She chuckled softly. "I'm really impressed, Jack. The Bluestone police work fast."

She could tell by his smile that her praise pleased him, so she was surprised when he said, "I was thinking the opposite."

"Why?"

"Because this investigation has been getting in the way of something I've wanted to do for a while now."

She couldn't have resisted asking the question in that moment if her life had depended on it. Not with Jack gazing at her, looking for all the world as if he'd been waiting forever to see her. Not when she already suspected she knew the answer. "What's that?"

"Kiss you."

He hesitated for the briefest of moments, giving her a chance to get away, though his intention was all over his face.

A chance.

Francesca didn't want to get away, had no more excuses to resist. So when he lifted his hand to her neck, guiding her toward him as he rose to meet her, she exhaled a tiny sigh and leaned into his touch.

Then his mouth was on hers, warm, demanding. Intimate. A kiss that shattered any illusion of distance between them, proved their mouths were meant to touch this way. A kiss that tasted, discovered, enticed.

Need awoke low in her belly, and she suddenly couldn't remember why she'd been resisting the way she felt for this man. There was just no denying the chemistry, and for the tiniest moment, Francesca let herself go, giving in to sensation, to the taste of him, the demand of his kiss.

His mouth was hot and hard against hers, as if she was the spark to his kindling. Jack trailed warm fingers down her throat, a caress that coaxed her even closer. She wanted to press against him, knew how he would feel against her. It had been so long since she'd felt alive. Too long. Thoughts scattered in the wake of sensation, all thoughts but one.

How she responded to him.

Jack wanted her. There was no mistaking his desire, his struggle between gentleman and rogue, between control and abandon. Francesca had forgotten how it felt to be desired as a woman, wasn't sure if she'd ever known this intensity, for every inch of her yearned in this moment, *wanted*.

He exhaled, a half breath, half groan, a sound all need and frustration. Sliding his hand down into the curve of her waist, he urged her forward, a position that would bring them closer.

She shifted enough to sink into his arms, unable to deny his urging and her own need in that moment, a need that smoldered through her like a fever. His breath broke against hers as he exhaled a low moan, the sound of pleasure as he anchored her close.

He felt familiar, but this time there was no icy snow, no threat of hypothermia. There was only heat. Nothing but the two of them in a quiet hotel room, far away from families and responsibilities and real life and sanity.

There was no longer an investigation, no question of ethics, no more excuses to fight an attraction that had been building since the moment she'd stepped off an elevator to glimpse a grown-up Jack Sloan.

There was nothing but desire.

And a chance.

Her hands fluttered around his shoulders for the barest instant, still hesitating before committing to the course, still pausing before she chose to go over the edge with this man, down a steep slope where she couldn't see bottom.

She'd gotten so out of balance that it was affecting every part of her life. But life was meant to be lived, a tiny voice inside reminded her. Wasn't that what she taught her daughter?

And hadn't that been the problem with her marriage all along?

So much wasted time.

Too much.

Francesca touched Jack then. A tentative touch at first, her fingers following the hollow of his neck, the warm contours of his skin. She felt the steady thrum of his pulse at the base of his throat, the hard curve of his shoulders beneath silky fabric, then the familiar shape of those strong, strong arms.

Arms so at ease with embracing, protecting, arousing… When had her robe slipped open? Francesca gasped aloud as her few working brain cells registered that only his shirt was keeping skin from touching skin.

Jack chuckled against her lips, a warm burst that felt somehow like a caress.

"This is even better than I imagined." His voice was throaty and low, a sound that filtered through the late-night quiet with the effect of a caress.

"Mmm-hmm" was all she could manage, and even that sounded breathless.

"I've imagined kissing you a lot." His gaze smoldered with the truth of his words, with pleasure. "Should never kiss the suspects. Law Enforcement 101. Now I see why."

"Why?"

"Too hard to keep a clear head. I'd have scratched you off the suspect list without investigating."

"Because you knew I wasn't guilty."

"I don't think it would have mattered."

She laughed then. She felt so comfortable with him. Once upon a time, she'd thought herself immune to Jack's charm, but that was before this moment when she lay in his arms on a comfy bed in a quiet bedroom.

No investigation. No ethical issues.

No distractions.

He was dressed, but she was not. Not appropriately, anyway. The tie around her waist had loosed, leaving her robe perilously askew and too much of her exposed with her skin all freshly showered and lotioned.

"I promised I'd behave." Running a fingertip along her temple, he tucked wet hair behind her ear. "I should go."

She knew what he was doing—giving her a chance to retreat, to think beyond the passion of the moment, to reevaluate.

A charming gentleman, she decided.

The rational part of Francesca's mind, the responsible part, the sane part, knew what she should do.

Tell him, "Sweet dreams," and send him on his way.

But the wild side, the wanting side, the side that was so incredibly tired of resisting argued that no charming rogue would ever come all this way, risk his career and reputation for her help to solve his case.

He didn't rush her, and the simple fact that he recognized a decision needed to be made reassured her. He didn't simply follow his impulse and plunge into a situation, which is what had always gotten her into trouble in the past. She'd had to learn to pause, take a deep breath and recognize the choices and consequences before rushing headlong into the moment.

A charming gentleman, definitely. Had there ever been a question?

So now it was up to her to decide whether he would get up from this bed or kiss her again.

She wanted to be kissed again.

So much.

A chance.

That's what she wanted, too.

"Do you have a place to stay?" she asked.

He smiled, a little sheepishly, and the expression enthralled her completely. "I meant to book a room. Really."

Tilting her head, she glanced at the display on the digital clock. "Nearly three in the morning. It would be a shame to pay for a whole night when it's almost check-out time."

He dragged his thumb along her lower lip, a glancing stroke that only emphasized their closeness. "It's so late they might not even have any rooms left."

"That's true." She pressed her lips to his thumb in a kiss of sorts, unable to resist the lure of the moment or the desire in his gaze.

"I want to make love to you, Francesca."

He held her gaze levelly, those dark eyes so honest in their need.

There were so many rational reasons to hand him a pillow and blanket and send him on his way.

But there was one reason that wasn't rational at all, but it was the most important argument of all.

She didn't want to waste more time.

Tonight was hers alone. They were in Chicago with no worries about the example she set for her daughter. No worries about who might notice they were spending the night together. She didn't have to let worries about tomorrow spoil the special moments she could live tonight.

She'd wasted so much time already.

Lifting her hand to his face, Francesca mimicked his touch, caressed his lower lip, amazed by how much one simple touch made her yearn.

"Yes." She breathed the word, another caress, excitement overtaking her when he smiled that classic Jack smile.

For her.

Then there was only this moment, no thoughts of the past, no concerns about the future. Not when Jack's expression mirrored her excitement.

"Francesca." Her name tumbled from his lips in a throaty growl, a sound that left no room for doubt about how pleased he was with her response.

Hooking his leg beneath hers, he flipped over her in a startling and athletic move. He supported his weight on his hands and gazed down into her face.

"You are so beautiful," he whispered.

And Francesca remembered what it felt like to be appreciated by the man who mattered.

Arching her back, she rose to press her mouth against an inviting kiss.

"I was afraid you wouldn't stop running," he whispered against her lips.

"I was a suspect."

"Yes, but you wouldn't even acknowledge what was between us." That dark gaze smoldered with intensity, and she knew he wasn't going to let her off the hook easily.

"No. I didn't want to read anything more into the situation. It was too complicated."

"And now?"

She couldn't stop the descent of her hands, feeling the solid strength of his back narrowing into his waist. The strength of a man who knew what he wanted, and intended to be honest about it.

He wanted *her.*

And she needed to be equally honest. "A chance, Jack. We have tonight—or what's left of it. I don't want to miss this time with you."

"So I'm your one-night stand?"

"Not if you're any good."

His laughter echoed between them. Curling his fingers around her neck, he dragged her close, until his mouth brushed hers in a sexy kiss that stoked the fire simmering deep inside.

"I guess I should appreciate you giving me a chance here."

Now it was her turn to laugh. "I'm not worried about tomorrow. I'm willing to take one day at a time." She swept her hands along his back, wanting to pull him close, resisting. "I just don't want to miss any more time."

Her reply seemed to give him whatever he was looking for because he stroked damp hair from her cheek and smiled down at her. "I better be good then, so I get invited back."

"Jack—" she burst out, but he captured her laughter as his mouth came down on hers again hard, demanding, a kiss that ended any discussion about what might happen next.

Their breaths collided with the promise of the moment, an exchange of breaths that let them drink in each other. All thoughts quieted beneath growing sensation. Spearing his fingers into her hair, he arched her neck to bring her more deeply into their kiss. Their tongues tangled, and they drank in the taste of each other, the growing need to get closer, ever closer, to stop the separation of where she ended and he began, to melt together as one.

Francesca was swept away by the demand of that kiss, by the feel of his hard body surrounding hers when he dropped down onto one elbow, his weight pressing into her. She could feel the length of his hard thighs against hers, the maleness that proved he wanted her as much as she wanted him.

She ran her hands along his body with an urgent freedom, explored the feel of each curve and hollow beneath his shirt. She welcomed the anticipation of knowing that beneath the silky fabric was a flesh-and-blood man who wanted her.

And he wanted her.

No question.

He wasn't nearly as patient as she, and Francesca sighed

aloud when he broke their kiss, rolling to his side and bringing her along with him. With his hands firmly on her waist and her bottom, he pulled her on top of him.

Where he could slide his hands beneath her robe.

The shock of his touch on her bare skin dragged a gasp from her lips. He wasn't remotely deterred and helped himself to a thorough exploration of her every curve.

He ignited sparks in the wake of his touch, trailing fingertips down her spine, along the sensitive sides of her breasts, over her hips, between her thighs.

She breathed his breaths, trailed her mouth along his jaw and against his throat, tasted the throbbing beat of his pulse, nibbled the warm hollow of his neck.

His hands picked up the pace, teasing her until she thought she'd go crazy, especially when her own exploration was hindered by his clothes, their position….

Cupping her bare bottom, he pressed her impossibly closer. His male hardness swelled against her belly and brought a groan to his lips. She arched her hips and ground against him again, a slow silken glide designed to win a response.

A tremor ran the length of Jack's body, and his grip tightened, holding her immobile for a breathless instant.

Then she fought fire with fire.

Scooting away, Francesca began an assault of her own. With a few no-nonsense motions, she unbuckled his belt and whipped it through the hoops.

He chuckled softly as she dropped it over the side of the bed where it landed with a soft thump on the carpet.

"You're not a neat nut, are you?" she asked, casting a sidelong glance over the bed.

"Not when there's a dry-cleaning service available."

She laughed.

Neither of them were children, so there was no room for

self-consciousness, no room for doubts, only the promise of the moment and the excitement of discovery. Francesca liked how comfortable she felt with him, feeling nothing but appreciated as she rose before him, completely naked when her robe slithered away to join his belt.

How could she care when he knelt before her, a proud display of absolutely gorgeous male, revealed by each vanishing piece of clothing?

She made the most of each tantalizing second it took to unbutton his shirt. He helped by unfastening the shirtsleeves, so she was free to slide the shirt down his arms, to press her mouth along his shoulder and blow warm breaths that heated the cotton of his undershirt.

He shuddered beneath her touch then gasped aloud as she slid her hands beneath his undershirt and dragged her palms over his warm skin.

"Oh, my, Jack." Each word escaped on a breath as she explored the defined lines of a very fit man.

Excitement overwhelmed her, and she suddenly didn't know what part of him she wanted to unwrap next.

Jack didn't give her a chance to decide, because his arms were suddenly around her, pulling her so close they were thigh to thigh and her breasts crushed against him.

His mouth was on hers again, kissing her while he murmured her name, a potent combination of abandon and control that literally stole her breath.

She couldn't stop from touching him, from raking her palms along his strong back, savoring the feel of his warm supple skin, the hardness cradled against her stomach, the wild excitement that spurred her to greater boldness.

Almost without conscious thought, she unfastened his pants and pushed them over his hips.

Not a boxer man.

Some crazy part of her let out a relieved sigh, and she

ran her hands over him, loving the feel of his tight butt in soft cotton, couldn't swallow back a laugh at her own expense.

Who got so aroused by tighty whities?

Francesca should have seen it coming. In one instant he was kissing her then the next his entire body grew taut. With a low growl, he tackled her, his weight pressing her backward into the pillows before she had a chance to resist. She went down in a boneless heap beneath him, and almost before she registered what was happening, he'd clamped his strong hands on her knees and slid her down the bed with a bold move.

Their gazes locked for one surprised instant as she realized exactly what he was about before he disappeared between her thighs with a smile on his face.

Oh. My.

That was the last semicoherent thought Francesca had before she was burying her face into the pillow to keep from crying out.

Oh. My. Oh, my. Oh, my, oh, my, oh, my.

Digging her fingers into his shoulders, she hung on for the ride. And when she went over the edge, she went hard. She gasped out loud as her entire body collapsed in pleasure.

The echoes of pleasure eventually faded, and she found Jack watching her, his hair tousled, his expression very pleased.

"I'm sensing it's been a while for you," he said.

She sighed, such a boneless move she earned a laugh. That irked her pride, so she made another attempt. "It's been so long, I can't remember if I've ever felt this way before. I would remember, wouldn't I?"

"You would."

He traced circles inside her thighs, so teasingly close to her most private places that she quivered beneath his touch.

"There's another one in there." Not a question.

"Not possible."

His grin flashed. "Trust me."

Oh, she did. She was in good hands with Jack Sloan. No question. And from the recesses of her passion-soaked brain, she remembered reading that unlike men, women hit their primes later in life. Did mid-thirties count as later?

She thought it might.

Then Jack brushed a sensitive place between her legs with his thumbs. She let out a gasp as her whole body quivered.

"Definitely another." He quirked an eyebrow as his face disappeared between her thighs again.

And that's when Francesca knew what was happening— Jack was being *good.*

"I'll invite you back," she said. "I promise. *If* I'm still alive."

"Oh, you'll be alive," came his muffled reply. "Trust me."

Francesca was in such trouble here.

She hadn't even gotten him naked yet.

Jack might be a charming gentleman everywhere else in his life, but he was pure rogue in bed.

And that was never as evident as when he brought her to pleasure again, and yet again, before allowing her a chance to catch her breath and recover enough to even undress *him.*

And when she finally did, when she got to run her hands over his breathtakingly, gloriously naked body, Francesca knew she was a goner. Big-time.

Because there wasn't another word spoken between them. No words were necessary. They came together, bodies becoming one as if they'd been waiting for the chance. And it didn't matter what came with the dawn.

Jack had his villain, and Francesca had proof that she was still a woman who could feel, a woman who could enjoy the moment with an impossibly irresistible man.

CHAPTER TWENTY-ONE

GERALD HAD INSISTED ON DRIVING Susanna to the airport himself. He was a nice man and always had been. Today, she felt very grateful.

"Please tell Betty thanks again for the delicious dinner last night. I can't imagine what the night would have been like sitting in my hotel room waiting for the ax to fall this morning."

"She'll be glad to know she distracted you. That's exactly what she wanted to do." His expression grew solemn, and suddenly Susanna could see how gray he'd gotten. The vital man who'd befriended her years ago when she'd become a part of the company really was getting old.

"I know you've had a lot on your plate these past few years, Susanna," he told her, never glancing away from the road as he wound through Chicago's lunchtime traffic toward O'Hare. "We've all been impressed with how you've handled yourself. I can tell you the firm has been tremendously pleased with the way your team has gotten things up and running. We've never had a smoother launch."

Susanna was pleased by his praise and her role in that smooth opening.

"I don't know what your workdays are like on the property," he said, "so I'm not sure what your relationship with Francesca is like, but she was a real pistol about these thefts. Flat-out told us she hadn't stolen anyone's identity and she knew you hadn't, either. From what your police chief told the board, Francesca has been telling him all along to keep on looking because he didn't have the right names on his suspect list."

Susanna was speechless. She finally forced out the epitome of lame responses. "She did?"

Gerald nodded. "Had nothing but good to say about your work. I thought you should know."

Of course he did. She'd thrown Frankie under the bus to keep suspicion off herself while Frankie had *defended* their innocence. Gerald cared enough to share this insider information, so Susanna would know her tarnished image would need some polishing in the days ahead.

"Have I told you how much I appreciate you lately?" She could barely get the words out around the swell of emotion choking her.

"You haven't." He finally glanced away from the road and met her gaze. She could see fondness sparkling in his warm eyes and felt very grateful for his friendship. "But I always like to hear how much I'm appreciated."

"You are. Very, very much."

"Ditto, kiddo. Ditto."

Gerald dropped Susanna off at the gate, leaving her alone to her thoughts, which followed her all the way home on the flight. Frankie hadn't thrown her to the wolves. And when Susanna thought about it honestly, she wouldn't have expected Frankie to do anything but what she'd done. Defend her people.

So why had Susanna been so convinced of Frankie's guilt? Not because of anything she'd seen at the office. Frankie hadn't done a thing suspicious since the day she'd walked onto the property. Yet Susanna had convinced herself that Frankie's professionalism must have been a diversion to hide her underlying dishonesty.

Why had she been so eager to believe the worst?

She needed to answer that question, but was thankful Jack hadn't run his investigation the same way or else she might be behind bars right now.

What disturbed her even more than looking bad in front of corporate was her own prejudice. In hindsight she saw what had happened. Her anxiety about work combined with Karan's crusade against Frankie had proven deadly. Susanna had jumped on the bandwagon the way she had in high school.

Hadn't she grown up at all?

She didn't like the answers that awaited her on those familiar roads leading to Bluestone. Not one bit. And when her cell phone rang with a call from her mother-in-law, who was taking care of Brooke and Brandon, Susanna flipped open her cell, relieved for the distraction.

"Hey, Mom. Everyone okay?"

"Oh, yes. No problems," her mother-in-law said. "I just wondered what time you'd be back."

"I'm outside of town now. Need me to pick up anything?"

"I'm figuring out whether or not I needed to make arrangements to pick up Brooke. Dad's not home yet from his Elks meeting, which means they're playing cards, and he won't sail through that door until after eleven. Brandon fell asleep already, and I didn't want to leave him alone."

"Where's Brooke?"

"At the lodge. She wants to be picked up at ten."

"What's she doing there?"

"Some sort of event. I'm not really clear on the details. I figured you'd know. She's been working on it practically around the clock ever since you left. She went over after school to set up, but she called to let me know so there wasn't a problem."

But there was a problem. Glancing at the digital display on her dashboard, she frowned. Ten, on a school night? Her daughter obviously hadn't expected her home from Chicago yet.

"Let Brandon sleep," Susanna said, "if you wouldn't mind getting him off to school in the morning. I'll take care of getting Brooke home."

"You're sure, Susanna?"

"I'm sure. Relax and enjoy the rest of your night. I appreciate all your help."

"Everything work out okay in Chicago?"

That was code for *Are you off the hook yet? Because everyone in town is talking.*

"Everything worked out just fine." Even saying the words lifted her mood. "All is well. Our resourceful police chief caught the real thief. And as it happens, our property wasn't the only one hit."

"Good for Jack. He's always been a good boy."

"Well, he deserves a trophy this time around, as far as I'm concerned. All right, Mom. I'm on my way to get Brooke. I'll call in the morning to talk with Brandon before school."

Susanna disconnected and headed toward the lodge, racking her tired brain to remember what was on Monday night's activity calendar. She couldn't come up with anything except bridge club and the current events discussion. And neither of those would necessitate a weekend of frantic preparations.

As soon as she stepped inside the main lobby, Susanna knew something big was happening. Glittery stars and bright red hearts hung in profusion from the ceiling. Silver garland had been draped over nearly ever surface in the main lobby, including the doorways. It looked as if Otis's holiday decorations storeroom had exploded.

And if this crazy mélange of Christmas and Valentine's Day decor wasn't enough, music poured from the direction of the banquet room adjoining the restaurant. Lori, the night clerk, sat at the desk, sipping some sparkling beverage—not champagne surely—from a plastic flute. She was decked out in what looked like a bridesmaid's dress.

"What on earth is going on?" Susanna asked.

Lori raised her plastic flute in salute. "Shame on you. You're not dressed for the prom. Did you even bring a date?"

"I didn't even know prom night was on the calendar."

"You didn't?" Lori frowned. "The girls were here all weekend setting up."

The girls? Brooke…Gabrielle Raffa. "That's what I heard. What manager's on duty?"

"Jerry. But everyone's here. Well, everyone but you and Francesca. They've all been helping pull this together." She pointed toward the banquet hall and gave a sheepish shrug. "Just follow the music."

Susanna was nothing short of amazed at the sight that greeted her in the banquet room. The entire place looked like a scene from some cheesy prom horror flick with foil stars hanging from the ceiling and strobe lights spinning. Roberto had been recruited as deejay, and big band music poured from the karaoke system that Rachel, the activities director, normally used during the monthly sing-a-long.

Residents were all decked out for the event. They sat at tables positioned around the dance floor, and Susanna spotted a number of staff members ushering drinks from inside the restaurant where a buffet table had been set up. The dance floor was packed. Couples swayed among small clusters of friends, and all appeared to be having a great time.

A song ended to laughter and applause, and as Roberto

introduced the next, perceptively giving folks enough time to make their way back to tables safely, Susanna headed toward Rachel who'd just emerged from the restaurant.

"Don't you look lovely?" she said, pointedly eyeing Rachel's scarlet taffeta formalwear.

With a laugh, Rachel twirled on her heel and sent the flared bottom of the dress ballooning around her ankles. "Isn't it glorious? I wore it on New Year's Eve. I'm so glad for a chance to wear it again. Cost a bloody fortune."

No doubt. The deep scarlet hue complemented her creamy skin and dark hair. "You look like Snow White."

"Don't think I'll be meeting Prince Charming in this crowd, though." She gave a deep sigh. "When did you get back?"

"Haven't been home yet. Came to collect my child."

"She's around here somewhere. She and Gabrielle are the belles of the ball tonight."

No surprise there. "So how did this all come about?"

Rachel met her gaze and looked thoughtful. "Tonight's Quinta's sixty-eighth high school reunion. You know she's not well, and since Teddie got sick, there was no way they could make it to New Jersey. Can you believe she has never missed a reunion? Not one in all these years. Isn't that amazing?"

"Completely."

"She was pretty upset. Everyone's been trying to cheer her up, but the poor thing hasn't been able to talk about anything else. She cried all through dinner the other night." Rachel waved a hand and motioned all around them. "So the girls came up with this idea to surprise her. Apparently prom was the theme of this year's reunion."

Susanna's immediate response to her daughter being lumped in again as one of "the girls" with Gabrielle Raffa wasn't positive. But she took a deep breath and asked instead, "Francesca knows?"

"You don't think any of us would have authorized this without her approval?" Rachel grimaced. "I called her before she even got to the airport the other day. But we pulled it off. It was a total surprise to Quinta. You should have seen her when she realized what was going on. She was in floods."

Scanning the crowd, Rachel pointed to a table close to the dance floor. "Look at her now. She's beaming. Gabrielle and Brooke have been taking pictures with their cell phones and sending them to one of Quinta's friends at the reunion. She's been sending pictures back. It's a total riot." Rachel pointed to the dance floor. "Oh, there's your daughter now."

Susanna followed her gaze to the dance floor where she spotted "the girls." Brooke wore her homecoming finery from the dance at the start of the school year and Gabrielle a simple sheath dress in bright red. Neither girl seemed to be so much dancing as dodging walkers and canes to keep the elderly prom-goers from colliding. And they were laughing. Even from this distance, Susanna could tell there was a lot of laughter happening on that dance floor.

She could also tell the exact moment Brooke realized her mother was in the room because the laughter stopped.

To her credit, Brooke knew better than to stall the inevitable confrontation. After the song ended, and those dancers who'd needed help returning to their tables had been settled, Brooke made her way across the room.

"How much trouble am I in?" she asked.

Susanna considered her reply carefully. "Why don't you first tell me what's going on?"

Brooke launched into a tale about how Quinta was too old to go to her zillionth class reunion, basically translating the details that Rachel had already shared.

"I know you don't want me hanging around with Gabby, Mom," Brooke said, addressing the problem head-on in a way that both surprised and pleased Susanna. "But Tara and her clones keep making snotty cracks about Gabby's mom stealing. They're being horrible, and it's totally not fair."

"So you're standing up for her?"

"Like I'd ever go along with Tara." Brooke's gaze narrowed at even the suggestion. "You should give Gabby a chance, Mom. She's really cool. This whole idea was hers."

Guilty as charged. Susanna hadn't given *Gabby* a chance. She'd written her off as Frankie's daughter no questions asked. The same way she'd written off Frankie.

Susanna switched gears. "Making tonight happen took a lot of work, didn't it?"

Brooke shrugged. "It was fun. We raided Otis's storeroom. Ohmigosh, it's totally, like, the party warehouse. There was so much cool stuff we couldn't decide what to go with, so we used everything. It's not a problem, so don't worry. We promised Otis to pack everything back so he wouldn't have to do it himself. Rachel and Roberto offered to help, too, so it won't take forever. The place will be back to normal tomorrow."

Brooke was excited and seemed to have covered all the bases. That in itself was a pleasant surprise, a glimpse of responsibility and work ethic and thoughtfulness for the lodge employees who had helped her.

Glimmers of the mature and lovely woman Brooke would one day become shone so brightly that Susanna found herself smiling.

"So am I grounded forever?" Brooke tried not to sound hopeful.

What to do, what to do? Susanna met her daughter's gaze and considered her response, struck by the parallel to her own situation with Frankie.

Instead of following the crowd, Brooke had stood up for what she believed was right—even without her mother's support. From the look of things tonight, "the girls" had accomplished something good. They'd thought about others and taken action in a responsible way.

What more could a mother possibly ask for?

"No, you're not grounded forever," Susanna said, not missing Brooke's excitement and deciding right then and there to look for more of these moments in their relationship. "I didn't tell you not to hang around with Gabby. I suggested that you think seriously before encouraging a relationship. If you believe she'll make a worthy friend, then I trust your judgment. I'll give her a chance. You both did a really nice thing tonight, and I'm very proud of you."

To Susanna's complete surprise, Brooke launched herself forward and gave Susanna a big squeeze-y hug just like she'd done when she'd been younger. Then she spun on her heel and took off. "Got to help the old people dance. Prom's almost over."

"You look beautiful, by the way," Susanna called after her.

"Thanks," Brooke tossed back over her shoulder. "You should dance, Mom. Mr. Shaw has been talking about how hot you are."

Susanna ignored that, but scanned the crowd for Mr. Shaw, a bad boy if ever there was one. She spotted him on the dance floor in the middle of a crowd of ladies, naturally.

Making a mental note to avoid that side of the room, she spotted Brooke, who'd caught up with Gabby again. Their exchange was animated and casual, and Susanna watched them, realizing that she had a choice here, too.

The next time Karan called on a rant about Frankie, Susanna could choose not to go along for the ride. That didn't mean she had to give up her best friend. It simply meant she was responsible for making choices that wouldn't hurt others or leave her feeling so horrible about herself. And who knew? Maybe in the process she might find opportunities to diffuse Karan's prejudice, too.

What had Skip always said?

Be part of the solution, not the problem.

She glanced upward with a smile. "Well, hon, you always said they'd help us become better parents along the way. Looks like better people, too."

CHAPTER TWENTY-TWO

JACK HAD ALWAYS BELIEVED that when he found the right woman he'd know. Nothing mysterious, just a gut feeling— one that served him well in the other areas of his life. He'd never second-guessed his position, had defended himself more times than he could count, had always believed there was a woman who'd be suited to him and his life—the perfect woman *for him.*

As he drove to Bluestone, he considered what to do now that he'd found her. Frankie was *his* perfect woman. He knew it in his gut, had suspected she was different from the moment they'd officially met.

He'd wanted this woman. Period.

But finding her didn't mean he had a clue about what came next. That much had been clear as he'd stood in O'Hare Airport, watching Frankie disappear beyond the gate, frustrated because he hadn't been able to swap his ticket for a standby seat on her flight, irritated to waste time they could have spent together.

Finding her had only been the first step.

Getting her to give him a chance had been the second.

As far as Frankie was concerned they'd enjoyed an incredible "break from reality" and tomorrow would work itself out. Jack didn't want to leave so much to chance. He didn't want to be her break.

So what came next?

After seeing her with her family, Jack knew she wouldn't be inviting him into her reality without being convinced he was reality material. His own past was biting him in the ass, and he could almost hear his mother chanting, "How do you expect any girl to take you seriously…"

His cell phone rang, a welcome distraction from his overworked thoughts, until he glanced at the display and saw his mother's cell number.

"What are the odds," he said into the quiet interior of his car and flipped open the phone. "Hello."

"Jack." His dad's voice shot over the line. "Your mom and I are hoping you can help us out."

"Sure. What's up? Gus-Gus?"

"No, thank God. He's still hanging in there if you can believe it. He refuses to leave your mother, and I told him there's no way she's going with him."

Jack laughed.

"Your grandfather needs to be picked up from Grey-wacke Lodge at ten. You anywhere around?"

Jack actually pulled the phone away from his ear and stared at it before asking, "What's Granddad doing there?"

"Some function or another. Judge Pierce had to make an appearance but didn't want to go alone. He recruited your grandfather. I remembered what you'd said about the place and encouraged him to go even though your mom and I had this board meeting at the credit union. The judge picked him up and they had supper together first. It was good for him to get out."

"I can't believe he actually went."

His dad laughed. "The judge doesn't take no for an answer. Come to find out he doesn't drive at night, either. Michaela's on death watch until we get back, so I thought I'd give you a try before sending a taxi. You know Granddad. If he gets it into his head we put us out, he won't leave the house again."

No argument there. "Tell Mom I'm glad Gus-Gus is okay. Don't worry about Grandpa. I'll be there at ten." Even sooner if he could make it.

"Excellent. Thanks, Jack."

"No problem, Dad. No problem at all."

Jack disconnected the call and found himself smiling as he glanced at the clock and hit the accelerator.

Some things were meant to be.

That was the only explanation there could be for arriving at Greywacke Lodge to find Frankie's Jeep double-parked in the front and the main lobby looking the town square decorated for the holidays. *All* of them.

The event board read: Reach for the Stars.

A quizzical glance at the front desk clerk dressed in formalwear brought the explanation "Prom night."

Jack nodded, understanding why Judge Pierce hadn't wanted to make a solo appearance at the event. Jack remembered his prom, but had no clue whether or not Frankie had attended.

On impulse, he considered the fresh floral spray on one of the sideboards in the main lobby before plucking a bright orange flower from the arrangement. Some sort of daisy, he thought. Then he went to join the party.

Had the age demographic of the party-goers been about six decades younger, the banquet room at Greywacke Lodge could have been hosting any high school dance. Gaudy decorations. Blaring music. Lots of dancing and laughter. He spotted his grandfather and the judge, deep in discussion over port at a corner table.

He noticed Susanna, a wallflower, as she watched the party from just inside the entrance.

"Brings back memories, doesn't it?" he said.

She glanced up at him in surprise then smiled wistfully.

"It does. Only we were the court back then. Tonight they crowned Quinta and Ted Flood."

Jack could see the requisite archway, but couldn't spot the king and queen in this crowd. He did spot a few people on the dance floor he knew. "Is that Brooke? When did she grow up?"

Susanna grimaced. "Overnight, it seems. Got back into town to find out she was one of the hosts of tonight's shindig."

"I see." And he did. Wrapping an arm around her shoulder, he pulled her close in a one-armed hug. "Been a rough couple of days. You okay?"

She leaned into him, as if drawing strength. "Thanks to you, I'm fine. You're my hero."

Her new hero, maybe. There was a missing hero very present in the room. Jack pressed a kiss to the top of her head. "So you'll forgive me?"

"Only if you forgive me. I've been acting like a big butt-head, as Brooke would say."

Jack laughed. "Nothing to forgive, Susanna."

They lapsed into a companionable silence, taking a moment to savor the mended fence. But Susanna looked so wistful, a woman with a lot on her mind.

He nudged her shoulder. "You really didn't think I'd let Skip's best girl fry, did you?"

That got a smile. "Not unless you wanted him to haunt you. Or for our kids to show up on your doorstep the next time they needed a hot meal or a ride."

"You guys seem to be hanging in there."

"We're okay." She smiled softly. "Some days better than others. Prom night has me reminiscing."

"We had a lot of good times back then." Too many of them hadn't been memorable enough to have weathered the passage of time, but there were also those worth remembering.

"At that age I didn't imagine there was a limit. Skip and I thought we had our whole lives ahead of us. We planned to rear our family then retire and travel and host big family gatherings at our summer home on the Sound." She exhaled a sigh. "If we'd have realized our time was limited, we could have made so many different choices. We'd have lived more instead of putting off our dreams. "

Another easy silence fell between them, a thoughtful silence filled with realizations and cautions. Jack understood exactly what Susanna was saying. Her family hadn't had enough time with the man they loved. She shared nothing more than conventional wisdom, but somehow, in this moment, it applied to his life in a way it never had before.

Nobody had a clue what tomorrow would bring. He saw proof of that daily in his line of work. But limitations on the future had never felt personal. Not even when he'd lost Skip, one of his best friends. Not until today when Frankie had given him a kiss and entrusted their *chance* to fate.

Tomorrow will work itself out.

He wasn't okay with that. His work might not lend itself to a white picket fence and two point five kids, but Jack wanted memorable.

"How would you have prioritized differently?" he asked.

"We would have definitely taken that vacation to Florida for a sunny Christmas instead of building an addition on the house. Maybe we'd have even accepted that job promotion to California. Think about all the quality time we'd have had together without our families and friends around. It would have been just us creating a whole new life together."

She sounded so sad that Jack slipped his arms around her shoulders again and pulled her close.

She glanced at the flower he held. "That a corsage?"

"Not very impressive, is it?"

"If you like gerbera daisies."

Jack twisted the flower between his fingers. "That's what this is?"

Susanna nodded. "Who's the lucky lady?"

"Francesca."

Susanna inclined her head and glanced out at the dance floor where Brooke and Gabrielle were teaching Frankie some dance steps to some amusing results.

"I don't know her as anything but a director, Jack, but she's a really good one."

Jack smiled, knowing Susanna's admission was a blessing of sorts, one that put the past where it belonged. "Get a good night's sleep. I promise there won't be any officers showing up on your doorstep tomorrow."

"Thanks to you. You better get that corsage to your date before it wilts."

Jack smiled at that, and took Susanna's advice, bypassing his grandfather who was still deep in conversation, and heading toward the dance floor.

"Ladies, mind if I cut in?"

"Jack?" Frankie's eyes widened when she recognized him, and to his profound pleasure, she actually blushed when he handed her the daisy. At least it looked like a blush in the shifting dance floor lighting.

"Hey, Uncle Jack." Brooke popped up on tiptoe and kissed his cheek.

"Hey, kiddo. You're getting way too gorgeous. I'm going to have to assign you a patrol."

"Please don't say that to Mom. She'll want you to."

He laughed. "Good evening, Gabrielle. Nice to see you again. Mind if I dance with your mother?"

Her green eyes lit up with mischief. "She's all yours, Chief Sloan. Go for it."

"Gabrielle Concetta," Frankie said, but her daughter was already disappearing into the crowd.

Jack slipped an arm around Frankie's waist and pulled her close for a dance more suited to the Golden Era music than the one she'd been attempting to learn.

Frankie tucked the daisy into her lapel, where the long stem hung comically. She didn't seem to notice or care. "What brings you here?"

"I missed you."

She narrowed eyes that sparkled in the flickering light. "Really, Jack."

"My grandfather's here."

"Is he? Where?"

"With Judge Pierce. If you don't mind, I'd like to introduce you."

Their gazes met. He wasn't sure exactly what he saw in those beautiful gray eyes—a mixture of excitement and uncertainty maybe—but he knew she understood that he wanted to introduce her to his family for a reason.

"I want my chance here in Bluestone, Francesca," he said simply. "I want to be part of your reality, Francesca. Not a break from it."

Because somewhere along the line tonight, he'd figured out what he wanted. And for the first time in memory, Jack was excited about what the future would bring.

They could figure out the logistics of two demanding careers, his and hers. He'd always believed his career didn't lend itself to committed relationships. He'd seen so many marriages fail under the ongoing demands of law enforcement. But Jack found himself considering those relationships that had stayed the course and endured.

And there were some. He suspected the real trouble lay with his views and his commitment. As Susanna, and his parents, had pointed out, work was only one part of life.

Or should be.

"I want someone to miss me if I don't come home at

night, someone who depends on me. Someone to love me like you do."

"You sound very sure of that, Jack."

"I am." He pulled her closer. His body remembered the feel of hers, the warm promise between them. "I want you and Gabrielle to make some extra room in your family for me. And who better to be a stepfather to a beautiful teenage girl than the chief of police?"

She leaned against his arm and gazed up at him with such excitement. "That's definitely in your favor."

And when she smiled her dazzling smile and said, "I'd like to meet your grandfather." Jack knew he wouldn't have too hard of a job ahead. Not if he opened himself up to the unique possibilities tomorrow could bring. They'd figure everything out. Together.

Frankie was, after all, *his* perfect woman.

EPILOGUE

Over a year later

ONE GLIMPSE OF BLUESTONE Mountain in full summer bloom reminded Francesca of exactly why her hometown was so special. The sun shone from a clear, cloudless sky, sparkling over the lush mountainside in one of those uniquely exquisite Catskill days that, viewed from the lodge's restaurant, was nothing short of breathtaking.

She'd slipped from the banquet room to catch her breath after one too many dances, a stolen moment to watch family and friends enjoying a day that couldn't have been more perfect.

Her wedding day, and the future looked as bright as the sunny vista outside.

Though it was her second marriage, it was her first wedding. Jack's, too. Nothing but a "real" affair would do, Gabrielle had insisted, complete with a white dress—a Nonna original as it turned out.

Nonna had had faith. She trusted that Francesca would one day come to her senses and had intended to be ready. So she'd beaded a bodice and packed it carefully away....

Francesca had gone to pieces while unwrapping the heavy satin where delicate beads and sequins twinkled up at her, each exquisite row hand-sewn with so much love.

She, Nonna and Gabrielle had designed a dress worthy

of that bodice. A good thing since most of the BMPD had shown up in their dress blues to stand honor guard for their chief at a wedding that had turned into a full-scale event.

Nonna had given her away and Gabrielle was maid of honor. Kimberly, Judith and Stephanie had traveled in with their families from Phoenix to stand beside Gabrielle as bridesmaids.

They'd all been partying nonstop ever since the guests had started arriving. Since she and Jack hadn't wanted the traditional rounds of showers, bachelor/bachelorette parties and rehearsal dinners, the days preceding the wedding had been filled with simply enjoying time with people they cared about.

Jack's parents had thrown open their apartment in the city to host a grand tour of Manhattan that culminated in the hottest show on Broadway. They'd had to charter a bus to get everyone there and back again.

Francesca should have been exhausted, but the wave of love and excitement still carried her along. She scanned the crowd and caught sight of Gabrielle dancing with Stephanie's son, who'd grown to be more than six feet tall in the time they'd been away from Phoenix.

Life with her beautiful daughter, who'd recently turned seventeen, had been a little less tumultuous lately. Gabrielle's interest in boys was at an all-time high—evidenced by the way she'd been keeping in touch with Stephanie's son—and she considered her mother dating the police chief common ground, which had opened up the lines of communication between them in ways that were all good.

Francesca had been getting to know her daughter as she matured into this incredible young woman, and their relationship was changing subtly. They'd spent quality time together as Gabrielle had learned to drive. They'd had long philosophical conversations while they'd worked on selling Nonna's house.

And after Gabrielle had gotten an after-school transportation aide job at the lodge's nursing center, she'd been showing up more and more often in Francesca's office with invitations to grab lunch or drop by Nonna's for coffee. Lately they'd been slipping away on weekends to tour colleges for the upcoming year.

Francesca embraced each and every one of these bittersweet moments, knowing she was living on borrowed time. She wanted to build a solid foundation for the years ahead, hoping Gabrielle would include her family no matter where her interests led her.

With any luck they wouldn't lead her as far away as a third-world country.

Even Francesca's ex-husband, Nicky, had come through in his own way. The girlie-girl had left him long ago, and in the failed relationships since, he'd discovered a newfound appreciation for the daughter who loved him no matter what. They e-mailed often nowadays, sharing their love of music and everything Mexican.

Nicky had even text messaged Gabrielle before the wedding and asked his daughter to kiss the bride.

"That was really nice of your dad. Send him a hug for me," Francesca had said, and was rewarded by a beaming smile.

Life was good.

And never better when she caught sight of her handsome new husband, dressed sharply in his uniform. He came to a complete stop when he saw her, a slow smile transforming his handsome face, that famous Jack Sloan smile, for her alone.

His gaze raked over her and his expression was one of such pleasure, such appreciation, that he literally stole her breath.

He covered the distance between them in a few long strides. "Mrs. Sloan."

"Chief Sloan."

"Hiding from all the confusion?"

She just smiled as he came close and drew her into his arms. Melting against him, she savored the familiar feel of his embrace and the warmth of the sun streaming through the windows.

"Your grandmother and my grandfather actually got up from that table, to dance."

"I told you, they're becoming friends. Who knew?" Francesca had witnessed firsthand how well Jack's grandfather had been settling in since his move to the lodge, a decision that had startled, and pleased, everyone who cared about him.

"Nonna wants to know if we want to take the china home with us tonight or wait until we get back from our honeymoon. I had no clue what to tell her, but I got the feeling it was code."

She chuckled. "You're very smart, you know."

He caught her hand in his and raised it to his lips. Brushing a warm kiss across her knuckles, he fixed those dark eyes on hers above their clasped hands, and promised all his love in a glance.

"May I have this dance, Mrs. Sloan?"

"I'd like nothing better." Francesca nestled against him as he rested his cheek on the top of her head. They swayed to the music pouring from the banquet room, so content for this stolen moment, just the two of them together.

"So," he whispered into her hair. "You going to tell me about that code, or is it a secret?"

She tightened her grip around his waist and exhaled a sigh that got lost in the curve of his neck. "It means that life doesn't get any better than this."

* * * * *

*Rancher Ramsey Westmoreland's temporary cook
is way too attractive for his liking.
Little does he know Chloe Burton came to his ranch
with another agenda entirely....*

That man across the street had to be, without a doubt, the most handsome man she'd ever seen.

Chloe Burton's pulse beat rhythmically as he stopped to talk to another man in front of a feed store. He was tall, dark and every inch of sexy—from his Stetson to the well-worn leather boots on his feet. And from the way his jeans and Western shirt fit his broad muscular shoulders, it was quite obvious he had everything it took to separate the men from the boys. The combination was enough to corrupt any woman's mind and had her weakening even from a distance. Her body felt flushed. It was hot. Unsettled.

Over the past year the only male who had gotten her time and attention had been the e-mail. That was simply pathetic, especially since now she was practically drooling simply at the sight of a man. Even his stance—both hands in his jeans pockets, legs braced apart, was a pose she would carry to her dreams.

And he was smiling, evidently enjoying the conversation being exchanged. He had dimples, incredibly sexy dimples in not one but both cheeks.

"What are you staring at, Clo?"

Chloe nearly jumped. She'd forgotten she had a lunch date. She glanced over the table at her best friend from college, Lucia Conyers.

"Take a look at that man across the street in the blue shirt, Lucia. Will he not be perfect for Denver's first issue of *Simply Irresistible* or what?" Chloe asked with so much excitement she almost couldn't stand it.

She was the owner of *Simply Irresistible*, a magazine for today's up-and-coming woman. Their once-a-year Irresistible Man cover, which highlighted a man the magazine felt deserved the honor, had increased sales enough for Chloe to open a Denver office.

When Lucia didn't say anything but kept staring, Chloe's smile widened. "Well?"

Lucia glanced across the booth at her. "Since you asked, I'll tell you what I see. One of the Westmorelands—Ramsey Westmoreland. And yes, he'd be perfect for the cover, but he won't do it."

Chloe raised a brow. "He'd get paid for his services, of course."

Lucia laughed and shook her head. "Getting paid won't be the issue, Clo—Ramsey is one of the wealthiest sheep ranchers in this part of Colorado. But everyone knows what a private person he is. Trust me—he won't do it."

Chloe couldn't help but smile. The man was the epitome of what she was looking for in a magazine cover and she was determined that whatever it took, he would be it.

"Umm, I don't like that look on your face, Chloe. I've seen it before and know exactly what it means."

She watched as Ramsey Westmoreland entered the store with a swagger that made her almost breathless. She *would* be seeing him again.

Look for Silhouette Desire's
HOT WESTMORELAND NIGHTS
by Brenda Jackson,
available March 9 wherever books are sold.

Devastating, dark-hearted and...
looking for brides.

Look for

BOUGHT: DESTITUTE YET DEFIANT

by *Sarah Morgan*

#2902

From the lowliest slums to Millionaire's Row...
these men have everything now but their brides—
and they'll settle for nothing less than the best!

Available March 2010
from Harlequin Presents!

THE WESTMORELANDS

NEW YORK TIMES
bestselling author

BRENDA JACKSON

HOT WESTMORELAND NIGHTS

Ramsey Westmoreland knew better than to lust after the hired help. But Chloe, the new cook, was just so delectable. Though their affair was growing steamier, Chloe's motives became suspicious. And when he learned Chloe was carrying his child this Westmoreland Rancher had to choose between pride or duty.

Available March 2010 wherever books are sold.

Always Powerful, Passionate and Provocative.

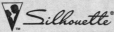

REQUEST YOUR FREE BOOKS!

2 FREE NOVELS PLUS 2 FREE GIFTS!

HARLEQUIN®

Super Romance®

Exciting, emotional, unexpected!

YES! Please send me 2 FREE Harlequin® Superromance® novels and my 2 FREE gifts (gifts are worth about $10). After receiving them, if I don't wish to receive any more books, I can return the shipping statement marked "cancel." If I don't cancel, I will receive 6 brand-new novels every month and be billed just $4.69 per book in the U.S. or $5.24 per book in Canada. That's a saving of close to 15% off the cover price! It's quite a bargain! Shipping and handling is just 50¢ per book in the U.S. and 75¢ per book in Canada.* I understand that accepting the 2 free books and gifts places me under no obligation to buy anything. I can always return a shipment and cancel at any time. Even if I never buy another book from Harlequin, the two free books and gifts are mine to keep forever.

135 HDN E4JC   336 HDN E4JN

Name	(PLEASE PRINT)	
Address		Apt. #
City	State/Prov.	Zip/Postal Code

Signature (if under 18, a parent or guardian must sign)

Mail to the **Harlequin Reader Service:**
IN U.S.A.: P.O. Box 1867, Buffalo, NY 14240-1867
IN CANADA: P.O. Box 609, Fort Erie, Ontario L2A 5X3

Not valid for current subscribers to Harlequin Superromance books.

**Are you a current subscriber to Harlequin Superromance books
and want to receive the larger-print edition?
Call 1-800-873-8635 today!**

* Terms and prices subject to change without notice. Prices do not include applicable taxes. N.Y. residents add applicable sales tax. Canadian residents will be charged applicable provincial taxes and GST. Offer not valid in Quebec. This offer is limited to one order per household. All orders subject to approval. Credit or debit balances in a customer's account(s) may be offset by any other outstanding balance owed by or to the customer. Please allow 4 to 6 weeks for delivery. Offer available while quantities last.

HSR10

SILHOUETTE

SPECIAL EDITION

FROM *USA TODAY* BESTSELLING AUTHOR
CHRISTINE RIMMER

BRAVO FAMILY TIES

A BRIDE FOR JERICHO BRAVO

Marnie Jones had long ago buried her wild-child impulses and opted to be "safe," romantically speaking. But one look at born rebel Jericho Bravo and she began to wonder if her thrill-seeking side was about to be revived. Because if ever there was a man worth taking a chance on, there he was, right within her grasp....

Available in March
wherever books are sold.

SSE65511

HARLEQUIN
Ambassadors

Want to share your passion for reading Harlequin® Books?

Become a Harlequin Ambassador!

Harlequin Ambassadors are a group of passionate and well-connected readers who are willing to share their joy of reading Harlequin® books with family and friends.

You'll be sent all the tools you need to spark great conversation, including free books!

All we ask is that you share the romance with your friends and family!

You'll also be invited to have a say in new book ideas and exchange opinions with women just like you!

To see if you qualify* to be a Harlequin Ambassador, please visit www.HarlequinAmbassadors.com.

*Please note that not everyone who applies to be a Harlequin Ambassador will qualify. For more information please visit www.HarlequinAmbassadors.com.

Thank you for your participation.

BAP09BPA